THE
SILVER
STRAND
LEGACY

ERITIS BOOK I

T.E. STOUYER

ISBN 978-1-9999649-3-1

"The advance of genetic engineering makes it quite conceivable that we will begin to design our own evolutionary progress."

ISAAC ASIMOV, *The Beginning and the End*

ERITIS

PART ONE

Chapter 1 – The Storm

The night sky was grim. Dark clouds melted into a pouring rain that battered the ground relentlessly. Trees were shaking, as if frightened by the fierce gale racing through the forest. At times, flashes of light slithered through the thick veil of darkness, each one a prelude to the ferocious roar of thunder.

In the distance, streams of electricity connected the skyline to the horizon, linking the heavens and the earth. A reminder, or perhaps a warning, that all of nature's parts are interconnected, and that any significant change in one will inevitably affect the others.

Deep inside the forest, a vast compound stood in defiance of this tumultuous portrait, an oasis of calm in the storm. At its center was a modern glass-and-steel building flanked by two squat concrete structures. The compound was surrounded by a tall metallic fence, and signs posted at regular intervals warned of the terrible fate awaiting all would-be trespassers.

From the outside, the facility appeared abandoned. There were no lights filtering through the black-tinted windows, no sounds arising to challenge the rumblings of the storm, and no movements which could not be attributed to the strong winds.

Then, all of a sudden, on the tail end of a deafening thunderclap, the compound sprung to life. An alarm siren resounded throughout the forest, and powerful projectors flooded the entire property with light, revealing a hangar farther back near the fence, and a military helicopter parked in front of it.

Answering the call of the siren, a large contingent of soldiers swarmed out of the two smaller structures. The men proceeded to surround the main building, splitting up into small groups positioned at equal distance from one another. The maneuver was accomplished with remarkable efficiency, and with almost no communication between them. It was clearly a well-rehearsed exercise.

Meanwhile, inside the main building, the scene unfolding in the second-floor control room presented a stark contrast to the organized deployment taking place in the courtyard.

The control room looked like it belonged on the set of a science-fiction movie. It was a large circular booth fitted with a variety of sophisticated equipment. The lone piece of furniture was a semicircular panel placed at its center, opposite a large bank of monitors.

Seated at the panel, a man was frantically typing on a keyboard while his colleague bounced around the room to check on the various instruments.

The alarm signal inside the control room consisted only of a blinking red light. And since very little of the buzzing from the siren outside filtered through the walls, the two men could communicate without having to raise their voices.

"What happened, Paul?"

"I'm not sure yet," said the man sitting at the console. "Hmm …"

"What?"

"I don't know how, but the audio and video feeds have been shut off in some areas. Even the motion sensors are down." He paused for a moment. "It's like there's no power anymore."

"No power? What about the backup generators? They should have taken over."

"I know, George, I know, but for some reason they haven't." Paul pointed to his right. "Try pulling up the grids."

George rushed to an instrument panel on the wall and pulled up an electronic blueprint of the facility overlapped on a grid map. "Yeah, I can confirm it. We've got some power outages."

"Where?" Paul asked.

"Grids sixteen to twenty have gone dark. There's partial visibility in grids thirteen to fifteen. Everything else remains unaffected."

The technicians were baffled. The facility's power source was cut off from the outside world and was comprised of a triple redundancy system designed specifically to prevent this sort of incident.

"Let's run a full diagnostic of the power systems," George suggested.

His colleague ran the command on his computer.

"You're not going to believe it," Paul said when the result came up on his screen. "The systems didn't lose power. They were overloaded."

"What? Are you sure about this?" George asked, sounding skeptical. "That can't be right. Check again."

"I'm telling you, the generators are fried!"

"How could this happen?"

"No idea."

"Could it be an accident?"

"Not a chance. Each system is independent from the others. For this to be even remotely possible, someone would have to find a way to link—" Paul stopped short.

"What's the matter?" George asked.

"The grids ..."

"What about the grids?"

Paul didn't answer, and instead kept staring at the grid display with growing apprehension.

"Look, if you know something, tell me," George pressed. But then it hit him. "Wait a minute … grids sixteen to twenty. Those are the sublevels."

"It's *them*," Paul said in a trembling voice.

George stared at the grid. His pulse had already been running high since the alarm had sounded off, but it spiked at the mere thought of what Paul had suggested. His heart was now beating so fast he felt like it might jump out of his chest. He rushed back to the main console. "Quick, we need to reroute power from the control room systems. Maybe we can reactivate the electronic locking mechanisms in the affected areas."

George took a seat next to his colleague and wasted no time implementing his plan. If their fears turned out to be justified, they would have very little time to act. Paul understood this as well; he too now feverishly applied himself to the task. For the following minute, the only sound inside the room was that of the fast clicking of fingers flying over their keyboards, until a gruff voice appeared out of nowhere to interrupt the string of clicks. "What's the status?"

Startled, the two technicians swiveled around in their chairs and saw a man standing in the doorway, half-covered by the shadows. They had been so absorbed in their task they hadn't heard the code being keyed in, or the door slide open. They hadn't even noticed that the alarm and the footsteps in the outside corridor had become clearly audible. They sat motionless, their eyes fixed on the intruder as he emerged from the shadows.

"Oh, it's you, Mr. Jenkins!" said George breathing a sigh of relief. "You gave us quite a scare."

"The status!" the man repeated in a dry tone.

"Ah, yes … of course …"

George had always felt a bit uncomfortable around Jenkins. It wasn't because Jenkins never smiled or because his steely dark eyes never seemed to stop glowering. It was something else, something about his general demeanor that George found strangely unsettling.

"Let's see," the technician continued, "we've lost all power on the lower levels. There is partial functionality on the ground floor and on sublevel one. Everything else checks out fine."

Jenkins took a moment to process the information. Then, he pulled out a small walkie-talkie from the pocket his black jacket and spoke into it. "I'm ordering a total lockdown effective immediately. No one gets in or out."

"Understood, sir," a voice crackled on the other end.

Jenkins put the walkie-talkie back inside his pocket and turned to George. "Continue."

"We think something overloaded the circuits. When you arrived, we were about to attempt a bypass to restore partial power to the affected areas."

"Won't that compromise the control room?" Jenkins asked.

"No, our systems are isolated from the rest of the compound, including our power source. There is no foreseeable risk. The only problem is we won't be able to restore power to all the lower levels, but we should be able to—"

"Never mind that," Jenkins interrupted. "Just concentrate on getting the ground floor operational, and on reactivating the security measures."

George looked unsure. "But ... members of our staff are still trapped down there. If we don't—"

"You have your orders!" said Jenkins.

George shot a frustrated look at his colleague.

Paul glanced back at him as if to say, *We'd better do as he says.*

George sighed. He had spent enough time around Jenkins to know it was pointless to try to sway him. As the technician sat back in his chair, he recalled the first time he had been brought to the facility. Jenkins had been introduced to him as the person in charge of all security matters and the one who had the final say during emergencies. The current situation definitely qualified as an emergency. The only way to override Jenkins was to contact his superiors on the outside. And that could take a while.

Those military types are all the same, George thought. *They're so narrow-minded, it's damned near impossible to get them to see things from a different perspective. Of course, the fact they're a paranoid bunch doesn't help matters either.*

"Keep me updated on your progress," said Jenkins as he headed for the door. "And kill the alarm."

Jenkins stepped out into the hallway, where a group of soldiers was waiting for him. He called them to attention. "Lieutenant, tell all units to hold their positions. No one is to come inside the main building. We'll wait until power is restored. I've called for additional personnel. When they arrive, we'll secure each floor one by one. For now, the order is to maintain a perimeter and contain the prisoners, nothing more."

"Sir, what if one of them gets out?" the lieutenant asked.

"Shoot on sight."

The lieutenant was surprised by his commander's reply. None of the soldiers had ever laid eyes on the prisoners—they didn't have the necessary clearance. Others were responsible for security inside the main building— guards from a private group that reported directly to Jenkins. Once in a while, the soldiers would see batches of those men arrive and leave in unmarked vehicles, but they had no real contact with them. The only sure piece of information the soldiers had regarding the prisoners was their number: eight.

The lieutenant had always wondered why it was necessary to mobilize so large a force on a simple watch duty for a mere eight prisoners. Most soldiers assumed it was because they were protecting some top-secret spies or informants, but that was pure speculation on their part. One of the soldiers' favorite pastimes when inside their barracks was to try to guess the identities of the people kept in the lower levels of the main building. Whoever they were, the number of resources devoted to their incarceration and protection suggested they were of great value, which was why the order to *"shoot on sight"* came as a surprise to the lieutenant. Not a single intruder had been spotted, not a single shot had been fired, and the men had been quick to deploy to their assigned positions around the compound. The situation appeared to be well under control.

"You don't want us to apprehend them?" the lieutenant ventured.

"Absolutely not!" Jenkins barked. "Make sure everyone is clear on this. We only need to keep them in."

"Understood, sir. But how are we supposed to recognize the prisoners?"

"Don't bother with details. If you see someone you don't know, shoot them."

The soldiers exchanged uneasy glances.

"Erm ... what if it's one of the scientists?" the lieutenant risked. "Or a member of the private security team? We're not too familiar with those guys either."

"I don't care! Now, return to—" Jenkins stopped and pricked up his ears.

With the alarm turned off, the hallways had become much quieter. And now, a faint but distinctive sound was making its way to them.

They all stilled and focused as they tried to identify its source.

"It sounds like an engine," someone hazarded.

A transmission came in on Jenkins' walkie-talkie.

"Mr. Jenkins! Come in, sir."

He answered right away. "What is it?"

"Sir, a helicopter has been spotted leaving the compound at high speed."

"Shoot it down!" Jenkins shouted.

"We tried," the voice replied, "but it was already out of range."

7

"How could they get up there so fast?" Jenkins muttered to himself as he hurried back into the control room.

Paul and George were still sitting at the main console, working on the power issue.

Jenkins ran over to them. "Track the transponder on the prototype helicopter."

The technicians looked up in surprise.

"The prototype?" George said. "It's all the way up on the roof."

"Yeah," Paul added. "Besides, it can't fly yet."

"Do it now!" Jenkins growled.

With a few keystrokes, Paul conjured up a radar image on a monitor. The image showed a detailed map of the area, and on it was a red dot moving away from their position.

"What the hell!" Paul exclaimed. "It's moving. It's moving fast."

George was bemused. "Impossible. It's not supposed to be ready."

"*They* stole it," Paul whispered.

"How long before it's out of radar range?" Jenkins asked.

"At its current speed, about … ten minutes, give or take," Paul replied.

"Why didn't they remove the transponder?" Jenkins wondered aloud.

"The transponder is buried deep inside the circuitry," said George. "It was designed that way on purpose to make it difficult for anyone to tamper with it."

"He's right," Paul concurred. "It would take a long time to remove it without damaging the adjacent components."

George scratched his head. "I still don't understand how they could have

8

taken it."

Jenkins wasn't the type to make rash decisions, but time was now of crucial importance. A decision had to be made based on the available information. And although he didn't like the idea of leaving the compound in the middle of a lockdown, he believed the situation here was stable enough. The lockdown had been implemented in a timely manner. All his men needed to do was stay put until reinforcements arrived. Right now, the highest priority was to make sure the prototype helicopter didn't get away.

"Call the hangar," Jenkins told Paul as he hurried to the door. He signaled two soldiers to come inside. "You two are to remain here and keep this room secured."

"I have the hangar on the line," said Paul.

Jenkins returned to the console. "Put it on speaker."

"Brett here," a voice said.

"Get the chopper ready," Jenkins ordered over the com line. "We're going after the prototype." Without waiting for an acknowledgment, he ended the communication and turned to George. "Stay here, and don't open the door for anyone. There's no telling who might still be out there."

"The prototype is a combat-type model," George remarked. "It's big enough to carry eight people."

"That doesn't mean they're all on board," Jenkins countered. "These two soldiers will remain here with you," he added, nodding at the sentinels by the door. "In the meantime, follow my previous instructions. Restore power to the ground floor and lock everything down."

"Very well," said George without trying to hide his frustration. He kept his eyes on Jenkins as he walked away and noticed him whispering something to the soldiers before leaving the room.

George wasn't happy about abandoning the people in the lower levels. It was one thing to leave the guards down there to maybe have to deal with the remaining prisoners—that was part of their job—but the scientists …

9

Unfortunately, there wasn't much he could do. He had no doubt Jenkins had posted the two sentries inside the control room for security reasons. But he suspected it was also to keep an eye on him and Paul, to make sure they followed orders.

George shot a quick glance at the soldiers. They both had the same stern, uncompromising look on their faces. *No point in trying to appeal to their sense of decency.* "Well, you heard him," he said, turning to his co-worker. "Let's get to work."

Paul winked at him. "Sure thing."

The message from George's tone had been clear. They wouldn't abandon their trapped colleagues. They would try to find a way to help them without the guards noticing.

Chapter 2 – Explosion

Jenkins arrived at the hangar accompanied by six soldiers. As requested, the helicopter was getting ready for take-off. Moving against the wind blasts from the propeller blades, Jenkins and his men hunched as they boarded the aircraft. The two pilots were already running their final checks.

Jenkins put on his helmet and activated his microphone.

"Are you sure about this Mr. Jenkins?" the lead pilot asked. "It's dangerous to fly in this weather."

"I don't care if it's raining grenades, Brett. We're going after them."

Moments later, the helicopter lifted off the ground.

Back inside the control room, George and Paul were working assiduously under the scrutinizing gaze of their *protectors* when someone started punching keys on the security pad outside.

Startled, the two sentries took a quick step back and raised their weapons.

The technicians froze, and their eyes slowly shifted towards the door.

"Who's there?" one of the soldiers shouted.

No reply came.

Paul broke out in a cold sweat. The blood drained from his face and his hands started to shake.

Seeing his colleague on the verge of a panic attack, George tried his best to reassure him. "Don't worry, Paul. Only three people have the code: you, me and Mr. Jenkins. As you know, it's a twelve-digit number, not something you can find by randomly pressing—" George never got to the end of his sentence. His jaw dropped to the floor at the sight of the door sliding open.

"Are we still getting a clear signal from the transponder?" Jenkins asked.

"Yes, sir," Brett replied. "We're still tracking it."

"What about the *Rafale* planes?"

"Our contacts in the French military have confirmed they're on an intercept course. They should reach the target soon."

"Their standing orders are to engage on sight, correct?"

"Yes, sir."

"Good," said Jenkins.

Even though he was relieved to hear the French military had scrambled its fighter jets, Jenkins still wore a pensive frown. The few minutes spent in the back of the helicopter had afforded him time to analyze the situation, and something was troubling him. It was like a nagging doubt repeatedly knocking on a door in the back of his mind. *This whole thing is happening way too fast,* he thought. He knew when it came to *them*, he should expect the unexpected, and assume the impossible could become possible. But he couldn't imagine how they had been able to reach the roof so soon after the alarm. Not only that, he also couldn't help thinking there was something odd about the theft of the prototype helicopter. They had tricked everyone into thinking the prototype wasn't operational yet—even though it was—which meant they had been planning their escape for a while. So why not disable the transponder? Granted they couldn't have known about the fighter planes on standby at a nearby base—very few people knew of this arrangement. Still, Jenkins was unable to shake the feeling that something was off.

His reflections were interrupted by Brett's voice on his headset.

"Sir, the fighter planes have a visual on the target. They're getting ready to engage."

Jenkins gazed out of the window.

Seconds later, a large explosion illuminated the night sky.

"Sir, the French report the target has been destroyed," the pilot confirmed.

"Get us over there," said Jenkins in an uncharacteristically shaky voice. He couldn't believe the chase had been brought to such a swift conclusion.

By the time the helicopter was hovering over the scene of the explosion, the *Rafale* planes were already on their way back to their base.

Jenkins leaned against the window to peer down into the forest, but it was too hard to see through the rain and past the smoke. "Land this thing!" he ordered, his eyes fixed on the flames dancing beneath the trees.

"Roger!" said Brett. He, like his co-pilot, welcomed the decision to return to the ground—neither of them had been thrilled about having to fly in this weather.

After circling the area a couple of times, the craft landed in a clearing about two hundred feet away from where the prototype had gone down.

Jenkins instructed his men to stay alert as they jumped out of the helicopter and headed into the forest, weapons and flashlights in hand.

When they arrived at the wreckage, the rain had already extinguished most of the flames, thereby making it easier to examine the carcass.

On quick inspection, Jenkins saw nothing but charred debris and scraps of metal. "Spread out!" he told his men. "But maintain visual contact at all times."

After scouring the surrounding woods, Jenkins and his men had found no trace of a single passenger.

"Sir, maybe they parachuted out before the explosion," a soldier suggested.

Jenkins thought about it. *No, something else is going on here.*

He decided to abort the search and ordered his men back to the landing site.

When the group arrived at the helicopter, Jenkins climbed into it and told the pilot to patch him through to the control room.

As Brett was attempting to establish communications with the compound, one of the soldiers called everyone's attention to a set of headlights shining through the trees in the opposite direction of the crash site.

Jenkins jumped out of the helicopter and squinted at the lights. They were close and heading straight for them. He was about to signal his men to spread out into a defensive formation when he realized the lights were those of a convoy. "Stand down," he said.

Moments later, an army jeep and three trucks entered the clearing.

As soon as the convoy stopped, soldiers poured out of the trucks and rushed into the forest. A tall man in uniform stepped out of the jeep and approached the helicopter.

Jenkins went to meet him. "Capitaine Le Grand, what are you doing here?"

The man stopped, looking puzzled. "Mr. Jenkins, we're here to help you in your search, of course."

Jenkins frowned. "You and your men were supposed to go to the compound and assist in implementing the lockdown."

"But the lockdown has been lifted," Le Grand replied, looking more and more confused. "The prisoners have escaped, non?"

Jenkins was livid. "Lifted? On whose authority?"

The French captain looked at Jenkins like he was crazy. "Uh … on yours. I spoke to Control myself."

"And you didn't think to verify this with me?"

14

Le Grand became defensive. "Why? You yourself were already engaged in the pursuit. Clearly there was a breach."

The captain had a point. There would have been no reason for him to question the information he had received from Control. Especially since it confirmed what he already knew: Jenkins was giving chase to a group of escapees, and two fighter jets had been dispatched.

Jenkins spun on his heels and hurried back into the helicopter. "Were you able to get control on the line?" he asked the pilot.

"I've been trying … but I can't seem to get through."

"Take us back, right now!"

Jenkins felt a knot tighten in his stomach. The fuzzy doubts that had been floating around in his head were slowly starting to take shape. He had the distinct impression the situation was slipping away from him. Like a block of ice melting inside his hand and turning into freezing water that sent chills throughout his body as it seeped through his fingers.

Capitaine Le Grand watched, incredulous, as Jenkins' soldiers boarded the helicopter in a hurry and took off without a word of explanation.

When Jenkins returned to the compound, he found it in a state of total disarray.

The higher floors of the main building were engulfed in flames. Soldiers ran around in all directions, some trying to contain the fire while others carried men in white blouses to the adjacent structures. Vehicles rolled in and out of the front gate, and dog units were combing the forest just outside the fence.

Jenkins stood on the grass a long time, gazing at the chaotic spectacle. Once his shock subsided, he ran to the main building entrance and grabbed one of the unit leaders by the collar.

"Evans, what the hell is going on here?"

15

"Sir, there was an explosion. We're evacuating the staff and dealing with the fire."

"Evacuating? I gave clear instructions no one was to leave the building."

"But the explosion—"

"The lockdown takes priority!" Jenkins shouted.

"But sir, Control informed us the lockdown was lifted since the prisoners had escaped. They asked us to rescue the scientists and put out the fire."

Jenkins was so enraged he wanted to strangle Evans on the spot. He sent the unit leader on his way and ran into the building, along with the six soldiers who had been following him.

Once they were inside, Jenkins stopped. The lobby looked like a war zone. The air was dusty and filled with smoke—but it was still breathable. The floor was littered with rubble and broken glass from the explosion.

Under the flickering lights, Jenkins spotted a group of soldiers in respirator masks who were evacuating injured people from the lower levels. But as he observed them, Jenkins noticed something peculiar. He marched up to one of the soldiers. "Where did you find these people?"

The soldier turned around and froze, surprised to see Jenkins back so soon. "Sir?"

"Which level did you find them on?" Jenkins pressed.

The harshness of Jenkins' tone shook the soldier out of his stupor. He promptly removed his mask. "Sorry, sir. We've gotten as far as sublevel five. We found them on the various floors as we went down."

"What is their condition?"

"They've suffered minor burns and injuries, but nothing too serious."

"Why are you only evacuating medical and research personnel? What about the guards?"

16

"All the guards we've come across so far were dead, sir. We're prioritizing."

"All of them?"

"Yes, sir."

Jenkins clenched his jaw. This was the worst possible scenario.

He left the soldiers to continue with their rescue efforts and led his men across the lobby and up the staircase.

When Jenkins' group arrived in the second-floor corridor, the scene before them was pretty much what he had expected. There were bodies of dead guards scattered all over. Some had been shot or stabbed, while others looked like they had perished in a terrible car accident.

Jenkins and his men continued past the bodies and made their way to the control room.

The door was open.

Jenkins rushed inside. The two soldiers he had left on guard duty lay motionless on the floor. Paul and George were also down, next to the control panel.

Jenkins instructed his soldiers to check on the four men while he examined the security pad. There was no sign of tampering. *How the hell did they get in?* he wondered.

"Sir," one of his men called out, "the civilians are alive."

"And the guards?" Jenkins asked.

"Both dead, sir."

Jenkins frowned. It was the same report the soldier in the lobby had given him. Every armed man had been killed, but the non-combatants had been spared.

"Wake them up," Jenkins ordered, nodding at the technicians.

George was the first to regain consciousness. He looked around, dazed and disoriented.

Paul woke up next. "Ouch ... my head hurts," he muttered, still lying on his back.

"Yeah ... mine too," said George as he sat up and tried to get his bearings.

"Snap out of it!" Jenkins barked.

George looked up at him. He was still struggling to regain full use of his senses. "Mr. Jenkins ... you're back. What happened?"

"*That* is what *you* are going to tell me."

"Ah! We were attacked!" said Paul in a flash of lucidity.

"Yes," George confirmed. "They came here ... they attacked us."

"How did they get in?" Jenkins asked.

George's gaze mechanically homed in on the keypad by the door. With great effort, he was able to pull the blurry images scrambled inside his head back into focus. "They knew the passcode ... they also had a key card. They simply walked in. How did they know the code?"

"What happened then?" Jenkins pressed.

"I'm not sure," George replied. "I think the guards opened fire ... something hit me on the head ... next thing I know, I woke up and here you were."

"Same here," said Paul as he rubbed the small bump on his head.

Realizing he wouldn't extract any worthwhile information from the two survivors, Jenkins had them taken away to be checked out by a doctor.

Then, he stood still and took stock of the situation.

There was no longer any doubt. The prisoners had somehow taken over the control room during his absence. From here, they had created enough chaos and confusion to escape unnoticed. It was a safe bet they were gone by now, but they couldn't have gone too far yet.

There was no time to waste.

After he had ordered everyone out, Jenkins pulled out his cell phone and dialed. While the line was ringing, he glanced at the digital clock on the console in front of him. It was a quarter past ten.

It took four rings before someone picked up on the other end.

"Yes?"

"I'm sorry to disturb you at this hour, Mr. Leicester," said Jenkins, "but it's urgent. We've had a breach."

Chapter 3 – Secret Meetings

The city of Paris is surrounded by a large dual loop beltway called the *Boulevard Périphérique*. Believed to be one of Europe's busiest highways, the *Boulevard Périphérique* can get very congested during rush hour. However, under normal conditions, it's a convenient way to move around Paris. There are no traffic lights; access in and out of the city occurs at one of thirty-four junctions called *portes—or gates*.

At around 4:20 the following morning, a car arrived at the *Porte d'Auteuil*, in the southwest part of Paris. The car pulled up in front of a flower shop on a side road close to the main intersection. The driver turned off the engine and stepped out of the vehicle. He was a round older man with thinning hair. His tight khaki pants, green-striped yellow shirt, and brown jacket exhibited a blatant disregard for fashion, whereas his well-trimmed mustache and neat gray beard indicated a certain attention to grooming.

Standing on the pavement, the man carefully surveyed his surroundings through the small pair of glasses perched on the tip of his nose. The streets were deserted, as was typically the case at such hour in that part of the city.

He stayed close to his car, nervously fiddling with his keys as he waited. He imagined himself in one of those movies where spies exchange coded messages during secret meetings at night. And when the occasional vehicle drove up past the main intersection, he would look on, holding his breath, until it drove away.

After a while, he checked the watch on his wrist.

It had been four minutes—though it had felt several times longer.

"Professor!" a woman's voice called in a loud whisper.

Startled, the old man jumped and dropped his keys.

A woman and a man emerged from the shadows and approached him. They both looked to be in their mid-twenties. They had on black army boots that seemed one or two sizes too big, and dark blue military jackets which fit them even less. Underneath the big boots and large jacket, each wore a skin-tight black outfit reminiscent of a professional diver's suit.

The woman was of medium height, with a slender body and long dark hair running down her back. She spoke in a soft and measured voice. "Sorry, we didn't mean to scare you."

"You're here. You're really here!" said the old man, his voice trembling with excitement.

The young man moved closer. "Hello, Professor!"

He was a bit taller than her and could have easily passed for a Bollywood actor.

The professor gazed at them with teary eyes. "My children, I can't believe it. When I received your message … I didn't dare to hope." He closed his eyes and smiled with contentment as he gave each one a heartfelt hug.

"It's not safe to stay out in the open like this," the woman said.

"Yes. Quite right," the old man agreed. He turned around and picked up his keys. Then, the three of them quickly climbed into the vehicle and drove away.

At the same time, a few miles north-east, in the Eighth District of Paris, a dark SUV pulled up in front of a limestone building.

A man wearing blue jeans and a black sweater stepped out of the passenger side and walked into the building. As soon as he passed through the glass doors, he was stopped by security agents in dark suits. He had been expecting them. Without a word, one of the agents extended a hand towards him. The man reached for the gun tucked in the back of his jeans and handed it over. Another agent approached and scanned him with a hand-held metal detector. Once the agents were satisfied he wasn't carrying any other weapons, they moved aside to let him through.

The man walked across the lobby to a set of elevators, pressed the button, and waited. Although he had not seen or heard anything during his short walk, he could sense there were more security agents lurking in shadows and lying in wait behind closed doors.

The elevator arrived with a chime. The man stepped into the carriage and rode up to the top floor.

More men were waiting for him at his destination, where he underwent another round of thorough inspection. Once it was over, a security agent escorted him along the hallway to a double door.

The agent knocked.

"Come in," a voice said.

The agent opened the door but remained outside.

The man entered a conference room with no windows and a large oval table that took up most of the space. He spotted Patrick Jenkins standing at the far end of the room. Three people were seated at the table, facing Jenkins. One of them, a clean-shaven man with grayish hair and a matching-colored suit, called out to him in a posh British accent.

"Mr. Carson, I'm glad you could make it on such short notice. Please, join us."

Carson glanced back as the door closed behind him, before walking over to them. "Good morning, Mr. Leicester."

Andrew Leicester checked the shiny gold watch on his wrist. "I suppose 'good morning' is correct." He then started the introductions. "This is Karl Schaffer and Nathalie Renard," he said, indicating with the man and the woman seated on either side of him. "Karl, Nathalie, this is Mr. Randall Carson. He's an old associate of mine, and he's worked with Mr. Jenkins on numerous occasions in the past."

22

Carson glanced at Jenkins and greeted him with a quick nod. Jenkins responded in kind.

"I'm afraid we've started without you, Mr. Carson," said Leicester. "To summarize, we had an incident at our facility near the French-German border. Mr. Jenkins can fill you in on the details later." Leicester leaned back in his chair and crossed his legs under the table. "Please continue Mr. Jenkins."

Jenkins resumed his report. "Once I realized Control had been compromised, I left Capitaine Le Grand and his men to proceed with their search and returned to the facility. Upon arrival, I confirmed the lockdown had been lifted."

"Who gave the order to lift the lockdown?" the woman asked in a strong French accent. Her tone was curt and antagonistic. She was eyeing Jenkins from behind a pair of glasses that looked too big against her long gaunt face.

"The unit leaders had received instructions directly from Control," Jenkins replied.

"And no one thought to verify those orders with you?"

"They knew I was in pursuit of the stolen prototype. Besides, they were given the correct authorization codes."

"Please go on," said Leicester.

"The compound was in a state of total chaos. A search was underway in and around the premises, and the main building was being evacuated. There had been an explosion. No doubt to create an added distraction. Anyway, I went up to the control room and confirmed it had been breached."

"How?" the woman asked.

"They knew the passcode and had a key card. Like the technicians said, they simply walked in."

Leicester was surprised. "The technicians are alive?"

23

"Yes," said Jenkins, "as were all the scientists. Only guards and soldiers were killed."

"Odd," said Leicester. "What do you make of that?"

Jenkins let out a faint sigh. "I'm not sure. Maybe they only killed those who tried to stop them from escaping. Or maybe they're sending us a message: Stay out of our way and we won't cause you any trouble."

"Or maybe they were taunting you," Renard croaked.

"Perhaps," said Jenkins.

"It doesn't matter!" Schaffer declared, breaking his silence at last. He spoke with a raspy voice and a slight German accent. He had thick eyebrows and his dark brown hair shot off in every direction, like a frozen firework explosion.

Up until now, Schaffer had seemed content to stare into space as he sat sunk into his chair with his hands buried deep inside his long black overcoat. He had been facing away from the others the entire time and still hadn't bothered to look at them as he spoke. All eyes converged on him, expecting he would elaborate on his comment. But it soon became clear from his demeanor that, at least for the time being, those three words would constitute the sum total of his contribution to the conversation.

"I thought this place was equipped with state of the art security," said Renard, pursuing her unrelenting criticism of Jenkins. "It certainly costs us enough money for it."

"It is," Jenkins confirmed. "There are over a hundred soldiers and private security personnel posted in and around the compound at all times. The grounds are equipped with cameras, motion sensors, and heat sensors. Of course, the most sensitive areas are in the lower levels of the main building, access there is highly restricted. The whole of sublevel one serves as a buffer security zone. On the floors below, there are armed sentinels posted at every point of entry, and all main access doors are electronically sealed and fitted with a number of security measures: key card access, palm print scan, retinal scan, voice authentication, etc. Even the scientists complained it was too much trouble just getting around."

"So how did they escape?" Renard asked.

"Our engineers are still looking into it. Preliminary reports suggest they may have used the weather."

Renard wasn't sure she had heard him correctly. "The weather?"

"Yes. Lightning to be exact. They rigged the circuitry and redirected lightning strikes to short out the power systems, including the back-ups. Soon after that, we heard the prototype helicopter flying away from the base. I decided to give chase and called for air support."

"What did Capitaine Le Grand report back from the crash site?" Leicester asked.

"They didn't find any bodies. Or any other trace of the prisoners."

"We prefer the term subjects, Mr. Jenkins."

"Of course, sir."

Renard frowned. "Are you trying to tell us the damn thing flew itself?"

"Yes, I'm guessing it was either remote-controlled or on auto-pilot."

"I was under the impression the prototype wasn't operational yet," Leicester remarked.

"That's what we were led to believe. The prototype is highly computerized. Our engineers are now speculating that its unsuccessful launches were not due to a mechanical issue as we previously thought, but rather to some sort of software block. The priso … the subjects must have planted some kind of virus."

Nathalie Renard erupted in anger. "What were you doing all this time? Wasn't anybody watching these people? I'm beginning to think they could have built a spaceship down there without any of you noticing."

Jenkins ground his teeth.

"Come now," said Leicester, turning to Renard. "It may be tempting to lay all the blame at Mr. Jenkins' feet, but the truth is we should all have been more vigilant. It hasn't been a year since you were appointed France's representative on this project following the tragic accident which claimed the life of your predecessor. And while I'm sure you've familiarized yourself with all relevant files, you cannot yet truly comprehend what we are dealing with."

Renard leaned back in her chair and crossed her arms over her berry-colored sheath dress. "If you say so, Andrew."

Patrick Jenkins was a career soldier and a pragmatist, the kind of man who preferred to focus on the problems in front of him rather than mull over past decisions. "Should I assemble a team to track down the fugitives?" he asked.

Even though Jenkins' suggestion had come in the form of a question, it was more a rhetorical question than an actual inquiry. The answer, he thought, could not have been more obvious, which was why he, like all the others in the room, looked as though the floor had just vanished from under his feet when Leicester replied, "Not yet."

Renard nearly fell out of her chair. Before Jenkins could ask the reason for this incomprehensible objection, she was already complaining to the Briton. "Not yet? You want to wait? Are you insane, Andrew?"

"My dear Nathalie, please calm down," said Leicester. "We can't afford to make any rash decisions. There are certain delicate aspects of this situation which we need to take into consideration."

Renard stared at him wide-eyed. She could not believe what she was hearing. "Karl, talk some sense into him, will you?" she said to her German counterpart.

But to her astonishment, Schaffer sided against her. "Andrew's right. We can't have Mr. Jenkins and his men running around in the streets. We cannot risk exposure. The project is too important."

"Indeed," said Leicester. "We need to proceed with extreme caution. Someone else should lead the search for the fugitives, someone who'll be free

26

to move around in the open. This will allow Mr. Jenkins to operate more discreetly, thereby protecting his anonymity, and ours. We'll need to procure the services of professionals, people who are reliable but also expendable, in case things take a turn for the worse. They would also have to be outsiders, with no connection to any of us."

Outnumbered two to one, Nathalie Renard did not insist further. She didn't like the idea of delaying the search, but she understood the need for discretion given the stakes. Having calmed down a little, she asked her associates, "And just how long do you imagine it will take us to find the sort of people you described?"

A smile flickered across Leicester's lips. "As it happens, I may already have a solution."

Chapter 4 – Proceedings

Later that day, at 5:18 p.m., a black limousine with diplomatic plates pulled up in front of a building inside the US military facility Joint Base Andrews, located in Maryland.

A soldier approached the limousine and opened the rear passenger-side door. A tall man in an expensive-looking gray suit alighted from the vehicle. He was greeted by a small man in a blue suit and by an officer in uniform.

"Good morning, Mr. Leicester!" said the small man. "You probably don't remember me. My name is Matthew Hall. We met during your last visit to Washington, at Senator Stanton's house. I was working as his aide back then."

"Of course, Matthew. I trust you've been well."

"Very well sir, thank you. This is Major Harris!"

The major extended his hand. "Pleasure to meet you, Mr. Leicester."

"Major." Leicester shook the officer's hand and then turned to Hall. "Has it started?"

"Yes, about twenty minutes ago. The general was eager to get on with the proceedings."

"Has he been briefed yet?"

"No, sir." The former aide exchanged an uneasy look with the officer. "As you know Mr. Leicester, this is very unconventional. The major and I thought it best to wait until you arrived."

"Hmm … I suppose there's no harm in it," said Leicester. "Quite the opposite, in fact."

"I'm sorry, I don't follow," said Hall.

"It may be easier to persuade our friends after they've had first-hand experience of the general's … resolve in this matter."

"I see what you mean, sir."

"Shall we go?" said Leicester.

"Of course, this way please." Major Harris steered the two visitors inside the building.

The proceedings in question began with a preliminary hearing to determine whether or not a court-martial could, and should, be held. A panel of five officers, led by Brigadier General John McKenner, presided over the session.

Through the years, McKenner had acquired a solid reputation for being an intransigent hard-liner. He believed in following the rules and was notorious for his aversion to compromise. So it came as no surprise to the people who knew him that he had used all of his influence to find himself at the head of this particular panel.

Inside the hearing room, opposite the panel of judges, two smartly dressed men were seated at the table of the accused, listening to an officer's detailed account of the events that had brought all of them here.

At the end of the officer's testimony, McKenner glowered at the accused. "You're already aware of the charges against you. Now, after hearing the captain's report, do you have anything to add in your defense?"

The man sitting on the right leaned towards the microphone placed in front of him. "Yes, General. As the captain mentioned, my team located the drugs and weapons cache and was successful in destroying it. But after the explosion, enemy reinforcements arrived faster than anticipated. Our escape route was blocked. We were forced to search for an alternative route back to the rendezvous point where we had agreed to meet with the captain and—"

"Why weren't the captain and his men with you?" the general interrupted. "You were supposed to complete the mission together, were you not?"

"After we surveyed the site, I re-evaluated our plan of action."

"Why?" McKenner asked in a forceful tone.

"The place was too well guarded. More than the intelligence report had estimated. I decided it was best to send in a smaller unit, one who could sneak in under the cover of darkness. The unit consisted of myself, my second-in-command, and my explosives expert, who is sitting here with me today." He paused to collect his thoughts. Some of the officers on the base had obtained permission to attend the closed-door session. They sat in rows of benches behind him, listening with ardent interest. Even without looking back, the accused could sense the deep hostility they harbored towards him and the co-accused. He tried his best to ignore them as he resumed his explanation. "We were able to find a new route to the meeting point. But it caused us to approach from a different direction than the captain had been expecting. And the enemy was right on our six. We were coming in hot. The forest was dense, it was dark … I guess some of the captain's men got jumpy when they spotted us. Next thing we knew, they opened fire on us, and—"

McKenner thumped his fist on the table. "And your man ended up killing a United States Army soldier and wounding two others."

"He didn't mean to do it. They never gave us a chance to identify ourselves."

"Mr. Kincade!" the general growled. "As a former officer yourself, I'm sure you understand that the actions of your men in the field are ultimately your responsibility."

"Yes, General. I do."

"Good. Now, I would like to hear from the man next to you."

Kincade leaned back in his chair and shot a concerned glance at the co-accused to his left. Even sitting down, the man was an imposing figure. His perfectly shaved head glistened under the ceiling lights as he leaned forward towards the microphone. He looked up at the officers on the podium and waited.

After a while, the general frowned and said, "Well?"

"Well what?"

"Don't you have anything to add?"

"Not really."

McKenner was so infuriated by the man's cavalier attitude that veins were starting to bulge on his neck and forehead. It required every last bit of self-control in his body to keep from ordering the entire team be thrown in jail without further deliberation. But the general was determined to maintain the integrity of the proceedings. "Did you know whom you were firing at?" he asked.

"Yeah," the big man replied. "I shot the guys who were shooting at me."

The audience grumbled in disbelief.

Kincade squeezed the armrests of his chair in frustration. He wondered if it wouldn't be less damaging to snatch the microphone away from his tactless comrade.

"You admit to having deliberately returned friendly fire?" the general pressed on, still half-stunned.

"What's that?" the huge man asked.

The entire panel, including McKenner, stared back at him with puzzled gazes.

"Friendly fire," the man repeated, "what's that?" But seeing that the fog of confusion was still heavy over their eyes, he attempted to dissipate it. "Look, I don't know about you, but when someone starts shooting at me … we're not friends anymore."

The general was speechless, as were all the other members of the

31

assembly. This was simply not an answer they had ever expected to hear. The utter lack of remorse from the accused was not something any of them had ever considered.

But soon, the initial shock gave way to anger.

General McKenner, in particular, was beside himself with rage. "Do you think this is a joking matter?" he yelled. "I will personally see to it the both of you serve the maximum sentence for this. As for the rest of your team, they will not—"

The general was interrupted when Major Harris barged into the room. The major ran up to the panel and paused to salute. "I have an urgent message for you General."

McKenner glowered at him. "Can't you see we're in the middle of a session?"

"My apologies, sir, but I was instructed to deliver it right away."

A little intrigued, the general nodded for the major to approach.

McKenner took the piece of paper handed to him and unfolded it. The room fell silent as he began reading the document. But as the general's eyes traveled down the sheet of paper, his expression gradually changed. By the time he reached the end, he looked like a man who had been condemned to the firing squad. He glared at the major. "What's the meaning of this?"

The major leaned down and whispered something in his ear.

After a long pause, General McKenner announced an adjournment to the proceedings without offering any explanations. Baffled gazes bounced around the room as the General shot up from his seat and left at a hurried pace.

Major Harris walked over to the accused. "Come with me please."

Escorted by four soldiers, Kincade and his comrade followed the Major out. He led the group up a staircase to a room one floor above. Once there, the Major opened the door and waved the accused inside while the four soldiers stood guard on the outside.

After the Kincade and his companion had gone in, the Major closed the door and left.

A man in casual attire that showed his trim and athletic figure was waiting inside.

"Doc, what are you doing here?" Kincade asked him.

"They moved me here ten minutes ago and told me to wait for you guys. How did it go with the general?"

Kincade spun around and glowered at his companion. "Why don't you ask this idiot?"

By any common standard, Kincade would be considered taller than average—with a muscular body forged through years of rigorous training. But despite his more than respectable frame, he was dwarfed by the colossus planted in front of him.

Kincade stared up at a towering mass of bones and muscles on top of which rested a polished head. A head whose hard but smooth features were evocative of a bust carved out of solid rock by some skilled sculptor. *Rock*. Incidentally, that was his nickname—the name given to him by the other members of the team. It had started as a joke, when he had won a bet that he could crack open a coconut with his head. From that moment on, the name had stuck with him. He didn't mind. He had gotten used to it over time.

The giant put on an innocent air. "What did I do this time?"

Kincade was furious. "What the hell were you thinking back there?"

"Hey, you said to tell the truth," Rock protested.

"No one told you to be a smart-ass."

"Hehehe! I don't know, I think they were starting to warm up to us."

"You think this is funny?"

The big guy bowed his head and apologized. "All right, I'm sorry, Nate."

Despite the dire nature of their situation, a fleeting smile passed across Doc's face as he observed the interaction between his two comrades. Unconsciously, Kincade had narrowed the distance between him and the giant, thereby emphasizing their considerable size difference. Watching Kincade berate the hulking figure was like watching a child scold an adult.

Kincade sighed and moved away. "Forget it. What's done is done."

"I wonder what that interruption was about," said Rock.

Doc looked intrigued. "I was going to ask you. How come the hearing was so brief? An interruption, was it?"

"Some kind of emergency," Kincade replied. "An officer showed up with an urgent message for the general. Next thing we know, the trial is adjourned and they take us here."

"Must have been serious," said Doc. "McKenner's been itching to send you both to jail, and maybe even the rest of us along with you."

Rock shrugged. "Today … next week … what difference does it make? It's not like they're going to forget about us."

Kincade rubbed the stubble on his chin. "Still, we should call in a few favors and see what we can find out about this document."

"Favors?" said Rock. "From who?"

Kincade raised an eyebrow. "You've spent how many years in the military again? Didn't you make any other friends?"

"Uh … no."

Kincade facepalmed. "Why do I even bother? Anyway, I can think of a couple of guys who still owe me one. I'll see if—"

"That will not be necessary, Mr. Kincade. I can tell you what you want to know."

Chapter 5 – Unexpected Offer

A man was standing in the doorway with his hands inside his pockets, smiling. He waited a moment, seemingly amused by the dumbfounded looks directed at him. Then, he stepped into the room and motioned to the soldiers standing guard outside to close the door.

"There. Now we can have some privacy."

Kincade sized up the visitor. "Who are you?"

"My name is Andrew Leicester," the man replied. "And you are Jonathan Kincade, former lieutenant colonel in the United States Marine Corps, dishonorably discharged about four years ago, and at present the leader of a group of … shall we say *contractors*? Your team handles various types of assignments in the more challenging parts of the world, ranging from security for high-value officials to black ops interventions."

"You can use the word *mercenaries*," said Kincade. "We don't mind."

"Of course," said Leicester. "And if I'm not mistaken, these are two of your associates." Leicester walked over to Doc. "Mr. Hulin Chen, doctor and former captain in the Army of the People's Republic of China. How do you do?"

Doc greeted him with a nod.

"I must confess," said Leicester, "I'd be curious to hear about the circumstances which have led you to join this particular group. That information was not in any of our files."

"It's a long story," said Doc.

"I'm sure," Leicester replied. He moved over to Rock. "Our files, however, do contain ample information about you. Richard Reinhart, former

Marine. You served seven years under the command of Lieutenant Colonel Kincade and ended up being discharged alongside him and three other men in your unit. About a year later, the five of you and Mr. Chen decided to band together. You've been working as mercenaries since." He turned to Kincade. "Would you say this information was accurate?"

"Pretty much," said Kincade. "Now what do you want? Did General McKenner send you?"

Leicester laughed. "No, I've never had the pleasure of meeting the general."

"Then I'll ask again. What do you want?"

"From what I gather, you currently find yourselves in a bit of a predicament."

"I guess that's one way to put it," said Kincade, "but it still doesn't answer my question."

"I have a proposition for you. A job, if you will."

The three captives stared at the Briton with conflicting sentiments. They didn't know whether to laugh at his ridiculous statement or to get angry at him for making light of their *predicament*, as he put it.

Rock walked over to the visitor. "It's Andrew, right?"

Leicester gazed up at him and gave a slight nod.

"For a guy who seems to know so much, it looks like you missed the part about us being busy for the next … what, fifteen to twenty years. I guess you haven't heard, but the Army wants to offer us an all-expenses-paid vacation at one of their top-class establishments."

Leicester brushed off the objection. "That won't be a problem, Mr. Reinhart."

The room immediately fell silent.

From the moment he had walked in, Leicester had been wearing the

36

same knowing smile. And nothing, it seemed, could make him part from it, not even for an instant.

Is this guy for real? Kincade asked himself as he observed Leicester. Under normal circumstances, he would have dismissed the bold claim as either an idle boast or a tasteless attempt at humor. At which point the Briton would have found himself unceremoniously thrown out the door—or the window—for his troubles. But fortunately for Leicester, the fact that he was standing there in the first place gave him all the credibility he needed.

Even though Kincade and his team were no longer soldiers, McKenner had used all of his influence to have them treated as such. He had insisted on handling the matter internally, citing the secret nature of their mission and the fact that Kincade and his men had spent years in the military.

This is a crime against soldiers committed by their fellow soldiers, the general had argued.

As a result, following their incarceration, the mercenaries had had very little contact with anyone. Only a handful of people had been allowed to meet with them, and they had all been Army personnel, including the lawyers. Leicester was the first civilian they had seen in over two months.

There's no way this guy's a lawyer, Kincade thought, gazing at Leicester. So why had this civilian, a British citizen, been allowed to talk to them in private?

Whatever the answer was, Kincade imagined it would still fall a long way short of securing his team's release. A wary frown formed on his face. "Are you claiming to be able to get us out of this mess?"

"Yes," said Leicester, "but that would be up to you."

"Meaning?"

"As I said, I have a job for you. If you agree to take it and manage to complete the mission, all charges against you will be dismissed."

"Just like that?" said Doc.

"Just like that."

37

"You make it sound simple," said Kincade.

Leicester laughed again. "Oh, I assure you, Mr. Kincade, it wasn't. But despite McKenner's passionate arguments, the fact remains you and your men are no longer soldiers. That's all the leverage someone like me needs to pry you away from the general's sphere of influence. Having said that, we did have to make quite a few concessions to your government in order to reach this agreement."

"Who's 'we'?" Doc asked.

"I oversee a special branch of the UK government, working in close collaboration with similar branches in other countries."

"That didn't sound vague at all," Rock said in a sarcastic tone.

"And the concessions?" Kincade asked.

"I'm afraid I can't get into those details," said Leicester. "But I can tell you that your government stands to gain a lot from this deal. You would be doing your country a great service by accepting my offer."

"You mean the people who are trying to lock us up?" Rock remarked.

"Point taken, Mr. Reinhart. I was merely appealing to Mr. Kincade's sense of patriotism."

Sense of patriotism, huh? How many times have I heard those words? Kincade wondered.

At his core, Jonathan Kincade was still a soldier. He had enlisted at a relatively young age and had never looked back. He recalled how, as a new recruit, notions of right and wrong had seemed so clear to him. And how, like many others, he had been so quick to throw around slogans about democracy and freedom, all the while lacking the wisdom to appreciate their true meaning.

However, years of traveling around the world, experiencing different cultures, and fighting in various conflicts had chipped away at his naiveté. He had in no way become a cynic. But he had learned to see the world for what it

38

truly was: *a work in progress*. A portrait painted in various shades of gray, in which it was sometimes hard to discern where *right* ended and where *wrong* began.

He still believed in the values instilled in him as a young man. But too often he had seen people in power use those beliefs and ideals to further their personal agendas. They would cloak themselves in the mantle of patriotism in order to manipulate the masses, all the while pursuing their own selfish goals.

Following his discharge from the military four years ago, Kincade had spent several months working as a security advisor for a high-profile firm. He had found the job through his former commanding officer, and after a shaky start, he had eventually adjusted to his new career quite well. It was far less perilous than his previous occupation. And the money didn't hurt either. His life looked set to go down a smooth new path, until a chance encounter had caused it to take an unexpected turn.

He remembered it had been hot that night. But a cool breeze had slithered through the city, tempering the summer heat. Kincade had opted to walk home instead of using the Metro as he normally would. It had been a really long day, most of it spent trying to accommodate the unreasonable requests of a difficult client. He had decided to take a stroll through the streets, hoping the fresh air would help vent the day's frustrations.

Kincade hadn't been walking for very long when someone called out to him from across the road. He immediately spotted Rock—never a difficult task, even in the larger crowds. The giant was accompanied by two familiar faces: Armando Da Costa and Sean Riley. All three had served under Kincade's command for many years. And like him, all three had been discharged from the military following a diplomatic incident during which they had chosen to side with Kincade in defiance of orders and regulations.

The trio insisted their former commanding officer join them for a drink. He agreed and accompanied them to a popular bar.

The four men spent most of the night reminiscing about their years of service and dredging up old anecdotes.

39

They parted ways just before dawn, leaving Kincade with barely enough time to get a couple of hours' rest before heading back to work.

Seeing his men again had filled Kincade with a sense of nostalgia. He had been glad to spend time with them, but he had also picked up on something else. Whenever he had asked the trio about their plans for the future, their answers had been vague and uneasy.

Since the day of their sentencing, Kincade had made it a point to keep in touch with the four members of his unit who had been discharged alongside him. Each time, he would insist they not hesitate to contact him if they ever needed anything, and each time they would claim to be getting by just fine. He knew at least one of them did. He had met up with the fourth member of the group, Benjamin Green, two weeks prior, and had been pleased to see that the former major was doing well for himself. But after the previous night, Kincade realized the same could not be said for his other former subordinates. He kicked himself for not noticing sooner. After all, it should have come to no surprise to him. A soldier's life was all this bunch had ever known. They couldn't be expected to seamlessly transition into civilian society. Rock and Da Costa in particular. Those two were severely lacking in the most basic social skills.

Kincade felt responsible. It was because of him they had abruptly been thrust into this new life for which they were so woefully unprepared.

Two days later, he quit his job.

He gathered his men and proposed that they form a team of *freelancers*.

The men were all reluctant at first, sensing Kincade had made the decision for their sake rather than his own.

But Kincade was adamant. "I'm doing this with or without you guys, but I'd rather have people I trust watching my back."

And thus, their mercenary team was formed.

Hulin Chen—whom they called *Doc* because he was a medical officer— joined them two weeks later.

Kincade and Chen shared a long and complicated history weaved with threads of improbable events and unusual circumstances. Their friendship had always been a tricky proposition due to their standings in their respective countries' armed forces. But it had endured nonetheless. Kincade used to joke it could be fun to bet on which one of them would be the first to mysteriously vanish off the face of the earth someday. Oddly enough, Doc saw the humor in it too. The only reason they never made the bet was that the loser wouldn't be around to pay up.

It was after receiving a cryptic message from Doc Chen that Kincade and four of his men had taken that fateful covert trip to Hong Kong. Their decision had kicked off a series of events resulting in a major diplomatic incident which had ended up changing the lives of all those involved.

"I take it from your silence you're considering my offer," said Leicester.

Kincade looked up. The Briton was staring at him, waiting, smiling.

On the face of it, the choice was an easy one. Just about anything was preferable to jail. Common sense dictated they accept Leicester's proposition. But experience had taught Kincade that when something sounded too good to be true, it usually was. He walked up to Leicester and stared him straight in the eye. "What's the catch?"

"I understand your skepticism," said Leicester, "but there's no catch, except that it's a complex and dangerous assignment. One which requires the utmost discretion."

"OK," said Kincade, "let's hear it. What exactly is this assignment?"

"You understand, of course, there's very little I can share with you at this time."

Kincade nodded. "I understand."

Leicester started ambling around the room. "For several years now, the British, French and German governments have been collaborating on a special project."

"Special how?" Rock asked.

"I'm afraid I can't divulge that information."

"Figures."

"I'll get straight to the point," said Leicester. "We had a breach last night. Eight of our scientists ran away from the secret facility where the project in question was housed."

"Ran away?" Doc noted. "Were they being kept there against their will?"

"Most people involved in the project were confined to the facility for security reasons."

"I see ... what is it you want from us?"

"Simple. Track down the scientists. Bring them in."

"That's it?" Kincade asked.

"That's it."

"Even if we agreed to this," said Doc, "wouldn't they be long gone by now?"

"No," Leicester replied.

"How can you be so sure?"

"They're searching for an item, Mr. Chen, a very important item. It was hidden some time ago by a former associate of mine. It's believed to be somewhere in Western Europe. They will not go far until they've found it."

Kincade was perplexed. "If that's true, it should be easy for you to track them down yourself. You seem like a guy who has people to handle this kind of stuff. Why come to us?"

Leicester sighed. "As it turns out, Mr. Kincade, our options are far more limited than you might think."

"How so?"

"Only a handful of people are aware of the project's existence, even within our respective governments. It's a … an off-the-books project if you will. And for good reason, I assure you." Leicester marked a pause to choose his words. "Our runaway scientists are in possession of top-secret information. And the item they're searching for is also of a very sensitive nature. We would prefer not to involve the police. Even our own secret services cannot be trusted to handle this matter. All it would take is one curious department head, or one overzealous agent, and the entire project could be compromised. The fugitives are aware of this, which is why they can afford to stay close and look for the hidden item."

Kincade and Doc exchanged a furtive glance. They wondered about the reason for all this secrecy, and about the nature of this *sensitive item*. But they knew better than to ask.

Leicester didn't notice their silent consultation, or at least pretended not to. "The good news," he continued, "is that we can expect them to confine their movements to Western Europe. This will give us an opportunity to apprehend them, which is where you come in. Your—"

"Hold on," Kincade interrupted. "If you can't trust your own secret services to handle the matter, what makes you think you can trust us? What if we come across this *important information* you seem so concerned about?"

"Ah, yes. She said you'd ask me this," Leicester replied.

"She?"

"Yes. My top analyst ran a full profile on your team. Incidentally, she's also the one who recommended you to me."

"Anybody we know?" Kincade asked.

"No. You don't know her," Leicester replied.

Kincade's brow twitched. For the first time since he had shown up, a hint of uneasiness had filtered through the Briton's façade.

"Why did she recommend us?" Doc asked.

"Two reasons," said Leicester. "One, because your profile suggests you will be far more interested in securing this deal than in meddling in the affairs of some foreign nations."

"That's for damn sure!" Rock exclaimed.

"Even so," said Doc, "you'd still be taking a risk."

"Perhaps," Leicester replied, "but it's a calculated one. My analyst assures me we can rely on your discretion. She doesn't believe you to be motivated by greed, which I think is a rare quality for people in your line of work. And since you're not formally affiliated with any government, there would be no conflict of interest."

"You seem to place a lot of trust in that analyst of yours," said Doc. "I find it interesting because you don't strike me as the trusting type."

"I'm not," said Leicester.

"And the second reason?" Kincade asked.

"Simple. We believe you to be a very capable group."

"Yeah, well … we have our moments," Rock boasted.

Leicester was amused by the comment. "I'm sure you do, Mr. Reinhart." The Briton made his way to the door. "I wish I could grant you ample time to consider my offer, but time is of crucial importance for this mission. I have business back in Washington but Mr. Hall will remain here, on the base. You can get in touch with me through him, or through Major Harris. I leave for London at seven o'clock tonight. I'll expect your answer by then. I do hope you accept, in which case we'll meet again soon."

With that, the Briton left.

The three captives stared at the closed door for a while, until at last, Kincade said, "And here I thought our day couldn't get any more interesting. What do you guys think?"

44

"I say we go for it!" Rock exclaimed. The excitement in his voice was almost palpable. The prospect of avoiding prison altogether was more than he had ever hoped for. He couldn't believe their luck. The strange British guy had thrown them a rope, a way out of the very deep hole they had been trapped in for the past two months.

Kincade thought the same, but he also couldn't help but wonder about the real cost of such a bargain. He knew there would inevitably be a heavy price to pay once they reached the other end of the providential lifeline.

Doc moved closer to him. "I'm thinking the same thing you are, Nate. There has to be more to it than Leicester let on. But we don't really have a choice, do we?"

Kincade sighed. "No, I guess we don't."

As the two men stood facing each other, pondering the unexpected offer, Rock moved between them and spread his massive arms over their shoulders. A wide contented grin stretched across his face. "Come on guys, let's go catch some geeks!"

Chapter 6 – Ghost

"*Danke.*"

The old man took the change handed to him by the woman behind the cash register and put it in his pocket. He then picked up his bag of groceries and started walking away.

"*Auf Wiedersehen!*" she called out as he passed through the sliding doors.

He gave her a timid wave and exited the convenience store.

I should have put on a coat, he thought as soon as he stepped outside. It was cold in Berlin that night, and his green short-sleeved shirt and khaki pants provided little protection from the chilled breeze.

He stopped to gaze up at the night sky. Not a single star had managed to pierce through the thick layer of clouds; only a blurry moon struggled to fend off the dark mist.

The cold wind picked up, calling the man's attention back to more earthly concerns. He started moving again at a hurried pace.

Five minutes later, he arrived in front of his apartment building. As he reached for his keys, the door opened and an old lady came out. She was his first-floor neighbor.

She greeted him in her usual formal manner. "*Guten Abend, Herr Schmidt.*"

"*Guten Abend, Frau* Krause," he replied.

Schmidt. It had been many years since he had first started using the name, and yet it still sounded strange to his ears. He checked his watch. It was 8:30 p.m. *Regular as clockwork,* he thought. Frau Krause always walked her dog twice a day at the exact same times.

She left the door open for him and strutted off with her poodle.

Schmidt went in and turned to the bank of mail slots to the left of the entrance. He opened his box and retrieved a stack of letters. After sifting through them, he tossed a couple of leaflets into the recycling bin at his feet, closed the mailbox, and pulled on the staircase door. The building was fitted with an elevator but he preferred to take the stairs. It was an old habit of his, a way of adding a little exercise to his daily routine.

He climbed up to the third floor, walked over to the apartment at the end of the hallway, and turned his key inside the lock.

The door opened into a narrow entrance hall. He switched on the lights and locked the door behind him. There was a small table along the wall. He tossed his keys onto it, between a small plant and a science magazine, and proceeded into the apartment. As he walked past the kitchen, he dropped the grocery bag on the floor and continued into the living room. There, he sank into the sofa, turned on the television, and started going through his mail.

Moments later, as he was looking over his first bill, he heard a noise behind him.

It had seemed to come from the bedroom.

Startled, Schmidt whipped his head around and peered into the dark opening. Was someone there? Had he imagined it? Maybe the sound had come from outside, or from an adjacent flat.

He sat motionless and listened.

After a while, just when he had convinced himself he had been mistaken, he heard the floor creak inside the bedroom.

There was no denying it this time. Someone *was* there.

Was it a thief?

The intruder had to be aware of his presence. And yet he had chosen to remain hidden. Perhaps he was still hoping to avoid discovery.

Schmidt knew the field of vision from the bedroom into the living room was somewhat limited, so the intruder couldn't have had a clear line of sight to him. His plan was simple: Act normal, pretend to go into the kitchen, and then quickly grab the keys and run out of the apartment.

He worked up the nerve to get up and walk nonchalantly towards the kitchen. It took a lot to keep from peeking back at the bedroom, but he never did. A few more steps now. Good, there was still no indication the intruder suspected anything. All of a sudden, the old man dashed into the entrance hall and reached for the keys on the table, all the while keeping his eyes on the bedroom door.

But when his fingers scraped against the wooden surface and closed in on themselves, his heart skipped a beat. He pulled his gaze down to the table and was left horrified by what his eyes showed him, or rather, by what they *didn't show*.

The keys were gone.

Patrick Jenkins and Randall Carson walked out of a limestone building.

A black sedan was parked at the front, waiting for them.

As they approached, a man wearing a black suit and red tie stepped out of the front passenger side. "Mr. Jenkins, Mr. Carson, it's a pleasure to meet you both. My name is Mark Stanwell. I'm Mr. Leicester's assistant."

The two men barely acknowledged the assistant as they slipped into the back of the vehicle.

Not sure how to interpret their reaction, or lack thereof, Stanwell hesitated a moment before returning to his seat at the front.

Once everyone was inside, Jenkins signaled the driver to get the car moving and then turned to Stanwell. "Do you have the files?"

The assistant twisted his body around, hindered by his seat belt. He had intended to start off the conversation with an icebreaker, as he liked to do.

48

But a quick look at the two men's closed faces told him neither of them was in the mood for pleasantries. He opened the flaps on his briefcase, took out two beige folders, and handed one each to Jenkins and Carson. "This is everything we have on the mercenaries."

"When will they be here?" Jenkins asked.

"Tomorrow. The meeting is scheduled for 3 p.m. at Mr. Leicester's office."

Carson turned to Jenkins. "I still don't understand why Mr. Leicester insisted on bringing those guys in. We have enough people to handle this matter ourselves."

"It was the analyst," Jenkins said through clenched teeth. "She's the one who's been pushing for this. The meddlesome little…"

"Mr. Leicester does have a tendency to go out of his way to indulge her," Stanwell remarked.

Once again, the two men ignored him.

"At least they appear to be professionals," said Carson as he studied the files. "It should make it easier to work with them."

Jenkins stared at Kincade's photograph. "We'll see."

Schmidt was dumbfounded. The keys he had left on the table a mere moment ago had vanished.

A host of questions raced inside his head. How could anyone remove the keys without him noticing? Could his attentions have been so fixated on the bedroom he had missed it? And why would someone sneak up, grab the keys, and then disappear again? Why make their presence known in such a strange manner? Was it to scare him?

In any case, the fact remained: he was trapped inside his own apartment, and he wasn't alone.

Sensing danger closing in around him, he fumbled for the phone in his pocket to call for help. But as soon as he pulled it out and started dialing, he heard the rattle of keys.

He looked up, holding his breath.

A figure stood in the shadowy frame of the kitchen entrance. "We finally meet again, Professor."

At first, the old man saw little more than a lean silhouette with long limbs wearing a white shirt with rolled-up sleeves. But as the figure moved closer, a face gradually came into the light. It was a pale white mask, covered by falling blond strands.

Schmidt recoiled, his expression a mixture of shock and terror. A specter had materialized in front of him, a ghost rising from the abyss of his past to torment him. "Johann ..." he mumbled. "... Impossible."

"And yet, here I am. I've waited a long time for this."

The phone was still in Schmidt's hand. He shot a quick glance at it.

"That would only cut our reunion short," Johann warned. "It would be a shame, would it not? After all, we have so much catching up to do."

The old man's initial fear was starting to subside. He managed to quiet the trembling of his hands and put the phone back inside his pocket. He moved closer to Johann. Close enough to see his own reflection inside the young man's electric blue eyes. "I have nothing to say to you," he declared in a fit of defiance.

"It hurts my feelings to hear you say those words, Professor. Oh, I get it. You're upset because of my little prank. Sorry, I couldn't resist." Johann dangled the keys in front of the old man, hoping to bait him into a desperate attempt to grab them.

But Schmidt was all too aware of the futility of such an attempt. He didn't take the bait. He refused to give Johann the satisfaction. "Ah! Feelings?" He sneered. "You don't have any. You don't even know the meaning of the word."

Johann tossed the keys aside and grabbed Schmidt by the arm. "I think you have me confused with your little Asian doll. She's the one without feelings. Me on the other hand, if someone were to … oh, I don't know … keep me locked up for over two decades. I would have very strong *feelings* about it."

Johann's grip tightened, his fingernails starting to sink into the old man's flesh.

Schmidt grimaced from the pain. "You enjoy killing people. You're a monster."

A cruel grin distorted the pale mask. "Oh, I freely admit it. But I hope you don't consider yourself absolved of all responsibility. Tell me, Professor, who is truly to blame? The monster? Or the ones who created it?" The villain loosened his grip and leaned closer. "The seeds of all my evils are rooted in your conscience."

Schmidt felt the urge to protest, to defend himself against the accusation. But as he tried to speak, his words felt too hollow to provide an honest defense. In the end, he could say nothing. Despite his initial reaction, in his heart, he believed Johann had spoken the truth. He knew it. The burden of his guilt had weighed heavily on him over the years.

"You're right," Schmidt confessed. "I regret many of the choices we made … the choices *I* made. We wanted to better ourselves. We wanted to change the world."

"How noble of you," Johann scoffed.

The professor's eyes were brimming with tears of remorse. "We were blinded by our ambitions … our dreams. We should have taken better care of you. I'm sorry, my child."

"That's right, I almost forgot. You and the other relic liked to pretend we were your children. OK, *Dad*, since you skipped so many birthdays, I think I'm overdue for a little present."

The old man gave a confused look. "What do you mean?"

"Come now, do you think I came all the way here to reminisce about my childhood?"

"I thought you came here to kill me."

"Well yes, there is that," Johann said in a casual tone. "But under different circumstances, I would have saved you for much later on. No, the main reason I'm here is that I need you to help me find something. The recording of the last conversation between you and Adam, where is it?"

Schmidt felt his blood run cold. "How do you know about the recording?"

"Irrelevant," Johann replied. "Tell me where it is."

"No, I can't. What use is it to you anyway? Unless ..." The old man's eyes widened with a terrible realization. "You're trying to find Adam's last project. Why? What do you intend to do?"

Johann shrugged. "Don't ask me, I'm only following instructions."

"Instructions? ...You?" Schmidt doubted his ears. He knew better than anyone that Johann had always been fiercely autonomous. Even as a child, they had always struggled to keep him under control. And now, having somehow escaped, it was hard to imagine he would spend his new-found freedom doing someone else's bidding.

"I don't believe you," said Schmidt. "Whose instructions?"

"Mine," said a voice inside the apartment.

The old man spun around and was horrified at the sight of the man walking out of the bedroom. He was a Caucasian man wearing an unbuttoned dark suit. Despite the man's youthful appearance, thick silver-gray hair sprouted from his head like thin metallic wires.

It was yet another apparition. This was turning into a nightmare.

It hadn't occurred to Schmidt that anyone other than Johann could have escaped.

Johann frowned, displeased. "What are you doing Damien? We agreed I would take care of this."

"You're taking too long."

"I wanted to savor the moment."

"The moment's over," said Damien. His tone was cold and harsh.

"Fine," said Johann with a shrug of resignation. "But it seems our dear professor is a little reluctant to help."

Damien's emerald-green eyes locked on to the old man. "He will."

Chapter 7 – Non-negotiable

The following afternoon, seated on a couch inside his Paris office, Andrew Leicester was carefully stirring milk into his tea. He glanced up at Jenkins and Carson, who were seated opposite him. "Would you like my secretary to bring you a cup of tea?"

"No thanks," said Carson.

"I'm fine," Jenkins replied.

Leicester studied their faces as he continued to trace small circles with his spoon. "Gentlemen, I know you disapprove. You've already voiced your concerns regarding this matter."

"I don't like the idea of involving outsiders," said Jenkins, "especially this group."

"I agree with Patrick," said Carson. "Based on the information in his file, I'd say their leader is a bit of a *loose cannon*."

"We've been over this," said Leicester. "We need to limit our exposure. It would be better to have you both operate covertly for now." He took a sip from his cup and seemed quite pleased with the taste. "Besides," he continued, "our girl believes they can be helpful. And as I'm sure you'll agree, Mr. Jenkins, you'll need all the help you can get." Leicester took another sip. "Are you sure I can't interest you in a cup of tea?"

Both men shook their heads.

Moments later, Leicester's phone buzzed.

He stretched out his arm and pressed the speaker button. "Yes, Rachel."

"Mr. Stanwell and his guest have arrived," a woman's voice said.

"Good, show them in."

"Yes, sir."

Soon afterward, a knock came. Without waiting to be called in, the secretary opened the door and ushered two men inside.

Leicester stood up and went to greet them. "Mr. Kincade, I trust you had a pleasant trip."

"Sure," said Kincade as he looked around the opulent office. "What is it you do again?"

"I suppose you could say I'm a diplomat."

"A diplomat, huh?" Kincade said, sounding skeptical.

Leicester turned to his assistant. "I believe there are preparations to be made for tonight."

"Yes, sir", said Stanwell, "I'll get right on it." As he left the office, he walked past the secretary, who was still holding the door open, waiting.

"Will that be all, Mr. Leicester?" she asked.

"Yes, Rachel, thank you."

As she shut the door, Carson and Jenkins stood to greet their boss' guest.

Leicester made the introduction. "This is Mr. Jenkins, my head of security, and Mr. Carson, a long-time associate. Gentlemen, meet Mr. Kincade."

Kincade studied both men as he shook hands with them. He could tell right away they had a military background. Usually, he would feel a certain camaraderie towards fellow soldiers, but those two had a very unfriendly look about them. In fact, he even sensed a degree of hostility emanating from them, Jenkins in particular. *What's up with this guy?*

Leicester invited everyone to take a seat. "Now that everybody's acquainted, let's get started, shall we! Mr. Kincade, I understand one of your men is unavailable."

"In a manner of speaking. Ben—Benjamin Green—left the team a while back. He still lends us a hand from time to time, but since he wasn't involved in our last mission, he wasn't detained along with the rest of us."

"Will he be joining you at a later date?"

"No. I didn't ask him. I see no reason to drag him into this mess."

"Well, it's your decision," said Leicester. He went over to his desk and pulled out two blue folders from the top-left drawer. Then, he re-joined his visitors and handed a folder each to Kincade and Carson.

The folders contained seven sheets of paper. Each one had a photograph, similar to the ones found on identification documents, and some very basic descriptive information: weight, height, eye color, etc.

Kincade frowned. He had seen his share of classified profiles in the past, and he was pretty sure all of them contained far more information than this. One omission in particular caught his eye. "No last name?" he asked looking up at Leicester.

"I'm afraid those would be of no use to you," the Briton replied. "All of them have had their identities scrubbed a long time ago. You won't find any trace of them in any systems."

"I still don't see how it could hurt. I mean … maybe they have family or—"

Leicester shook his head. "Take my word for it. The family angle's a dead end."

Kincade and Carson exchanged a quick look. There was clearly something fishy going on there, but neither of them pressed the issue.

"Well, it's not much to go on," Kincade said, waving the documents. "How do you expect us to find these people? By posting an ad in the papers?"

"Don't worry, Mr. Kincade. I'm confident our analyst will be able to point you in the right direction. Your job will be to lead the search and help us neutralize the fugitives by any means necessary."

Kincade's gaze sharpened. "You want us to bring them in alive, right?"

"Ideally, we would prefer to have the fugitives returned to us safe and sound, yes, but should you find it too difficult to apprehend them … you're authorized to do whatever is necessary to stop them."

Leicester noticed that his directive had made Kincade and Carson uncomfortable. "Gentlemen," he insisted, "I cannot emphasize enough how crucial it is they not be allowed to find the item they're searching for."

Kincade said nothing. This was not what he had signed up for. Already, the vague apprehension he had felt when Leicester had first approached them was starting to return. "By the way," he said, "I thought there were eight of them. Why do I only have seven files?"

"Same here," said Carson.

"These are the people we need to focus on," said Leicester. "Do not concern yourselves with the last one for now."

More secrets, Kincade thought.

"Are these pictures recent?" Carson asked, leafing through the documents.

"Actually, I was wondering the same thing," said Kincade.

Leicester looked a bit surprised. "Yes. Why do you ask?"

"They look kinda young," said Carson.

The remark caught the Briton off guard. He was so accustomed to their faces, he had grown oblivious to that fact.

"Don't be fooled," Jenkins warned. "They're extremely dangerous."

Kincade raised an eyebrow. "Dangerous? I thought they were scientists."

57

"They are," Leicester confirmed. "But it's a bit more complicated than that."

Of course it is. Kincade was waiting for the other shoe to drop.

Leicester sighed. "As I mentioned during our first meeting, this project is highly classified. However, we have to balance this secrecy against the need to prepare you for the challenges ahead. You will both be briefed later tonight and will be given all the information required to complete your mission." He paused before adding, "But you will need to keep an open mind. For now, I will urge you to heed Mr. Jenkins' warning. Do not judge them by their appearance."

"Who will brief them?" Jenkins asked.

"The analyst," said Leicester.

"They're to meet with the analyst?" Jenkins asked, his voice rising to a higher pitch.

"She insisted on briefing them herself."

"And you agreed?"

Leicester exhaled. "You know how she gets." He fixed his gaze on Kincade and Carson. "When you meet with her, it is imperative you not reveal the full extent of your mandate on this mission. As far as the analyst is concerned, she will be helping you to bring the fugitives in, nothing more. Do not say, or do, anything that would make her think otherwise."

Kincade stared at Leicester with genuine curiosity. He recognized the strange expression he had seen on the diplomat's face back at the base, when he had mentioned his analyst for the first time.

Leicester noticed the American's gaze lingering on him. "She can be a little … difficult," he explained. "You'll see for yourself soon enough. Normally she resides in London, close to me. But I've had her moved to a house near Paris two weeks ago for another matter. The three of you are to go there tonight, since you'll be working together on—"

58

"Forget it," Kincade interrupted.

Leicester gave him a puzzled look. "I beg your pardon."

"No offense, but my team and I will handle this on our own."

Leicester's smile faded. "What you're suggesting is not possible, Mr. Kincade. Besides, Mr. Jenkins is uniquely qualified for this assignment. I think you'll find that without his help, your chances of success will be slim, at best."

"This is non-negotiable," Kincade declared in a curt tone. "He can help by telling us everything he knows. My men and I will take over from there."

From the corner of his eye, Kincade could see the angry look Carson was casting at him. But it was mild in comparison to Jenkins' intense glare.

From the very beginning, Jenkins had been ferociously opposed to the mercenaries' presence. As head of security at the compound, he felt he should have been the one to lead the efforts to track down the group of escapees. But even though it had been a hard pill to swallow, he had come to accept he would have to collaborate with these soldiers for hire. And now, the leader of those disgraced soldiers had the nerve to suggest he should be sidelined.

Jenkins felt his blood boil. He stood and growled at Kincade, "You think you and your little band can handle this on your own? You have no idea what you're getting yourself into!"

Kincade stood in turn and locked gazes with him. "That's our problem, not yours. Our number one rule is: we work alone."

Jenkins' demeanor was growing menacing.

Leicester felt the need to intervene in order to diffuse the mounting tension. "Gentlemen, please! We're all on the same side here." He took a deep breath. "I'm afraid I cannot grant your request, Mr. Kincade. There are those who believe we should not entrust such a delicate matter to you and your men in the first place. I was able to appease those voices of dissent because I assured them you would be working closely with Mr. Jenkins and Mr. Carson. Therefore, I would ask you to make an exception this time."

Kincade turned to him and calmly said, "Mr. Leicester, we've only made one such exception in the past. That was when we agreed to team up with the US military on our last job. I don't need to tell you how that turned out."

Without another word, Kincade made his way to the door. He placed his hand on the handle and turned to face the room. "I trust my team, no one else. Look, I'll make this simple for you. We'll meet with your analyst and talk with whoever else you want us to. But, either you agree to let us work alone, or you can book our seats on the next flight to D.C." Having delivered his ultimatum, Kincade walked out, leaving Leicester and the others stupefied.

The room was silent for a while, until Jenkins said, "He's bluffing. He knows what will happen if you rescind your offer."

Leicester smiled as he kept his eyes fixed on the closed door. "No, Mr. Jenkins, that man was not bluffing."

Chapter 8 – The Manor

At around 9:30 p.m. that evening, two dark SUVs drove past the barred metallic gates of an isolated property 80 miles south of Paris. The vehicles followed the long driveway all the way to a large mansion and pulled up in front of it.

As soon as the engines were turned off, Mark Stanwell stepped out of the front passenger side of the lead SUV. The driver followed him out and opened the back door for his passengers. Two men with their heads covered in black hoods were led out onto the smooth gravel.

At the same time, the driver of the second SUV mirrored the actions of his colleague, and three more black-hooded men appeared.

"You can take these off now," said Stanwell.

The huge man was the first to uncover his head. "It's about time!" he complained.

"Relax Rock," said Kincade as he removed his hood.

The giant grinned. "What can I say, Nate? I hate being kept in the dark."

"Again, I would like to offer my sincerest apologies," said Stanwell. "Protocol … you understand."

"Don't worry about it," Kincade told him.

Having regained the use of his sight, Kincade took a minute to get his bearings.

They were standing in front of a four-story manor set in the middle of a vast garden. Kincade had never seen such well-kept, and fancy-looking, grounds. Around him was a beautifully arranged collection of statues, colorful plants, neatly trimmed bushes, and small water fountains. He also noted that the garden was surrounded by a high wall, with rows of trees planted on either side of it—no doubt to guard against prying eyes.

The chants of nocturnal animals informed Kincade they were somewhere in the countryside. There was a light breeze carrying the scent of freshly cut grass, lined with the strong perfume of lilies growing near the mansion.

As the team gathered around Stanwell, Kincade noticed Doc Chen's furrowed brow.

"Everything all right Doc? You look upset."

"We're switching places on the return trip," he replied, sounding annoyed. "You get to ride with Sonar next time."

"Hey, what did I do?" one of their companions said in a high-pitched voice.

Sean 'Sonar' Riley was the team's communications expert. He looked like a lightweight boxer, and his red hair and beard hinted at his Irish descent. The others had nicknamed him *Sonar* because of his extraordinary hearing, which made it almost impossible for anyone to sneak up on him—a very useful attribute to have in the field.

"Are you serious?" said Doc. "You wouldn't shut up all the way here. Not even for five minutes."

"But we couldn't see anything," Sonar protested. "What else was I supposed to do to pass the time?"

"Come on Doc, I'm sure it wasn't that bad," Rock taunted. "Besides, you also had Da Costa with you, and he never says anything. That balances things out, right?"

The giant padded his comrade on the back as he mentioned him.

Like Kincade and Doc Chen, Armando Da Costa was a career soldier. Born of an American mother and a father from the Republic of El Salvador, he had joined the Army in his early twenties. There, he had been singled out for his sharpshooting abilities, which had eventually landed him in the special unit commanded by Kincade. Da Costa's personality was the polar opposite of Rock's and Sonar's. He tended to remain discreet and spoke only when he had something pertinent to contribute. He glanced up at the colossus with a disapproving expression and shook his head.

Doc wasn't amused either. "Oh, you think this is funny, do you?" he asked Rock. "All right, you and Sonar can ride together on the way back, just the two of you. You'll get to spend some quality time alone with your good buddy."

Rock suddenly looked worried. "What? Wait a minute … you can't do that. He can't do that, right, Nate?"

Sonar moved closer to them. "I gotta be honest, people. I'm not exactly feeling the love here."

All the while, Stanwell was staring at the mercenaries, his expression conveying a mixture of doubt and surprise. He began to question whether his boss had made a mistake by entrusting such an important task to this bunch.

Kincade noticed the assistant's perplexed gaze. "Don't mind them," he said. "Let's get on with it."

"… Oh, of course. Please, follow me."

As Stanwell led the group towards the house, Kincade spotted something far into the garden. He squinted at the darkness, trying to identify the object. It took him a few seconds to discern enough of its shape to realize what it was.

That realization brought him to a halt.

A swing? What's that doing here? he wondered.

"Is there a problem?" Stanwell asked when he saw that Kincade was lagging behind.

"No, it's nothing," Kincade replied as he caught up with the others.

The party arrived at a heavy wooden door, Stanwell went to an electronic panel to the side and keyed in a series of digits.

After a long beep, signaling the disengagement of the locking mechanism, the assistant opened the door.

The group entered a large vestibule with a marbled floor and a bright chandelier hanging from the ten-foot-high ceiling. Further inside, they could see a vast reception hall decorated like a small art gallery. The walls were adorned with paintings, admired by a sparse audience of statues and sculptures.

Sonar whistled, impressed. "Nice place!"

"Thank you," said Stanwell. "It was renovated after—" He cut short his explanation and started looking around.

"What's the matter?" Kincade asked.

"Strange," said the assistant. "Someone should have come to meet us."

"How many people are staying here?" Doc asked.

"Let's see … there's the analyst, her maid, the cook, and fourteen bodyguards."

"She's got a maid?" Rock noted.

"Not now," said Kincade. He turned back to Stanwell. "Is it possible they don't know we're here? This looks like a pretty big place."

Stanwell shook his head. "I don't think so. There are security cameras all over the property. Someone should have seen us when we drove through the gates. Besides, the people here were informed of our arrival." Stanwell motioned to one of the drivers. "You! Get on the com and try to contact someone."

The driver pulled out a two-way radio. "Walker, Jones, come in."

No one replied.

Stanwell was growing increasingly worried.

"It does seem a bit too quiet," Doc remarked. "Sonar, can you hear anything?"

The redhead moved a few steps ahead of the group and pricked up his ears while the others waited in silence.

After a brief moment, Sonar turned and said, "Nope, not a peep. Usually, when a place is this quiet, it means everyone's asleep."

"Or dead," Rock pointed out.

Even though the giant's remark was intended to be light-hearted, it quickly turned the atmosphere heavier. A creeping feeling of uneasiness spread throughout the entire party.

Without a word, Kincade drew his firearm. The members of his team and the two drivers immediately imitated him. It was more of a precautionary measure than an anticipation of danger, but it was enough to push Stanwell beyond his panic threshold. "The girl …" he muttered as he made a sudden dash for the staircase to their left.

Kincade barely had time to hold him back. "Wait!"

"What are you doing?" said Stanwell in a rattled voice. "If something happens to her … Mr. Leicester will have my head."

"Try to stay calm," said Kincade. "Tell me, where do you think she is? Where were you about to go just now?"

"To check her room," the assistant replied, regaining a little composure.

"Where's that?"

"On the fourth floor … the top floor."

"All right, hold on a sec."

After exchanging a few words with Doc, Kincade decided they would split into two groups. The drivers would assist Doc and Da Costa in

65

performing a rapid sweep of the house, while Sonar and Rock would go with Kincade, straight to the fourth floor, to look for the analyst.

"I'm going with you too," Stanwell told Kincade.

"Fine, as long as you do what we tell you."

The assistant nodded.

"All right, let's go!" said Kincade.

His group cautiously proceeded up the stairs, pausing on each floor to peek down the hallways. Once they reached the top floor, Stanwell pointed to a room inside the right corridor. Kincade took the lead as they made their way over to it.

When they reached the analyst's room, Kincade motioned Stanwell to stay back as he placed his hand on the door handle. Meanwhile, Sonar had begun counting down the fingers on his left hand, folding them one by one into a fist, and Rock had taken up position against the opposite wall, ready to ram the door if it turned out to be locked. The idea was to give whoever might be inside as little time as possible to react.

When Sonar's count reached zero, Kincade pressed down on the handle.

The door was unlocked.

The three mercenaries rushed inside, aiming their guns in all three directions—front, left, and right.

The room appeared to be empty.

Rock checked the bathroom. "Clear."

Sonar paused to eye the king-size bed covered with pink silk sheets and a purple duvet, before peeking under it. "Nothing here either."

Stanwell followed them inside and looked into the walk-in closet. "She's not here."

Kincade made sure both windows were locked and shot a quick look around the garden from his high vantage point. Everything appeared quiet. As his gaze reached the edge of the window frame, his attention was drawn to the curtains. Like the room itself, they were out-of-sync with the rest of the house. They were the same color as the duvet but with added yellow flower motifs. There were no paintings or statuettes inside the bedroom, only a chest of drawers and a big shelf stacked with complicated books.

"Where is everyone?" Stanwell muttered. His face was glistening with sweat. He felt the need to loosen his tie just to breathe easier.

Kincade studied the assistant. He looked like he was on the verge of a nervous breakdown, at which point he would become useless. "Focus!" Kincade said in a firm tone. "Where else could she be?"

"The maid … the maid's room," Stanwell mumbled. "She often goes there."

"Show us."

"It's on the other wing," said Stanwell as he led the group out into the corridor.

They retraced their steps and hurried past the stairs. Mid-way down the hallway, the assistant stopped and pointed to a room.

The mercenaries proceeded exactly as they had earlier.

That door was also unlocked. But when the trio burst in guns raised, there was a surprise waiting for them.

Rock was the first to spot her because of the direction he was facing when he rushed into the room. "Don't move!" he shouted, aiming his weapon.

When his two companions whipped their heads around, they saw a small Asian girl in the far-left corner, standing over an unconscious middle-aged woman.

Two men in dark suits were also lying face-down on the floor near the bed.

67

"Who are you?" Kincade asked. But as he took a closer look at her, he thought she looked familiar somehow.

Rock and Sonar had also fallen silent. Probably because they too were searching through their memories, trying to place her.

By the time Stanwell stood in the doorway and uttered her name, Kincade had already recognized her.

Mitsuki. One of the fugitives his team had been tasked with tracking down. Her presence there was so unexpected it had taken Kincade and his companions a moment to identify her.

"What are you doing here?" Kincade asked. "What happened to these people?"

She didn't say anything.

Seeing her in person reminded Kincade of the impression he had had when he had first examined her picture. Her oval-shaped face was devoid of all expressions, and her big brown eyes, while beautiful, seemed lifeless. Adding to that, her pale skin, bright red lips, and long silky black hair completed the illusion that one was staring at a porcelain doll, rather than at an actual person.

"Quick, shoot her!" Stanwell urged.

Rock raised an eyebrow at him, "Take it easy, man, it's not like she's armed or anything."

Kincade agreed. Mitsuki's skin-tight black outfit didn't appear to have any pockets or pouches in which to conceal a weapon.

"No, no," said Stanwell nervously, "this is very dangerous."

All three mercenaries gave the assistant the same odd look. They were surprised to see him so agitated.

"Honestly, man, chill," said Sonar.

But Stanwell didn't let up. "You don't understand—"

"Look," Kincade snapped at him, "we're not shooting an unarmed girl. So drop it. Besides, we need to find out what happened here." He went to the men on the floor and knelt down to check their pulses. Both were dead. Shot with their own guns from the looks of it. The weapons were still on the floor next to them.

Mitsuki watched him, silent and immobile.

Kincade motioned her to move back as he went to check on the woman at her feet. "She's alive," he said, feeling her wrist, "but it appears she took a hard hit on the head. I don't think she'll be waking up anytime soon." He picked the woman up and placed her on the bed. "I'm guessing this is …"

"The maid, yes," Stanwell replied offhandedly. "At least restrain her," he pressed, his eyes still fixed on the black-clad girl.

Kincade took another look at Mitsuki.

She remained still, with only her gaze jumping from person to person. He decided there was no harm in following Stanwell's recommendation, if only to keep her from running away. After all, capturing Mitsuki and her friends was the reason why his team was there in the first place. He tucked his gun into his pants and turned to his companions. "Cuffs."

Sonar tossed him a pair of handcuffs. He caught them and approached the young woman.

"I'm going to put these on you now," said Kincade in a non-threatening tone. "I promise we won't hurt you, so don't try anything stupid, OK?"

She extended her arms out and offered no resistance when he secured the metal bracelets around her wrists.

Then, Doc's group arrived. They all froze at the sight of the girl in black.

"Isn't that …?" Doc said.

"Yep," Rock replied. "We found her here with those three." He nodded at the two bodies on the floor and at the maid on the bed.

"See anything during your sweep?" Kincade asked.

"We found twelve bodyguards," said Doc. "All shot dead. We also found the cook. He's alive, but he suffered severe concussions."

"Well, I guess everyone's accounted for," Rock concluded. "Except for the one person we came to see."

"We'll keep looking," said Doc. "But first, we need to find out who took out those guards."

"Stanwell seems to think she might have done it," Kincade said, glancing at Mitsuki.

Doc gazed at the frail-looking girl. "Her? Are you joking?"

"Nah, you should have seen him earlier," Sonar said with a mocking smile. "He was shaking like a costumed dancer at a Brazilian carnival."

"We'll worry about her later," said Kincade. "For now, we still need to locate the analyst."

"Did you ask her?" said Doc, his eyes still fixed on Mitsuki.

"Sure," Rock replied, "but she's not much of a talker. I bet she'd get along great with Da Costa."

Da Costa didn't react to his comrade's comment, instead eyeing the prisoner from head to toe. She stared back at him, and the two examined each other at length, before finally looking away.

"See what I mean?" said Rock with a large smile. "You can almost hear the music."

But Stanwell wasn't in a joking mood. He took out his cell phone and stared at it with dread. His hands were shaking. He had put off calling Leicester up until now because there was still a chance the analyst could be found in one of the other rooms. But now that the entire house had been searched, he no longer had any valid reason to wait. The assistant imagined several different scenarios in which he informed his boss the analyst had gone missing. Not one of those scenarios ended well for him.

"Who are you calling?" Sonar asked.

"I have to report to Mr. Leicester," Stanwell said in a shaky voice. But as his finger closed in on the first digit, he froze and stared into space.

"Well, aren't you gonna call him?" Rock asked.

"The panic room ..." Stanwell whispered.

"Say again?"

"There's a panic room in the mansion," he said in a more audible voice.

Kincade frowned. "And you didn't tell us about this earlier because ..."

"I just remembered."

"OK, where is it?" Doc asked.

Stanwell shook his head. "I don't know. A few months back, I overheard Mr. Leicester and Mr. Jenkins discussing the security measures in this place. I wasn't really paying attention ... but I'm certain Mr. Leicester said something about a panic room ... a hidden chamber."

Kincade thought about it for a moment and said, "Tell me, Stanwell, who else comes here?"

"Huh?"

From the blank expression on the assistant's face, it was clear he didn't understand the question. So Kincade phrased it differently. "Those security measures ... are they just for the analyst, or do other people come here? Like Leicester, for instance."

"Oh, no," said Stanwell. "It's just for her. Mr. Leicester would never let anyone else use this house."

Doc knew what Kincade was getting at. The same idea had occurred to him. Their gazes crossed, and they said in one voice, "The bedroom."

It was the logical answer. If the point of all the guards, the cameras, and the blindfolds was to protect the analyst and her alone, it made sense the hidden chamber would be located in the one room meant only for her. Also, people are typically more worried about security breaches in the late hours of the night rather than in the middle of the day. Again, the bedroom is where you'd expect the analyst to be during that time.

Chapter 9 – The Analyst

The entire party headed to the analyst's bedroom with their prisoner in tow. But as they neared the staircase, Kincade halted. He thought it would be a good idea to take another pass at the floors below and double-check that nothing had been overlooked.

The task was assigned to Da Costa and Sonar. The two made their way down the stairs, while the others continued on to the east wing.

When the group arrived back in front of the analyst's room, the drivers were instructed to wait outside.

"Rock, you keep an eye on the girl," Kincade said, nodding at the prisoner. "The rest of us will—" He was interrupted mid-sentence as Stanwell bumped into him.

The assistant rushed into the bedroom, shouting, "Lucielle! Can you hear me? Are you in here?" No longer able to keep his composure, Stanwell began to inspect the walls frantically. But as his gaze swept across the room, he noticed the mercenaries giving him strange looks. "What? Why aren't you looking?"

"What kind of name is Lucielle?" Rock said, giving voice to the question hanging on each of his comrades' lips.

Stanwell grew even more upset. "I hardly think now is the time to worry about something like this. We have to fi—"

"Is that you, Mark?" a crackling voice echoed inside the bedroom, interrupting him.

The voice had been faint, as if distant, and it had seemed to come from the electronic panel on the wall near the bed. Kincade recalled seeing a similar device in the maid's room as well.

Stanwell hurried to the panel. "It's an intercom system used to communicate between the bedrooms." He looked over the device, not sure how to operate it. "Lucielle! Where are you? Are you all right?"

"I'm fine," the voice replied.

Stanwell could finally breathe again. He felt as though a boulder had been lifted off his chest.

Kincade was surprised to hear the analyst sound so poised given the circumstances.

"You're late," she reproached. But before Stanwell could respond, she moved on to her next question. "Are the mercs with you?"

The mercs? The three men looked at one another with raised eyebrows.

"Yes, they're here," Stanwell replied.

"OK, I'm coming out."

There was a loud click inside the closet, followed by the low rumble of a sliding wall. Then, the closet door opened and the analyst came out.

In the short time Kincade and his team had been at the manor, events had jumped from one twist to the next. So much so that Kincade had come to believe himself immune to further surprise that night. He could not have been more wrong. Nothing could have prepared him for the jolt he received when Lucielle emerged from her hiding place.

The head of Leicester's intelligence department, the person for whom all those security measures had been put in place, the analyst, was a child who barely looked old enough to go to the movies by herself.

Kincade was speechless. As was Doc. Even Rock, who never missed an opportunity to whip up a snappy comment, was stunned into silence.

"Lucielle, I'm really glad you're safe," said Stanwell, relieved as much for himself as he was for her.

She ignored him and walked straight over to Kincade. She tilted her head up and stared at him with her large emerald-green eyes.

As he stared back, Kincade's brain automatically registered the flowery white dress and the dark purple cardigan and leggings, as well as the doll she was holding. But it was her hair that drew most of his attention. She had long, silver-gray hair. It was like someone had taken a granny wig and fitted it onto her small baby-faced head.

The youngster then turned to size up Doc, and finally Rock. But as soon as her gaze landed on the hulking figure, she recoiled and pointed at him. "Watch out!"

Rock, like his comrades, was still grappling with the notion that this child was the analyst. Her sudden and inexplicable reaction only contributed to add to his confusion.

Kincade, however, realized she wasn't looking at the giant, but rather at the prisoner standing in front of him.

When Lucielle had exited the closet and walked to the center of the room, Doc had unintentionally shielded Mitsuki from her line of sight. She was only now laying eyes on the prisoner for the first time.

Wondering what caused the young girl to be so alarmed, Kincade shifted his attention to the captive. He immediately noticed something different about her. Mitsuki's eyes had come alive and were shimmering with intense concentration.

Also sensing a change in the prisoner's demeanor, Rock gazed down at her. "What's the matter wi—" He never got to the end of his question. The words fell back down his throat when he saw Mitsuki snap the handcuffs by pulling her arms apart in one swift motion.

Both Kincade and Doc looked on stupefied as they wondered from where inside her small frame Mitsuki had mined the strength to perform the impossible feat.

The same question was rattling inside Rock's head. While he was still frozen, asking himself how the petite woman had managed to break free from

75

her restraints, she delivered a violent kick to his midsection.

The force of the blow sent the giant tumbling through the door, until he bumped his head against the corridor wall.

With Rock out of the picture, Doc's self-preservation instinct spurred him into action. He was the next closest to the former captive and, as such, the one in the most imminent danger. Quickly, he drew his firearm from the shoulder holster under his vest. But before he could point it, Mitsuki's hand was also on the weapon. He tried to wrestle it away from her but was shocked to find he could not. Then, his shock doubled when she grabbed him by the collar and, with one hand, sent him flying half-way across the room. He crashed into Kincade, toppling him over.

Lucielle started running back to the closet. But Mitsuki was much quicker. She intercepted the youngster and tossed her onto the bed.

The instant Lucielle landed on the duvet cover, two detonations shook the room.

The two drivers had stepped in and fired at Mitsuki. But they had waited to get a clean shot so as not to hit the analyst. During that split-second hesitation, Mitsuki had spotted them and rolled away just before they fired.

The drivers wasted no time adjusting their aims.

Two more detonations followed in rapid succession.

This time the bullets hit their mark, but it was the drivers who collapsed on the floor. Mitsuki had shot them with the gun she had taken from Doc.

Having dropped it when his comrade had crash-landed into him, Kincade made a dive for his firearm. But just as he recovered it, he saw Mitsuki standing next to him, peering at him down the barrel of Doc's gun.

He gazed into her eyes.

There was no emotion, no hesitation.

Bang!

76

"What is it, Rachel?"

"It's time for your conference call with Mr. Schaffer and Mrs. Renard," a voice said over the speakerphone.

"Ah yes, thank you."

Sat at his desk, Andrew Leicester spun around in his chair to face a large TV monitor hanging on the back wall of his office. He took out a remote control from a drawer and turned on the monitor. The screen was split vertically down the middle, with the words '*Connected. Waiting for user*' displayed in font on either side.

A short time later, Nathalie Renard's image appeared on the right side of the screen.

"*Bonsoir*, Andrew."

"Good evening, Nathalie."

"Have the mercenaries arrived?" she asked, the tone of her voice conveying the full measure of her disdain. *Mercenaries* … the word itself left a bitter taste in her mouth.

"Yes, they're meeting with the analyst as we speak."

"I see."

Leicester watched her for a moment. "Regarding the analyst, I hope you understand why I had to pull her from your other case even though it was the reason we brought her to Paris."

"Of course, I understand. This takes precedence."

"Ah! Hello, Karl," said Leicester as Karl Schaffer appeared on the left side of the screen.

"I see you're both here," said Schaffer without returning the greeting.

Leicester smiled. He was used to the German's utter disregard for social conventions. He didn't mind. He thought of it as part of Schaffer's eccentric personality.

Nathalie Renard, on the other hand, was often irritated by the German's attitude. She viewed him as rude and arrogant, though she tended to keep that opinion to herself.

Without further exchange of pleasantries, she started the meeting.

"*Messieurs!*" she said. "First, I want to talk about the report I received this afternoon. Karl, have you learned anything new from the Berlin police regarding the body they discovered earlier today? Was it Professor Aleksandr Karpov?"

"Yes. He had been living in Berlin for the past few years under the name *Schmidt.*"

"I received a similar report," said Leicester. "I was told he died from a stab wound. Do the Berlin police have a working theory as to the motive for his murder?"

"Karpov had a hidden safe inside his flat," said Schaffer. "It was found open. The investigator in charge is proceeding under the assumption it was a robbery gone wrong. But we here know who was responsible for this."

"Indeed," said Leicester. "Still, I must admit, I'm surprised Damien was able to find him in such a short time."

"To think Professor Karpov was living in Berlin all along," said Renard, "hiding right under your very nose, Karl." She made the pointed remark with a mocking smile. She had often felt patronized by her two counterparts because of her *newcomer* status within the group. She particularly hated the condescending tone Schaffer always took with her, which was why she relished the opportunity to get back at him.

"Instead of trying to assign blame," said Leicester, "might I suggest we concern ourselves with the reason Damien went to find the professor so soon after his escape, and how it affects our plans."

"Agreed," said Schaffer. "This is an alarming development."

"It is," said Leicester. "Let's hope the analyst is able to find him in time, for all our sakes."

Chapter 10 – I Can Explain

Kincade turned away and raised his arms to protect his eyes from the flying shards of glass.

Just as Mitsuki had pulled the trigger, a bronze statuette had struck her on the wrist, redirecting her aim to the tall mirror on the wall and knocking the gun away from her. Everyone turned to the door, expecting to see Rock. But the giant was just now returning to the room. A young woman wearing the same skin-tight black outfit as Mitsuki was standing a few feet in front of him.

Rock waved his gun. "Don't move! Both of you."

The two women paid no attention to him. They seemed to be concerned only with each other as they faced off in the center of the room.

Doc and Kincade had now gotten back to their feet. Kincade raised his gun and repeated the command. "You heard him. Don't move!"

The women ignored him too and looked like they were about to pounce on each other. Then, all of a sudden, Mitsuki dashed straight toward the wall and, without slowing down, jumped through the window with her knees folded up and her arms crossed over her face.

"Is she nuts?" Kincade exclaimed. "We're on the fourth floor."

He and Doc hurried to the broken window and scanned the area near the house, expecting to see Mitsuki lying injured on the ground. But there was no trace of her.

"Over there!" Doc exclaimed, pointing further out into the garden.

Kincade raised his head and spotted her. She was running. He could hardly believe his eyes. Mitsuki had been left unscathed by the four-story-high

80

drop. And not only was she running, she was sprinting through the garden like an Olympic athlete.

"Damn, she's fast!" said Doc, whistling his admiration.

When Mitsuki reached the tree line, a tall, muscular black man dressed in the same strange outfit stepped out of the shadows and exchanged a few words with her. The pair then glanced back up at the window before disappearing into the trees.

Despite having seen the man for just an instant, Doc thought he had recognized one of the fugitives. "Don't tell me…"

"Yeah, that was Darius," Kincade confirmed as he turned around and faced the room.

The mystery woman was still standing in the same spot, immobile and looking non-threatening, similar to the way Mitsuki had behaved earlier.

"Arianne!" Lucielle exclaimed gleefully as she jumped off the bed and ran into the woman's arms.

Hearing the young girl call out the stranger's name only confirmed what Kincade had already realized. The woman's face was among the set of photographs handed to him by Leicester. But the fact that she and the analyst appeared to share a close bond came as a total surprise.

At that moment, Sonar and Da Costa came rushing into the room. First, they spotted the two fallen drivers at their feet. And as they turned to their comrades with question marks on their faces, they saw a silver-haired child pressed against the woman in black, except she was a different woman from before.

"What happened to the other one?" Sonar asked.

"Gone," said Doc.

"Who's the kid?" Da Costa asked.

"Jury's still out on that," Doc replied.

81

"And what's with the gray wig?" Sonar added.

Kincade was just as baffled. His head was bursting with confused thoughts. But even in the midst of his confusion, there was one point he was clear on: he wouldn't still be alive were it not for Arianne's timely intervention. So, at least for the time being, he assumed her intentions weren't hostile. He still had a host of questions for her, but those could wait. Right now, there was someone else far more deserving of a thorough interrogation. His eyes found Stanwell. The assistant had run into a corner at the first sign of trouble and had remained huddled there since. As Kincade started moving towards him, Rock, who was also marching in the same direction, shoved him aside.

Seeing the hulk closing in on him with a menacing air, Stanwell held out his palms in the futile hope of keeping him at bay. "Wait … Mr. Reinhart … please, wait …"

Stanwell's pleas fell on deaf ears. Rock grabbed him by the collar with one hand and squeezed his neck against the wall with such force he began to choke.

"What the hell was that?" Rock yelled, pointing at the broken window.

But with the giant choking him, all Stanwell could manage were a few unintelligible syllables.

Without lessening the pressure, Rock pointed at Arianne next. "And what the hell is this?" Then, again without waiting for an answer, he finally pointed at Lucielle. "And what the hell, man?"

Stanwell was still unable to answer. It was all he could do to simply breathe.

"Let him go!" Lucielle bellowed. "I can explain."

Her statement incensed the giant even further. "What are you talking about, 'you can explain'? You need to be explained."

"Let him go, Rock!" Kincade ordered, pulling on his comrade's arm.

Moaning under his breath, the giant complied. He loosened his grip and took a step back.

Stanwell crumpled on the floor, gasping for air.

Kincade crouched next to him and said, "What my not-so-eloquent friend is trying to say is: you'd better have a damn good explanation for all of this."

"Yeah!" Rock exclaimed, still feeling high-strung. "You can start with the midget."

Realizing he was talking about her, Lucielle's face turned red with anger. "I'm not a dwarf, you big ape. I'm eleven and a half."

"Eleven?" Kincade echoed at Stanwell, as if to point out the absurdity of that number.

"Eleven and a half," Lucielle corrected.

Doc turned to Stanwell, equally perplexed. "You mean to tell us your big-shot analyst is a child?"

"Wait a minute," said Sonar, "*she*'s the analyst?"

"I'm not a child!" Lucielle protested.

"You just said you were eleven," Doc countered.

"And a half," she corrected again, her tone growing impatient. "And I'm not a child."

"Shut up, kid," Rock told her in a dismissive tone, "the grown-ups are talking."

Lucielle looked like she was about to explode.

"Please, Luce, there's no time for this," said Arianne as she placed her hand on the young girl's shoulder to calm her down. She then approached Kincade and said, "Lucielle and I have to leave. Would you consider coming with us? I promise we'll explain everything."

"Are you crazy?" Rock exclaimed. "We're not going anywhere with you. Hell, it's you who's coming with us."

"Please, we need to hurry," Arianne pressed, ignoring the giant.

Kincade didn't reply and instead kept staring at her, as if considering her invitation.

After a while, his inexplicable silence became a source of concern for the others.

"Nate ...?" Doc said tentatively. "Don't tell me you're actually thinking about this."

"What's there to think about?" said Sonar. "I hate to admit it, but the big guy's got a point. This is crazy."

Of course, Kincade knew his companions were right. This was an unbelievably lucky break. Within minutes, two of the fugitives had literally fallen into their laps. And although one of them had pulled off a spectacular escape, the other was still standing before them. All they needed to do was apprehend her. Perhaps she could even lead them to her friends. If so, the odds of them completing their mission would jump from slim to promising.

So what's the problem? Kincade wondered, himself unsure of the reason for his hesitation. At first, he thought it was gratitude toward Arianne for saving his life. But as he delved into her clear hazel eyes, he began to realize it was more than that. Her gaze conveyed such honesty, such sincerity ... it was disarming. As paradoxical as it seemed, he felt he could trust this total stranger.

In the end, though, as Kincade weighed his options, it was the mind-boggling manner of Mitsuki's escape that tipped the scales in favor of his decision. It was clear Leicester had withheld essential—and potentially life-threatening—information from them. Granted, the meeting with the analyst had been set up so she could offer them additional explanations. But as Rock had pointed out, this so-called analyst required an explanation unto herself. Maybe they would have better luck getting straight answers from Arianne, who had promised to *'explain everything'*. At any rate, as long as they didn't let her out of their sights, they could always turn her in at a later time.

"Fine," said Kincade, "we'll go with you."

The rest of his team were stunned.

Doc pulled Kincade into the corridor, away from the others, and spoke to him in a hushed tone. "You're going to have to give me something here, Nate. Is it because she saved your life?"

"Part of it, yes," said Kincade in a matching low voice. "But I also think it might not be such a bad idea to hear what she has to say."

Doc gave him a dubious frown. "Yeah? What if she leads us into a trap?"

"A trap? You mean like what went down a minute ago?"

"I get your point, but it doesn't mean we should tempt fate a second time."

"Come on, Hulin. You saw the same things I did. That girl broke her handcuffs, kicked Rock's butt, tossed you like a pillow, almost shot me, and then superheroed her way out of a fourth-floor window. I've never seen anything like it!"

"Neither have I."

"That's my point. There's nothing routine about this job. We need to know what we've gotten ourselves into. If Leicester won't tell us, maybe she will," he added, glancing at Arianne.

Doc thought for a moment. "Are you sure about this?"

"Nope," Kincade replied with his usual candor.

Doc didn't press the issue further. He knew despite his flippant answer, Kincade was not the type to make impetuous decisions.

When the two men re-joined the group, the others could tell Doc was now on board too. And despite their strong reservations, all three held their objections. They were willing to abide by their leader's decision. As soldiers, they had been trained to follow orders once a decision had been made. But above all else, they trusted Kincade's judgment.

Stanwell, on the other hand, had a much harder time accepting the idea. "Have you taken leave of your senses?"

"Don't worry," said Kincade, "you're coming too."

"… What? Absolutely not," Stanwell protested. He broke into a nervous laugh. "I have no intention of accompanying you."

Rock dropped a heavy hand on his shoulder. "You heard him! You're coming with."

The assistant shot a worried look at the giant and gulped.

Kincade walked over to Arianne. "Can you help us make sense of what happened? How was your friend able to do all that?"

"I'm very curious about that too," said Rock.

"You'll have your answers," Arianne told them. "I promise, but not now. We should leave at once."

"What's the hurry?" Sonar asked, sounding suspicious.

"Jenkins and his men will arrive soon. We can't let them find us."

Kincade turned to Stanwell. "Is it true?"

The assistant shook his head. "I've heard nothing of this. Mr. Jenkins almost never comes here." He looked at Lucielle and added, "I get the impression he doesn't like you very much."

"The feeling's mutual," she said. "But he is on his way. My guess is he intended to show up at about the same time you did, which is why I made up an excuse with Andrew to have you brought in earlier than previously arranged." Her eyes homed in on Stanwell. "*Half an hour* earlier," she added, once again emphasizing their tardy arrival. "By now, Jenkins will be wondering why the guards have stopped checking in. I expect he will hasten his arrival. We should—" Lucielle stopped when she noticed the strange

86

looks the mercenaries were giving her. "What's the matter?"

"You talk kinda funny," said Rock. "You know ... not like a normal kid." In his own unique way, he had summed up the overall impression among his team as they had listened to the young girl speak.

"We have to go," Arianne urged again as she took Lucielle's hand.

"All right," said Kincade, "let's move."

They all made their way down the staircase. But once they reached the ground floor, Arianne turned away from the entrance.

"Hey, where are you going?" Sonar asked.

"We can't use Leicester's cars," she said. "They're fitted with tracking devices. There's a van parked outside, at the back."

"OK, lead the way," said Kincade after a brief hesitation.

They went past the reception hall, through the kitchen, and exited into the back garden. Arianne led the silent procession down a long pathway, continuing through the trees until they arrived at a thick metallic door.

"What now?" Kincade asked, gazing up at the ten-foot-high wall.

Arianne's eyes fell to Lucielle. "Do you have it?"

"Of course," the young girl replied, looking very pleased with herself. She pulled out a heavy key from a pocket in her doll's dress. "I took it this afternoon. I knew they wouldn't notice. No one ever uses it."

Arianne took the key and turned it inside the lock. Lucielle was right, the door hadn't been used in a while. It scraped against the ground as she pulled it open.

On the other side, a deserted road ran parallel to the wall for about forty feet before swerving away to merge with the highway.

"Hmm, I would have expected to see guards posted here," said Da Costa as he checked the surroundings.

"Yes. We took care of them," Arianne replied.

"We?" Kincade noted.

She stepped out onto the grass and waved across the road.

A white van emerged from the trees and pulled up next to them.

"Come on," said Arianne.

Rock made an overly courteous gesture, inviting Kincade to go first. "After you," he joked. "If it's a trap, I figure you should be in front."

"How considerate of you," Kincade replied as he led the group out.

As they approached the vehicle, the driver came out to meet them.

Kincade was no longer surprised to see the now-familiar skin-tight black outfit. He took one good look at the driver and said, "Ashrem, right?"

The man gave Kincade a friendly smile. "Yes, nice to meet you."

"Another one?" Rock said, also recognizing him from the pictures. "Do you all live here? I don't know why they thought it'd be hard to find you guys."

Lucielle ran over to him and jumped into his arms. "Ash!"

He knelt down and held her tight—like Arianne had done earlier. "Luce. I'm so happy to see you."

Once again, Kincade and the others were astonished by the apparent closeness between the analyst and the fugitives. They even used pet names.

"What's the deal with you guys?" Kincade asked Arianne.

"We'll tell you," she said. "Please be patient."

Stanwell, who had been quiet up until then, became agitated again. "Please, Mr. Kincade. You don't know what you're doing. There're two of them now."

"We mean you no harm, Mr. Stanwell," Arianne told him.

But her words did little to put his mind at ease. "Fine, do what you want," he told Kincade, "but at least let me go."

"Sorry, Stanwell, but I need you to come with us."

"Why? What could I possibly—"

Everyone turned to Stanwell, wondering why he had abruptly stopped talking.

As Kincade followed the assistant's gaze to the bushes across the road, he was able to make out three silhouettes lying on the ground.

"They were the ones guarding the back entrance," said Arianne.

"Are they dead?" Rock asked.

"Of course not," Ashrem replied. "They're unconscious."

Not inclined to take the young man at his word, Kincade crossed over to make sure.

He returned a few seconds later and nodded to the others.

"We'd better leave," Ashrem pressed.

"Yes, yes, we know," said Kincade, "we'll hold off on the questions until later."

Ashrem jogged around the van and hopped back into the driver seat. Doc sat up front with him while the rest of the group climbed into the back.

Once everyone was seated, Arianne turned to Stanwell. "I'm sorry, but we can't let you see where we're going. We need to cover your eyes."

Stanwell was outraged. "What? Just me?"

"Yes."

"Why? What about them?" he asked looking around at the mercenaries.

"We're asking them to trust us. We have to trust them in return."

"But that's … I don't even want to go with you," Stanwell protested.

Rock couldn't stop smiling. He had had a very unpleasant trip on the way to the manor and had profusely complained to Stanwell about the hood placed over his head. Now their roles were reversed. He was delighted to have the opportunity to get back at the assistant. He pulled out the black cloth they had used on him—he had kept it in his pocket—and covered Stanwell's head. "Sorry, buddy, but you understand, right?"

"You should tie his hands as well," Arianne suggested. "I'd rather make sure he doesn't try anything."

Rock didn't need a lot of convincing. His smile grew wider as he placed a pair of handcuffs around Stanwell's wrists. "Hehe! You heard the lady."

"Is everyone all set back there?" Ashrem asked.

"Yes, let's go!" Arianne replied.

The van rolled down the dark road and swerved off toward the highway.

Twelve minutes later, Jenkins was standing in the middle of Lucielle's bedroom, talking on his phone. "Almost all security cameras were disabled. We have very little footage. The maid's not fully lucid yet, but she described an Asian girl, in other words, Mitsuki.

…

Yes, sir, I'm certain the analyst is gone. So are the mercenaries. And your man Stanwell too.

…

The panic room was opened when I arrived. She went in, but for some reason she chose to come out.

…

No, I believe it was of her own volition. There are bullet holes in the walls and dead bodies lying around, but I found no signs of forced entry into the panic room.

...

I don't know, the reason is still unclear.

...

Someone knocked out the guards at the back entrance. I assume they all left from there.

...

Yes, sir. My men have already been dispatched.

...

Of course, I'll let you know the second we have something."

Jenkins waited for Leicester to cut off the call on the other end, and then slid the phone back into his pocket. Then, at the sounds of footsteps approaching, he turned to the door just as Carson showed up inside the frame.

"Anything new?" Jenkins asked.

Carson shook his head. "I can buy the analyst getting abducted ... but a group of experienced soldiers? That's a tough sell. I don't understand what Kincade and his men are up to."

Jenkins had a mean look in his eyes. "I intend to ask them."

Chapter 11 – Crime Scene

Detective Marie Heirtmeyer gazed at her reflection in the mirror. She was tired. It was almost 4:15 a.m., and she hadn't slept at all. Her eyes were red and swollen from crying too much.

As she stood there, absently staring at herself, she recalled the events of the previous morning.

She was already on her way to the police station when she received a call from her partner. They were to investigate a new crime scene. She didn't think much of it at the time. Having spent close to three years working as a criminal detective in a major city like Berlin, she had come to view crime as an unfortunate, but all too common, occurrence. Marie's partner had told her it would be faster to meet at the victim's apartment since it was on her way to the station. She pulled over and waited for him to send her the address.

Seconds later, his text arrived.

As soon as she read it, a shiver ran through her entire body. *It can't be.* She recognized the address. She knew the person who lived there. She had visited him two days earlier. *There must be some mistake,* she told herself as she stomped on the gas pedal.

It took Marie less than fifteen minutes to arrive at her destination—it should have taken her twice as long. She arrived well ahead of her partner, who had a shorter distance to travel. She had been to that address many times, so she knew all the shortcuts. And her driving had been so reckless it was nothing short of a miracle she had made it there in one piece.

Marie abandoned her car on the curb and ran towards the building. As she neared the entrance, two uniformed police officers moved to intercept her. Without slowing down, she flashed her badge and ran past them. She rushed up the stairs and hurried to the victim's door. Another police officer was standing guard outside. He tried to tell her something, but she didn't hear. She reached for the door handle … but then she froze, suddenly afraid to see what was on the other side.

She remained frozen for a while under the officer's befuddled gaze until, at last, she worked up the courage to go inside.

She stepped into the entrance hall, nervous and hesitant, and proceeded past the kitchen. But the moment she came into view of the living room, she stopped and gasped in horror.

There he was, lying on his side in a pool of blood. Professor Karpov.

"Oh no!" she muttered. "Professor …"

Two forensics technicians and a police photographer were collecting fingerprints and taking pictures, but none of them noticed the detective. They were focused on their tasks and had their backs turned to her.

Despite her shock, Marie's police training prompted her to scan the room. There were no signs of a struggle. Everything was in its proper place, except for the painting resting on the floor, and the hole in the wall where the painting was supposed to hang. The professor's safe had been opened.

Eventually one of the lab technicians noticed her. "Ah, Detective Heirtmeyer! When did you get here?"

She didn't reply. Her gaze was drawn back to the professor, but she didn't dare get close to him. "Is he…?"

"Dead? Oh yes, a Mr. Maximillian Schmidt. The poor guy was stabbed through the heart. I'm pretty sure it happened right here. It doesn't look like the body was moved. I'm guessing he was … uh … Detective Heirtmeyer? Where are you going?"

Marie had begun moving backward, one small step at a time. At first, she wasn't even aware she was doing it. Before long, she was once again standing outside the apartment, leaving the three men inside staring at one another, perplexed.

"Finished already, Detective?" the officer at the door asked.

She didn't acknowledge him as she closed the door, moving almost in slow motion.

"Detective …? Are you all right?"

When Marie's partner, Hans, arrived five minutes later, he found her sitting alone in the hallway near the staircase with her back against the wall and her face buried in her hands.

"Hey, you got here pretty fast," he said.

Marie brushed the golden locks away from her face and looked up at him. Her eyes were brimming with tears.

"What's wrong?" he asked, surprised to see her so distraught.

"Nothing, I'll be fine," she replied, getting back to her feet.

He touched her on the shoulder. "Come on, Marie, it's me. Tell me, what happened?"

"The man who lives here. I know him."

"You mean the victim?"

She nodded.

Hans hesitated a moment. "Who was he? How do you know him?"

Marie took a deep breath as she tried to collect herself. "He's a close friend of mine. I come to visit him often. I was here with him two days ago."

"Oh, Marie, I'm sorry," said Hans. He peered down the hallway. "Have the forensics people arrived?"

She nodded again.

"What are they saying?"

"He was stabbed," she said in a voice so weak he almost didn't hear. "And his safe was left open. Maybe the killer wanted to make it look like a robbery."

Hans cocked his head back. "Make it look like? You don't think it was a robbery?"

Marie straightened up and clenched her fists, as if she was preparing for battle. "Not for a second."

"How do you know? Did you pick up a clue?"

"No, I ... just trust me, there's something else going on here."

Although she could not explain it to her partner, Marie knew for a fact there was nothing of value inside the professor's safe. All it contained was some old documents and a few photographs. Any burglar skilled enough to break into this kind of safe would at least have some idea about what it contained before even setting foot inside the apartment. And if someone had forced the professor to open the safe, why kill him afterward? It made no sense to commit murder over some worthless old files. The only one who cared about the contents of the safe was the professor himself, and perhaps the people who were after him.

Hans gave his partner a searching look. "What are you thinking?"

Marie's eyes now burned with a quiet fury. "I'm going to find whoever did this, and I'm going to make them pay."

Hans felt a wave of uneasiness wash over him. Never before had he seen his partner look so determined and so vengeful. Perhaps it even scared him a little, but it definitely worried him a lot.

Chapter 12 – Father and Daughter

Marie was brought back to the present by a tingling sensation on her skin. In the mirror, she saw a tear roll down her right cheek. She opened the faucet and splashed some water on her face. It was cold, but she didn't care. She grabbed a towel hanging by the door and dried her face.

She returned to the bedroom, sat on the bed, and stared into space for a while. Her phone rested on the night table next to her. She picked it up. She opened the album application and scrolled through it, looking for a particular picture. When she found it, she lay on her back and held up the phone.

As she stared at the picture, her mind drifted back to the time it had been taken.

It was a Sunday, almost a year ago to the day.

Like every Sunday, she had gone to see Professor Karpov at his apartment. It was nice and sunny, so she suggested they go for a walk in a park. Of course, the old man obstinately refused at first. He was always reluctant to go outside, and he hated crowds.

But Marie wouldn't take no for an answer. "It will do you some good to get out in the sun for a change, Professor."

"All right, all right," he grumbled.

While the pair were strolling in the park, they met an old couple: Japanese tourists on a European tour. Since it was the couple's first visit to Berlin, Marie offered to take their picture as a memento of their trip. She ended up taking four or five. After she handed the camera back, the old woman offered to return the favor. Karpov wasn't interested. Marie, however, thought it was a splendid idea. She and the professor had known each other for almost two years, and despite having spent plenty of time together, she didn't have a single photograph of him. She took the professor by the arm and asked him to smile.

"Fine," he said, "just don't go posting it on the internet. I know young people like to do this kind of stuff these days."

"I won't, I won't."

"I mean it, Marie! Promise me," he insisted.

She was a little taken aback by his brusque tone, but she understood the reason for it. "I promise. You can trust me, Professor."

After taking a picture with Marie's phone, the old couple thanked her and her *dad* before moving on. The Japanese tourists had mistakenly assumed Marie and Karpov were father and daughter because of the apparent close bond between them.

Once, the professor had mentioned having had a family many years ago. Sadly, both his wife and daughter had died in a tragic accident. It was the only time he had ever spoken of them. He had told Marie his daughter would have been about her age if she were still alive, and that Marie reminded him of her.

Marie, on the other hand, was an orphan. She had never known her parents, nor did she have any brothers or sisters. In a way, there was a complementarity in those tragic parts of their lives. He was the closest thing to a father figure she had ever known, and she was the closest thing to a daughter he had left. It was one of the main reasons they had grown so close in such a short time.

Still lying on her bed, Marie's mind took her back to the time they had met, a couple of years earlier. She had knocked on his door while conducting a sweep of his building. She had been going through each apartment, hoping to find a witness to an assault and robbery that had taken place at a nearby store.

An unfriendly-looking old man opened the door and eyed the detective from head to toe. "Who are you?"

"Hello, sir, my name is Detective Heirtmeyer. I'm with the Berlin police."

97

He tensed up. "Police? What do you want with me?"

"Please calm down, sir. There was a robbery in a store across the street. I'm only here to take a statement. Can you tell me your name, please?"

"Schmidt. And I didn't see anything. Sorry."

"Wait!" Marie barely managed to hold the door back as he tried to slam it shut. She explained to him that she was questioning the people on his side of the building because it was the one facing the street.

Marie's first impression of Schmidt was that of a rude and unsympathetic old grump. He insisted he had neither seen nor heard anything and seemed eager to cut their conversation short. But Marie was stubborn. Despite his repeated efforts to get rid of her, she persevered. She remained polite and patient, but also determined. Of all the apartments she had checked thus far, his was the first where someone had answered the door, potentially making him the sole witness in the entire building.

"You must have at least heard the gunshots," she insisted.

"I told you, I can't help you."

"Please, the store owner was injured, and he might not make it. If there's anything you can tell me … even a minor detail could prove useful."

It was Marie's first real case since making detective a couple of months earlier. She had passed all the tests with flying colors, and her new colleagues had made her feel welcome after she had transferred to her new division. But in spite of all of this, she was beginning to have doubts regarding her decision to become a police detective. Thus far, it wasn't what she'd expected. She had made a great many sacrifices to earn her badge because she wanted to help victims and take down bad guys. In short, she wanted to make a difference. But all she had done in the past nine weeks was file paperwork and run errands to help others in *their* investigations. This was her first *major* assignment. Deep down, she felt she needed to solve it in order to prove herself.

Realizing she wouldn't go away, Schmidt agreed to let her in.

He invited her to take a seat on the sofa in the living room.

Marie took out a small notepad and a pen from her handbag. Then, in keeping with her training, she began with simple questions in order to make him less defensive.

The old man didn't respond to any of her queries. Instead, he studied her with a piercing gaze, like he was sizing her up.

"Mr. Schmidt?"

"I'll help you," he said. "But on one condition."

"A condition?"

"Yes, I want your assurance that my name will not appear in your report. In fact, don't mention me to anyone, not even your colleagues."

"Not mention you? I'm sorry, but procedure dictates—"

"Take it or leave it."

Marie wondered why this odd man was so intent on keeping his anonymity. *Is he a criminal?* Like most detectives, she was suspicious by nature, and Schmidt's strange behavior was raising a few red flags.

Sensing her hesitation, Schmidt promptly changed his mind. "Forget it! Please leave," he said.

"OK, fine. I won't mention you," Marie told him. She reluctantly agreed for fear of losing her single lead.

"I have your word?"

"Yes, you have my word. Whatever you tell me will be logged in as an anonymous tip."

Sensing that Schmidt was satisfied with her answer, the detective resumed her interview.

"Did you get a look at the culprits? Or perhaps the kind of car they were driving?"

Schmidt waved his hand. "Stop talking, please."

"I beg your pardon?"

"Stop talking," he repeated, "just listen. There's a young man who's been working part-time at the store for almost a year now. His name is Barnard. He seems like a nice young fellow, but from what I gathered, he's been having some financial difficulties for the past three or four months. It might have something to do with that flamboyant new girlfriend of his. Anyway, I went down to buy groceries earlier, and I saw two men sitting in a gray sedan parked down the block. When I came back, they were still there, waiting. I became curious and kept an eye on them from up here. A short time later, Barnard popped outside to make a call. I caught him exchanging a signal with the two men in the car. He went back into the store, and about a minute later, the two men followed in after him. They're the ones who robbed the place. If you want to find them, all you need to do is *grill* Barnard a little and he'll confess to everything. Like I said, he seems like a nice enough young man. I'm sure he feels bad about the owner getting shot."

Marie had listened in silence until he was done. She was staring at him with a strange expression. How could he possibly know all this? He had told his tale in one go, without pauses or hesitation, like someone reading a report. She couldn't help but think he had made up the entire story just to get rid of her.

The detective sighed. "I see you're not going to help." She put away her notepad and pen and got up. "Thank you for your time."

Surprised by her reaction, Schmidt followed her with his gaze as she walked away. He meant to say something to stop her, but he was too late. She was already gone. *Strange girl,* he thought. It didn't occur to him she hadn't believed a word he had told her.

Two days later, at around seven o'clock in the evening, Schmidt heard a knock on his door. It startled him. He wasn't expecting any visitors. Come to think of it, he never had any visitors. He tiptoed to the door and listened.

A woman's voice called out from the other side. "Mr. Schmidt! It's Detective Heirtmeyer. Could I have a word, please?"

He hesitated for a moment and then opened the door. "I didn't think I'd see you again. What do you want now?"

"How did you know?" she asked him.

"Huh?"

"About the robbery."

"Ah! I take it the young man confessed."

"He did. We ran out of leads, so I decided to follow your suggestion. As soon as I told Barnard there was a witness and mentioned the gray car, he crumbled. You were right. He must have been feeling quite guilty about the whole incident."

"Good." Schmidt smiled. "I told you he wasn't a bad person."

"You were right about the girlfriend too. It seems Barnard's been living beyond his means to keep up with her expensive tastes. He's up to his neck in debts."

The old man shook his head. "Young people these days." He suddenly gave Marie a distrustful look. "You didn't say anything about me, did you?"

"Not a word."

"Good."

"May I come in?" she said.

He frowned. "Why?"

"It'll just be for a minute."

He hesitated briefly and then stepped aside to let her in. "Fine."

They went into the living room and sat in the exact same spots as before.

"How did you know all of this?" she asked.

"I already explained it to you."

"You were telling the truth?"

"Of course."

She paused for a moment. "What made you start paying attention to Barnard?"

"I didn't."

Marie looked confused.

"I mean ... I didn't pay any particular attention to *him*," the old man clarified. "I tend to observe the people around me. Force of habit, I guess."

Marie was impressed. "Are you saying you deduced everything you told me about Barnard simply from watching him from time to time? This goes way beyond being observant, you know."

Being a detective, Marie could not fail to appreciate such a display of perception and reasoning abilities. In her experience, there were typically two kinds of people capable of such feats: brilliant detectives and brilliant criminals.

Schmidt gave her an uneasy smile. "Well, I suppose it also helps to be paranoid."

Marie too looked uncomfortable. "While we're on the subject ..." she said.

"Hmm?"

"You seem tense around police officers." She hesitated, not sure how to word it. "I mean ... I'm thankful for the help you've given me. In fact, I don't think we would have solved this case if it hadn't been for you. Both the owner and his wife were convinced their assistant had nothing to do with it. Oh, he's going to make it, by the way."

"Who?"

"The owner. He's going to recover."

"Good," Schmidt said again.

Marie's gaze grew insistent. "Well...?"

"What?"

"You're not in trouble with the law, are you?"

"Of course not." He laughed nervously. "Do you think I'd let detectives freely walk in and out of my apartment if I was wanted by the police? I simply value my privacy. Plus, I don't like interacting with people all that much."

"Really? I hadn't noticed," she joked.

They exchanged awkward smiles.

"Anyway," she said, "I'm sorry, but I had to ask."

"I understand. You're a detective. It wouldn't do for you to just stroll in and out of a criminal's home."

They smiled again.

After a brief period of uncomfortable silence, Marie stood up.

"Thank you," she said. She decided she had imposed on her host long enough. And this time, she made her proper goodbyes before leaving.

A week later, Detective Heirtmeyer stopped by the store to check on the owner's wife—her husband was still in the hospital. As she was walking back to her car, she bumped into Schmidt. He was on his way to have dinner at a nearby bar-restaurant. She asked if she could join him, promising to leave the detective behind. And a most unexpected thing happened. He accepted.

So, the unlikely pair went off to dinner.

Marie's motive for wanting to go with Schmidt could have been summed up in one word: curiosity. Intrigued by the way he had solved the robbery case, she hoped to get answers to the questions that had been nagging away at her all week. But after spending a couple of hours with the old recluse, she found him to be a completely different person from the one he had appeared to be. She realized his rude and cranky exterior was only a façade, a barrier he put up to keep people away. But now, for some unknown reason, he had chosen to let his guard down around her. She felt like she was meeting him for the first time. And what she discovered was a warm and kind man, who had a great sense of humor and was surprisingly easy to talk to.

As the night went on and two hours turned into four, Marie discovered that Schmidt's most remarkable quality was neither his acute sense of observation nor his unique capacity for deductive reasoning. No, it was his incredible knowledge. No matter which topic their conversation steered toward, he had a plethora of facts and arguments at his disposal. Never before had the detective met anyone this knowledgeable on so many unrelated subjects.

After that evening, Marie and Schmidt kept in touch. In the beginning, it was nothing more than the occasional phone call. Then, Marie began to stop by once or twice every couple of weeks. Eventually, her visits turned into a regular twice-a-week occurrence.

They would discuss all sorts of topics, from the most frivolous of subjects to the more serious matters. In time, Schmidt found himself looking forward to their long talks. The hours they spent together provided rare fleeting moments of escape from the prison of solitude in which he had confined himself all those years ago.

Marie also liked spending time with him. She would talk to him about her work and her private life. And he would always listen attentively and, on occasion, give her small bits of advice. In less than a year, their relationship had developed into a genuine friendship.

One day Marie was telling Schmidt about a difficult case that had the entire department baffled.

He offered to help.

She was reluctant at first. Revealing the details of an on-going investigation to a civilian was a serious breach of regulations. But she trusted him. She decided it was okay to bend the rules a little if it gave the police a better chance of catching a criminal.

Once again, Schmidt astounded her with his insight and brilliance. After three hours spent reading case files and questioning her on certain key points of the investigation, he managed to identify a promising suspect.

The detective followed up on his lead. A few days later, the police apprehended the culprit.

Following the arrest, Marie's colleagues showered her with accolades, and at the end of the day, invited her out to celebrate. She thanked them but declined their invitation. In truth, she didn't feel at all like celebrating. *Schmidt is the one who deserves all the credit,* she kept thinking. She was dying to tell them. She wanted people to acknowledge him. But she had vowed never to mention his name.

She felt like a fraud.

She went to Schmidt's apartment that same night to tell him she would never again rely on him to solve a case.

When the old man saw her morose expression despite the positive outcome of her investigation, he understood right away what she was going through.

"You're a very good detective, Marie. You're intelligent, observant and dedicated. You have the potential to be great. I can tell."

She sat on the sofa. "It's nice of you to say. Don't worry, I'll be fine."

He sat next to her and took her hand. "Marie, if there's one thing I want you to remember from all our talks, it's that we all need help from time to time. I know it's difficult for you to accept because you're an orphan, and because you've never had anyone you could depend on. But trust me, there's only so much any of us can accomplish alone."

"I don't know, Schmidt"—she always called him by his last name. "You

105

seem to have been doing fine on your own. I suppose it helps to be as smart as you are."

"Ha! I've had plenty of help in my time. I wouldn't be here today if I hadn't learned to accept it. And I think you know by now I haven't been doing that so great on my own."

"Yes, I know. I'm sorry for saying that."

"It's all right, Marie. But please, you have to let me help when I can, even if it's only a little. It means more to me than you realize. Not just because of you, but for myself as well. I never thought I'd get another chance to do something good for other people, a chance to make up for the things I've done."

From the moment she had walked into Schmidt's apartment, Marie had been in a sort of half-dazed state. It took a second for her brain to catch on to his strange comment. "What did you say? Make up for the things you've done? What did you mean?"

"Nothing. I misspoke."

Marie gave him a searching look. But she was too tired and too preoccupied to press him further.

"So, you'll let me help?" Schmidt asked.

"Sure, and thanks again. Truth be told, your help has been invaluable."

"Good," he said. "And for the record, I know certain people who are a lot smarter than I could ever hope to be," he added with a coy smile.

She glanced at him from the corner of her eye. "Now I find *that* hard to believe. Still, thanks for trying to make me feel better."

After that night, the bond between them grew even stronger, and it became easier for her to accept his help. She continued to visit him twice a week, each time encouraging him to go outside, but rarely succeeding, while he continued to help with some of her cases, especially ones where a serious crime had been committed. All things considered, Marie concluded, it was worth bending the rules a little, if only to catch just one more criminal, or to save just one more life.

And so, the days went by, pleasant and uneventful, until about six months later, when everything changed.

Chapter 13 – True Identity

It was a stormy night. But despite the awful weather, Detective Marie Heirtmeyer rushed to Maximillian Schmidt's apartment to share the good news. She'd finally caught him: a kidnapper of young girls whom the police had been tracking for weeks. It had been a tough case to crack, and she had done it without any help from Schmidt.

She arrived at his apartment out of breath and rang the doorbell a couple of times. There was no answer. She thought it was strange because she could see a faint light filtering out from underneath the door and she could hear the TV was on.

She waited a moment and rang the doorbell again.

Still no answer.

Marie wasn't the worrying type, but for some reason, she felt something was wrong. She reached inside her purse, took out her keychain, and used one of her keys to unlock the door. She and Schmidt had exchanged keys to their apartments a few of months back in case of an emergency—Marie's idea. Normally, she'd call ahead to make sure he was home, and not too busy, before showing up. But in her excitement, she had forgotten.

She opened the door and hesitantly proceeded inside. But as soon as she cleared the entrance hall she stopped in her tracks.

Sheets of paper were scattered all over the sofa and side chairs. Schmidt's jacket, which he usually hung by the door, was lying on the floor near the kitchen entrance, and his laptop was flipped open on the coffee table, amongst a pile of newspapers and folders. The detective had never seen Schmidt's living room in such a messy state. She had often teased him because his apartment always looked too neat and tidy. Nothing was ever out of place. She would tell him it was like no one lived there.

Next, her attention was drawn to the television. The volume was high, which was why she had been able to hear it from outside. There was a breaking news report about a French diplomat who had died in a car crash. Marie had heard about it over the radio on her way to the apartment.

She took a few more steps inside the living room and for the second time stopped dead in her tracks. She had spotted a small safe embedded in the wall on the other side of the television, in place of the painting that normally hung there.

Marie was stunned. She had been inside Schmidt's apartment dozens of times, but she'd had no idea this was there. And she would never have guessed it. She didn't think he possessed anything valuable enough to justify keeping it inside a safe.

Schmidt came out of the bedroom, dragging his feet, and with his head down as he read from an opened folder. He was so engrossed in the document, he didn't notice Marie's presence.

She was about to say something when he started mumbling to himself. She tried to make out what he was saying, but his voice was too low. The TV wasn't helping either. She could only pick up parts of his sentences.

"… Adam was right … Vice … We should have …"

The rest was swallowed up by the surrounding noise.

"Aah!" Schmidt shouted when he finally noticed the detective. "Marie … you scared me."

"Sorry. I rang the bell several times but you didn't answer … I got worried."

He eyed her with suspicion. "How did you get in?"

She gave a crooked smile and showed him her keys.

"Oh, of course …"

"What's going on?" she asked.

109

Schmidt glanced around and realized the state of his apartment required some kind of an explanation. "I, erm … I was looking for some old documents and, erm …"

Marie moved closer to him. "Please. I know you're trying to put on a brave face like you always do, but if you're in trouble, you can tell me. I want to help."

Schmidt stared at her at length. Then, he sighed and buried his face in his hands.

He remained like this for a while.

Marie took him by the arm and led him to the couch. "What's wrong? Tell me."

He exhaled heavily. "Before I met you, I only had two friends left in the world. One of them died tonight."

"Oh, Schmidt, I'm so sorry." She rubbed her hand on his arm to convey her sympathy.

He forced a faint smile. "Thank you."

She smiled back.

The following moments were a bit awkward for Marie. She knew Schmidt didn't want her to see him looking so miserable. She averted her eyes and let her gaze wander around the room. It landed on a photograph sticking out from the jumble of papers spread over the table. It was a picture of three middle-aged men laughing together. Two of them, she had never seen before. The man on the right, however, looked familiar. She focused on the picture, trying to place him.

Meanwhile, Schmidt observed her in silence.

"It's you!" she suddenly exclaimed. "You were much younger, but it's definitely you."

The old man said nothing.

"Do you mind?" she asked, leaning toward the table.

He shook his head.

Marie picked up the photograph. The man in the middle had on a blue-striped suit, but Schmidt and the man on the left were both wearing long white coats.

"Are you a doctor?" she asked.

"Not quite."

Marie's eyes remained fixed on the photograph. Something about it was bugging her. Then, she realized the man in the suit also looked vaguely familiar. She put down the picture, intending to ask Schmidt about him. But when she raised her head, the answer was staring at her in the face. Or rather, *she* was staring at it. It was him, on the television, the victim of the fatal car crash, the French diplomat whose face was on the news.

"Is he the friend you just told me about?" she asked.

"Yes. His name was Pierre Dumas. It's my fault he's dead. I knew it was too dangerous. I should have stopped him."

Marie gave a puzzled look. "What are you talking about? It's no one's fault. It was an accident."

"No, it wasn't," Schmidt sharply replied.

She pointed at the television. "It says right there, on the news …"

Schmidt slowly picked up the photograph, turned it over, and handed it to Marie.

There was writing on the back: Prof. J. Fournier, Mr. P. Dumas, Prof. A. Karpov.

"I don't … I don't understand," she stammered, her eyes riveted on the three names.

She waited for Schmidt to give an explanation.

He didn't.

She flipped the photograph over and examined it once again. She gazed at it for almost half a minute before she finally put it down. Her eyes locked in on Schmidt. "Who are you?"

"My name is Aleksandr Karpov. I was a research scientist in the Soviet Union during the Cold War, until my mentor and I were taken to the West."

Marie was gobsmacked. A mix of emotions rampaged inside her head: shock, confusion, distrust, anger.

She instinctively inched back as she voiced her indignation. "I trusted you. I confided in you … I even shared details of my investigations with you. You're telling me I didn't even know your name?"

"I'm sorry I lied to you, Marie," he said, his voice conveying genuine sincerity. "Some years ago, I was forced to go into hiding. I had to disappear and assume a new identity."

Marie thought back on the day she had met him. Her instincts had told her there was something odd about his behavior. She remembered wondering if he was some kind of criminal. And now, it turned out she might have been right.

"Why did you have to disappear?" the detective asked in the same tone she used during a suspect's interrogation.

"There are people looking for me."

"What people? Why are they looking for you?"

He closed his eyes and shook his head. "It's better if you don't know."

"Not a chance," she objected. She leaned forward and locked gazes with him. "Does it have anything to do with your friend's death?"

Realizing there was no way she was going to let it go, the old man resigned himself to answering her questions. "Yes. This is how they operate, with accidents or coincidences, always staying in the shadows, never drawing attention to themselves."

"you're certain it wasn't an accident?"

"I'm positive."

"Then we tell the authorities. I am a police detective after all."

He bowed his head, dejected. "I'm afraid it wouldn't do any good. They're far beyond your reach."

"Who's 'they'?"

The old man's body stiffened. It was like he had just received a shot of stimulants. "No, this I cannot tell you."

"Oh, come on!"

"I'm sorry. I can't."

"You're not getting off the hook that easy."

"No!" he snapped.

Marie jumped in her seat. Schmidt had never raised his voice at her before.

"I'm sorry I yelled," he said, having regained his composure. "Please try to understand. It's for your own safety."

They sat in silence for a long time.

Then, he took the young woman's hands and squeezed them to impress upon her the importance of what he was about to tell her. "I need you to promise me one thing."

She eyed him warily. "What?"

"Should anything happen to me, I need you to promise you won't take part in the investigation."

"Why would anything hap—" Suddenly she understood what he meant.

She pulled her hands back and shot a glance at the television screen. "Wait a minute ... are you saying ...? Don't even talk like that."

The thought of her friend falling victim to a similar *accident* had changed her anger into distress.

"Please, Marie, you must swear," he insisted.

"No, absolutely not," she said, her voice louder than she had intended. "If your life is in danger, we'll put you under police protection. We'll—"

"I told you, it wouldn't do any good. Those people have connections high up in the government. Involving the police might, in fact, lead them straight to me."

"Then you'll come live with me. At least you wouldn't be alone. I'll protect you."

"That's not an option. I've already put you in enough danger as it is. I was lonely ... and you reminded me so much of my daughter ... I didn't think. Anyway, it's too late for regrets. All I can do now is try to keep you as far away from all of this as possible. So, you have to promise me."

"I can't ... I won't ..." she said, her voice shaking. "I won't just sit around waiting for something bad to happen to you."

"No one's saying that. I don't intend to just give up. I've taken a lot of precautions over the years to make sure they wouldn't find me. It's obviously been working so far, and hopefully it will continue to."

"Right, of course it will," she said, trying to reassure herself.

"Don't worry. I've gotten quite good at staying invisible."

She forced a smiled. "Good. But what about the other man in the picture? Is he your other friend? Does he know where you are?"

"Who, Jerome? Yes, he's my friend. But he doesn't know where I am. And I don't know where he is. This way, if either of us gets caught, he won't be in a position to compromise the other."

"I see." She picked up the photograph and examined it again. "Are those same people after him too?"

"Oh yes!"

"And you have no contact with him whatsoever?"

The old man shot an involuntary glance at the laptop on the table.

"What? Is there something on the computer?" Marie asked.

"Well, we do have a way of getting in touch, though we've never used it. An old friend of ours set up two anonymous email accounts for us; one for Jerome and the other for me. But he warned us to use them only in case of an emergency."

Marie reached for the laptop and slid it closer. It was logged in to an email inbox. A new email was open, but its contents were empty. She took a long look at the destination address. "You were going to send him a message?"

"I considered it. But what would be the point? No doubt Jerome has heard the awful news. And after this, I'm not even sure he would respond. Living in hiding tends to make one paranoid, you know."

"If you're not sure about it, then don't write," she said. "You should continue to be as careful as you can."

"I know. Don't worry. I'll be all right."

The old man noticed Marie's gaze lingering over him.

"I'm sorry," she said. "It's just ... you look different ... older somehow."

"I'm just tired," he exhaled. "So very tired."

"Well, you're not alone anymore. You've got me now."

Her words seemed to genuinely bring him some comfort. "Thank you, Marie."

"All right, enough of all this sentimental stuff," she said. "I'll help you clean up this mess."

"No need to trouble yourself. I'll do it."

"No, no. It's no trouble, Sch—" She stopped mid-sentence.

"What is it?"

"I can't call you Schmidt anymore, can I? It'd be too weird now that I know it's not your real name."

"It was already weird using a last name."

"It's not the same," she said. "Anyway, I can't start calling you Karpov, or Aleksandr."

"Never," the old man told her.

Marie tapped her index finger on her lips. "Hmm … how about Alex?"

"Still too risky, I'm afraid."

"Ha! I know. You said you used to be a scientist. Is that why there's the title of professor before your name on the picture?"

"Yes."

"At the moment you're teaching night classes, and your students call you Professor, right?"

"Yes, they do …"

"Then I'll do the same. If I call you Professor, it'll be *real*, but it won't raise any suspicions because if anyone hears it, they'll think I'm one of your students."

He thought about it and agreed it wouldn't pose a problem. "Okay, if you prefer. I don't mind."

They exchanged a warm smile.

The old man knew, in truth, Marie didn't really mind continuing to call him *Schmidt*. But she sensed he had been carrying a great burden over the years. A burden made heavier by the secrets he kept, especially the one about his identity. And although his students called him *Professor*, they did so unaware of the word's true significance as it applied to him. But from now on, when Marie used the same word, it would have a different meaning because she knew the truth about him. It would be a way for her to help him reclaim a small piece of his true identity, and to help him cope with his self-inflicted isolation.

In less than ten minutes, the apartment was back to its usual immaculate state.

"I still can't believe there was a safe behind the painting all along," said Marie. "I never suspected a thing. Some detective …"

"Don't be so hard on yourself. You had no way of knowing. Besides, as you saw, there's nothing of value in it, just some old documents."

"Well, I suppose it's one more thing I'm going to have to get used to." Marie hesitated. "You sure you don't want me to stay over? I can sleep on the couch."

"Don't be ridiculous. I told you, I'll be fine. Off you go."

"OK. But remember, if you notice anything remotely suspicious, call me."

"I will."

"Promise?"

He smiled. "Hold on, weren't you the one who was supposed to make me a promise?"

"You're trying to change the subject. It's not going to work. Promise me you'll call at the first sign of trouble, even if you're not sure."

"I promise, I promise."

"Good. I meant what I said. I'm here if you need me."

"I know. Thank you."

"And if you change your mind about staying with me, don't hesitate. I'm told my sofa bed is quite comfortable."

He waved her away. "Just go home already."

Marie nodded and headed for the door. But half-way down the hall, she remembered something. "By the way, who's Adam?" she shouted.

The professor's eyes widened. "What did you say?" he asked in a low voice.

She returned to the living room. "Adam. I thought I heard you mention the name when I arrived earlier."

"Uh …no … I don't think I know anyone by that name. You must have misheard."

"Oh, maybe I did. Never mind then." She waved him goodbye. "Good night, *Professor.*"

"Good night."

After she had gone, the old man dropped on the sofa like a deflated balloon. Lucky for him, she had not been in a position to see his reaction when she'd mentioned the name *Adam*. Otherwise, she would certainly have caught the fear on his face. He let out a deep sigh of relief. "Phew! That was close."

The next day, Marie went back to the professor's place to check up on him. It was unusual for her to stop by two days in a row in the middle of the week, but the events of the previous night had been most unusual. She still felt awkward about the whole thing. The professor, on the other hand, was back to his normal self. His grief had temporarily made him feel vulnerable, and he had confided in her. But now, it was evident from his demeanor he had no intention of revisiting the subject. The message was clear: *We will go on as though nothing happened, and we will not speak of this again.*

118

And they never did. Their relationship continued as before, except she never again called him *Schmidt.*

Marie was still lying on her bed, half-awake, holding the precious photograph against her chest. Her mind was jumping from one memory to the next, re-living the moments she had shared with Professor Karpov over the short years, until, at last, she fell asleep.

Chapter 14 – Beginning

By the time Kincade's group arrived at their destination, day was breaking. The first rays of light were shooting up from the horizon, illuminating the stage in preparation for the concert of birds that preceded the morning sun.

The van pulled up in an isolated property about 16 miles from the town of Quimper, in Brittany. It had been a long drive from outside the south of Paris to the northwest of France.

"We're here," said Ashrem as he turned off the engine.

"And where exactly is 'here'?" Rock asked from the back of the van.

Arianne nodded at the black-hooded Stanwell.

Rock realized at once the foolishness of his question. Why bother to blindfold someone for an entire trip only to tell them where you are when you arrive. "Oh, yeah. I almost forgot about this guy."

"Where are we?" Stanwell asked. "What do you plan to do with me?"

"Shut up," Rock told him.

The assistant's neck was still sore from his earlier run-in with the colossus. Not eager to repeat the experience, he wisely decided to hold off on asking questions.

"Let's go inside," said Arianne.

One by one, the group disembarked from the vehicle. Rock was put in charge of Stanwell. He helped the assistant down and guided him by the arm.

Kincade paused to take a look around. They had parked inside a property surrounded by trees and green fields, and the air carried the scent of the nearby ocean.

In front of them stood a two-story house with white stone walls, slate roof tiles, and metallic shutters covering the windows. It was a nice and simple house in the quiet countryside.

Thirty feet to their right was a wooden shed with a dark blue car parked inside. It reminded Kincade of the barn at his grandparents' farm. He used to visit them in the summer as a kid. He had always enjoyed spending time with the animals there—the horses in particular. It felt strange that a shed in this foreign country could bring out those fond, but distant, memories from his childhood.

As the group neared the house, Sonar moved close to Kincade and whispered in his ear. "Nate, you sure it's wise to follow them like this? What if there's a welcoming committee waiting for us in there?"

In response, Kincade coolly nodded to Ashrem.

The young man was carrying Lucielle on his back. The long drive had been too tiring for her, so she had asked him for a piggyback ride. Ashrem was walking at a relaxed pace, a couple of steps ahead of Da Costa. His was not the attitude of a man on the verge of engaging in a violent confrontation. Besides, since the manor, it had been apparent that both Ashrem and Arianne cared a great deal for the young analyst. Kincade did not believe they would endanger her by starting a gun fight around her.

Arianne was the first one through the door, with Kincade right on her heels. He stepped onto the wooden floor and surveyed the entrance area. A long hallway stretched out in front of him. To the left was a small room with four chairs, a coffee table, and a liquor cabinet. To the right was a wooden staircase leading up to the second floor.

"Please, come in. Make yourselves at home," said Arianne as the others followed her inside.

"Hold on," said Kincade. "Da Costa and I will do a quick check around the house first. The rest of you stay put."

121

Neither Arianne nor Ashrem voiced a single word of protest. Kincade's caution was understandable under the circumstances. The mercenaries had already been more obliging than they had any right to expect.

"Of course," said Arianne, "but I should tell you—"

The ceiling creaked, interrupting her.

The mercenaries swiftly drew their weapons and aimed them at their traveling companions, and at the floor above them.

A round older man appeared at the top of the stairs. "Ah, Arianne, Ashrem, you're back. I was beginning to worry." He was wearing bizarrely-matched clothes. But even more peculiar was his lack of concern at the sight of strangers pointing guns at him.

"Someone else lives here," Arianne said, finishing her sentence.

The old man came down the steps. "I see you've brought back friends." He was smiling and cheerful.

Arianne made the introductions. "Everyone, this is Professor Jerome Fournier. Professor, these are the men sent by Leicester to capture us."

"I see … well, it's nice to meet you all," he replied, untroubled.

"Anyone else up there?" Doc asked, peeking up the stairs.

"No, it's just me, young man."

Doc gave Sonar a quick tap on the chest. "Let's go make sure."

As Professor Fournier watched the two men make their way up the stairs, a child's voice called to him.

"Hello, Professor."

The old man spun around and scanned the group. "Lucielle?"

The young girl had asked Ashrem to put her down and had been hiding behind Rock to surprise the professor. She stuck her head out and giggled before running to him.

He knelt down to hug her. "Oh, my dear girl. I didn't think I'd ever see you again. How are you? Have you been treated well?"

"Yes, Professor."

"Good. I'm so happy to see you." He put his hands on her shoulders and pushed her back slightly. "Let me have a look at you. My, you've grown. I can't believe you're eleven now."

"And a half," she corrected.

Rock rolled his eyes. "Argh, not again! Look, I hate to break up your little reunion, but we had a deal. Now I don't care who, but somebody better start explaining just what the hell happened back there."

The professor looked up at the hulk. "Did something happen to you, young man?" That was when he noticed the man in handcuffs with a hood over his head. "Why is—"

"Never mind him," Rock interrupted. "From now on, *we* will be asking the questions."

Kincade turned to Arianne. "He's right. We had a deal."

"Yes, we did," she said.

Doc and Sonar returned.

"All clear," said the redhead.

"All right, you guys wait here," said Kincade.

He and Da Costa proceeded down the L-shaped corridor, checking behind every door. Straight ahead, at the end, was a dining area with a long table and eight chairs arranged around it. To the left was a good-sized living room with two sofas, a big chair, two tall shelves, and a fireplace. On the other side of the house was the kitchen, a couple of bedrooms, and a door leading to the cellar.

Having completed their inspection, Kincade and Da Costa re-joined the group.

"OK," said Kincade, "we're good for now."

"Good," said Arianne. She invited everyone into the living room. "This way, please."

Da Costa discreetly tugged Kincade by the sleeve. He waited until the others were far enough away and whispered, "There's something off about these people. The old man didn't even flinch when he saw our guns, or when the girl told him who we were."

"I know what you mean," said Kincade. "They're acting a bit too carefree given the situation."

"That's what I'm trying to tell you, Nate. It's not an act. They don't feel threatened by us at all. Not even the kid."

Kincade rubbed the stubble on his chin. "Hmm … It's true we agreed to follow them here, but … they do seem a bit too trusting."

"Trust, eh? I guess that's one explanation."

"Why, you got another one?"

"Like I said … they don't see us as a threat."

Kincade thought about the events at the manor. He still had trouble believing that the frail-looking Mitsuki had been able to wreak such havoc. His carelessness had almost cost him his life. "I get your point. They may look harmless, but at the very least some of them aren't. We underestimated them once. Let's not make the same mistake again."

Da Costa nodded.

"Come on," said Kincade, "let's join the others."

"Ah, there you are," said the old man as Kincade and Da Costa walked into the living room. "I was just asking your friends if they wanted something to drink."

"No, thanks," said Kincade.

Da Costa shook his head.

Arianne sensed a change in Kincade's demeanor. "Is something the matter?"

"It's nothing."

"Yo, Nate. What should we do with this guy?" Rock asked as he tapped Stanwell on the head.

Kincade glanced at the captive. "There's a cellar across the kitchen. You and Sonar can stash him down there. And don't forget to take off his hood once he's tied up."

Ignoring Stanwell's complaints, Rock and Sonar escorted him to the cellar.

They returned shortly afterward and, rather than sit down, posted themselves by the doorway.

"Hehe, he's comfortable down there," Rock chuckled.

"All right, we're all here," said Kincade. He turned to Arianne. "Let's hear it. Who are you guys?"

"I suppose I should be the one to explain," said the professor. He stood in the middle of the room and began, "Back in the late 1970's, not long after the Vietnam War—"

"Hey, Pops!" Rock cut him off. "You can skip the history lesson. Just answer the question."

The giant had reached the limit of his patience; a sentiment shared by his comrades.

Sonar squinted at the old man with suspicion. "Are you trying to stall us or something?"

"If you could be a patient just a little bit longer," Arianne pleaded. "What we are about to tell you will make more sense if you hear the story from the beginning."

"Come on, guys," said Doc, "let's hear them out. And you, Professor, try to get to the point."

"Young people these days ... always in a hurry," Fournier lamented. "Anyway, as I was saying, after the Vietnam War, an unofficial branch of the American government, let's call it 'the Agency', put together a team to work on a special project. The team was led by a woman named Michelle Brainsworth, one of the world's most prominent scientists at the time. They were tasked with the development of new drugs to enhance soldiers."

"Enhance them how?" Doc asked.

"Physically. Strength, stamina, etc. But they were also interested in the psychological aspects. They wanted to make the soldiers more aggressive, and less prone to emotions such as fear or remorse."

"In short, they wanted to create their idea of a perfect soldier," Kincade summarized.

A light bulb went on inside Rock's head. "Aha! Then little miss superhero ninja was high on some crazy drug!" He turned to Ashrem and Arianne. "I'm guessing you two are doped up as well, huh?" He then turned to Lucielle with a wry smile. "Don't tell me they've got you on the same stuff too. That would be just ... wrong, man."

"What ...? No!" Lucielle exclaimed. "I'm not on drugs! And neither are they!"

"You're not?" said Rock, sounding surprised.

"If you would just let him finish," she said in an irritated tone.

"Don't raise your voice, Luce," Arianne chided.

The young girl pouted as she crossed her arms and sank deeper into the sofa.

126

"Go on, Professor," said Arianne.

"Ah, yes … after a great deal of time and effort, Dr. Brainsworth's team succeeded in creating a drug that produced the desired effects … more or less."

"Which is it?" Sonar asked. "Did it work or didn't it?"

"It did, to some extent. But like all scientists who embark on this type of research, Dr. Brainsworth was confronted with a major issue."

"What issue?" Sonar asked.

"Side effects, of course!" Professor Fournier motioned to some imaginary board, like a classroom teacher giving a lecture. "You can't just tamper with the body's internal functions without consequences. There's always a price to pay. The soldiers were stronger, as intended, and from what I've heard, most of them turned out to be quite mean. However, prolonged use of the drug resulted in other symptoms, like severe migraines, muscle spasms etc. A few subjects even died of cardiac arrest."

"I bet that put a stop to the whole thing," said Sonar.

Fournier wagged his finger. "Wrong. They kept going. The project had shown real promise. Plus, the soldiers were volunteers. They knew the risks. Even so, the variations in side effects were too significant from one individual to the next. And the longer the soldiers took the drugs, the more their bodies adjusted to them, which rendered the drugs less effective over time. You could say it was a partial success. Dr. Brainsworth worked tirelessly to resolve those issues, but to no avail."

"I thought you said she was some kind of big shot scientist," Rock commented.

"She was. But the simple fact is the human body has limits. You can bend the rules to some extent, but you can't break them. The body wouldn't survive it. As time went by, the Agency grew frustrated with Brainsworth's lack of progress. They were on the verge of shutting the whole enterprise down when Dr. Brainsworth approached them with an audacious new idea.

127

She believed they needed to change the parameters of the project itself. Advances in science and technology presented them with a different solution, one which would have been inconceivable a few years earlier: Genetic manipulation."

Those two words piqued the mercenary's interest.

Chapter 15 – Unnatural

"Genetic manipulation?" Doc echoed.

"Yes." Professor Fournier was pleased to see he had caught his audience's attention. "It makes sense when you think about it. If you can't push the human body beyond its limits, why not try to push those limits instead? Dr. Brainsworth was given a new mandate. She abandoned her previous research and redirected all of her resources in this new direction. It was, of course, as you say in English, easier said than done. Brainsworth had to rethink everything from scratch, starting with her team, and that proved quite a challenge. Genetic engineering was a new field at the time. She knew that in order to assemble the best possible group, she would have to enlist the help of scientists from other countries as well. One man, in particular, was considered vital to the success of the project. His name was Friedrich Engel. He was widely regarded as the world's leading expert in the field of genetics. But there was one problem. Professor Engel was a German citizen living in East Berlin, which, as you all know, was part of the Eastern Bloc."

Kincade smiled. "In the middle of the Cold War? Yeah, I can see how that would be a problem."

"Indeed. The idea made more than a few people nervous. Dr. Brainsworth had to push hard to get the Agency to go along with it. But in the end, she was able to convince them. Then came the hard part."

"The extraction," Doc guessed.

"Correct. They needed to find a way to extract Professor Engel without his knowledge."

"Why not try to contact him?" Sonar asked.

Fournier waved his hand like he was brushing aside a question from an overeager student. "Too risky," he said. "Very little was known about

129

Professor Engel on a personal level. The Agency had no idea if he would be receptive to their offer. What if he refused? Not only would they lose all access to him, they would also tip off the Russians to what they were trying to accomplish."

Still standing in the doorway with his arms folded over his chest, Rock drummed his fingers with increasing frequency. The long-winded explanation was chipping away at his last nerve. "Can we skip to the end already?"

Sonar, on the other hand, was fascinated and wanted to hear the story in detail. "Let the man finish," he said. "Never mind him, Professor, please continue."

"Oh, come on!" said the giant. "We just asked them who they were. I don't recall signing up for a lecture."

"Ahem, very well," said Fournier, "to cut the story short, they found a way to *acquire*, I believe was the term they used, Professor Engel. But as fate would have it, the professor was accompanied by his assistant at the time of the extraction. Well … I say assistant, but he was more like his protégé. A promising young Russian scientist named Aleksandr Karpov. He was a bright and kind man … with a …" His voice shook with emotion, and his throat tightened as he tried to fight back tears.

Ashrem moved closer to Fournier and gently rubbed his hand over the professor's back. "It's all right, Professor, take a moment."

Lucielle went to the old man and wrapped her arms around his waist in silence.

Sonar glanced up at Rock. "What did I miss?"

"You're seriously asking me?"

The other mercenaries were just as perplexed. Kincade turned to Arianne for an answer, but the tears in her eyes dissolved the words about to form in his mouth. She was staring at Fournier with a sad expression, and Kincade could see that she too was struggling to keep her own feelings bottled up inside.

In the end, it was Ashrem who provided the explanation. "Professor Karpov was murdered recently," the young man declared. "He was like family to us. He and Professor Fournier have known each other since before we were born."

"I'm sorry," said Kincade. "Murdered, you say? Do you have any idea who could have done it?"

Ashrem lowered his eyes. "It was killed by one of us."

Kincade was confused. "I don't understand."

"You will after you hear the rest of the story," said Fournier. He took off his glasses and dried his damp eyes with a handkerchief. Then, he stuffed the cloth back into his pocket and caressed Lucielle's hair. The silver-haired child responded with a warm smile and returned to her seat.

The old man cleared his throat and resumed his tale. "With the help of the British, the Agency smuggled Professor Engel and his assistant out of Berlin and eventually convinced them to help. I say *eventually* because it took a while before the professor was calm enough for Brainsworth to even present the project to him."

"I guess it's understandable," said Doc. "Anyone would be upset if they got abducted."

"No, it wasn't the abduction," said Fournier. "The Agency didn't know it at the time, but Professor Engel had a child. He had had a secret relationship with a librarian a few years prior. Sadly, the woman had fallen ill and died when the child was still very young. After her death, Professor Engel had arranged for his daughter to be adopted by a wealthy couple and made sure to keep his distance. He knew if people found out about his daughter, she would attract all sorts of unwanted attention because of his high-profile status; he didn't want that for her. Engel was furious because the abduction had made it look like he had defected, thereby putting his child in serious danger. If the state learned of her existence, they would use her as a bargaining chip to get him back."

Jerome Fournier paused to make sure his audience was still following.

131

"Ultimately, Professor Engel agreed to work with Dr. Brainsworth on the condition her employers did everything in their power to retrieve his child. But I believe his decision may have also been influenced by his scientific curiosity, which was no doubt sparked by the prospect of working on such an innovative project. The professor's protégé, on the other hand, was far less open to compromise. Alek—Aleksandr Karpov—was young and an idealist. For him, the idea of working with the Americans and the British was unthinkable. Thankfully, his devotion to Engel was such that, in the end, he reluctantly agreed. Later on, though, he confessed to me he had intended to share all findings with his government at the first opportunity. In any case, Dr. Brainsworth had assembled her new team and was ready to begin."

"I assume Engel and his assistant were asked to go to the US," said Kincade.

"They were," said Fournier, "but Professor Engel wouldn't hear of it. He wanted to remain as close as possible to his daughter, to make sure the Agency would keep their word. He insisted the team work from London instead."

Kincade raised an eyebrow. "Hmm, it must have been a tough sell."

"Oh yes. But Dr. Brainsworth had made it clear the success of the project hinged on Professor Engel's cooperation."

"I hope he was worth all the trouble," Sonar remarked.

"He was," Fournier said. "Whenever the team ran into a seemingly unsolvable problem, Professor Engel would come up with a solution, or a way around it. He understood the human genome better than anyone else. The techniques he used were unheard of at the time. He was an exceptional scientist. So was his protégé. Dr. Brainsworth was quite impressed with the young Karpov. She understood why Engel had taken him under his wing. Thanks to them, the team was able to make significant advances in the first year alone. Within two years, they had reached the testing phase."

"They actually found a way to manipulate people's DNA to enhance them?" Doc asked in a dubious tone.

"Yes! Well, in theory at least. In reality, things were a lot more complicated."

"How so?"

"They performed the procedure on groups of fertilized eggs divided into large batches. Each egg was then implanted into a surrogate mother for—"

"Why so many?" Sonar interrupted.

Fournier meandered around an invisible box as he gave his explanation. "Since they would have to wait for the babies to be born, they couldn't afford to run the experiment one egg at the time, or to wait nine months before making the next batch. Instead, they produced a new batch every three months for the following three years."

"Whoa! That's a lot of babies!" Sonar exclaimed.

Fournier looked hesitant. "Um… actually … as it turned out, none of the first batches lasted long enough to reach the fetal stage. And it was the same for the following groups."

"Why? What went wrong?" Kincade inquired.

"No one knew. Perhaps the genetic alterations were too extensive, turning the eggs into something too … unnatural. The team tried to exploit the knowledge gained after each failure to adjust the protocols used in subsequent batches, but nothing worked. Dr. Brainsworth and Professor Engel had become convinced the entire procedure needed to be revised. Then, the unexpected happened. Four embryos from the last group, Batch-12, defied the odds and survived. Day after day, week after week, the team continued to monitor them, waiting for something to go wrong. But it never did. They developed into healthy babies."

"What was different about those four?" Doc asked.

The old man shrugged. "Again, no one had a clue."

"Maybe it was just luck!" Rock suggested half-jokingly.

"Doubtful," Fournier replied. "The fact they all came from the same batch indicated there was some other factor at play. Something had improved their chances of survival."

Kincade sensed the professor was holding back. "Anything else you're not telling us?"

Fournier's gaze bounced around the room as if afraid to land on anyone. "The truth is there was another ... event, which steered the team away from the idea of an accident. A horrific event." Fournier paused and took a deep breath. "The four surrogate mothers of those four babies died on the delivery table. It was very strange. As though the children had literally siphoned the life force out of them. Even to this day, we still can't explain it."

"Creepy," Sonar commented.

"Against Dr. Brainsworth's objections, the Agency decided to try the procedure again. Only this time, they ran it on an even larger scale. They gathered hundreds of women for the next group, hoping to get even more babies."

"Let me guess," said Kincade. "No one told those new surrogate mothers what to expect if the experiment actually succeeded."

Fournier shook his head. "No. Since no one could predict with any certainty what would happen to them, the higher-ups decided it was an acceptable risk given the time, money, and resources they had put into the project. They were determined to see it through."

"Did it work?" Doc asked.

"I am pleased to say it didn't. Their next batch had a zero percent success rate. And it was the same with all subsequent batches. No surrogate mother needed to be put in harm's way. Even Professor Engel was baffled. They had recreated the exact same conditions and followed the exact same procedures."

"If they did everything the same, shouldn't they get the same result?" Sonar asked.

134

Fournier had been expecting the question. "Aha! You'd think so, wouldn't you? But it doesn't really work that way. How can I explain this …?" He scratched his head, trying to come up with a simple way to make his point. "Sometimes people make an analogy between genetics and cooking, a loose analogy, mind you, but the point is valid nonetheless. For example, imagine you have a recipe for a marble cake. You will never bake the exact same cake twice, even if you follow the same detailed set of instructions. This applies to genetics as well. You never quite get the exact same result. And when it comes to DNA, even the slightest change in certain genes can have a major impact in long run. Add to that an absurdly high number of possible permutations, and things can get very complicated."

Unlike his redheaded comrade, Doc had grasped the gist of the professor's explanation and was eager to hear the rest of it. "What happened next?"

"The team was stumped," said Fournier. "All attempts to reproduce their one successful experiment had failed. No one could figure out why those four babies had survived when all the others had not. Meanwhile, as the babies grew up, the scientists ran all manner of tests on them. But it was impossible to make a conclusive determination because they were still too young. Therefore, the decision was made to halt the project and wait until the subjects were old enough to be accurately evaluated." The professor marked a brief pause. "The wait was shorter than anticipated. By their fifth birthday, all four children were already displaying promising abilities."

Strange glances passed between the mercenaries.

Even Rock straightened up. "What kind of abilities?"

"For one thing, they were ridiculously strong for their size. This had been the main goal of the genetic manipulation all along, but no one had dared hope it would work to such an extent. Professor Engel had also intended for his process to result in a higher bone and muscular density in the subjects. And it did. They weren't just stronger, but also much tougher than the average individual. This was crucial. Otherwise, they would have ended up hurting themselves."

135

"Why?" Rock asked.

"Because if a person were somehow able to punch a wall with the power of a sledgehammer, they would make a hole in the wall, sure, but they would also break every bone in their arm."

"Strong *and* tough, eh?" said Kincade.

Fournier nodded. "Yes. Speed and reflexes were improved as well. Hmm … what else? Ah, excellent hand-eye coordination. That one was a surprise."

Rock chuckled. "Hehehe. It's starting to sound like a vampire movie."

Sonar poked the giant with his elbow. "Try to be serious for once!"

"Serious? Come on, man. There's nothing serious about any of this."

Rock wasn't the only one having trouble accepting the old man's outlandish tale.

"I'm with the big guy on this one," said Doc. "I find it hard to believe you can go around manipulating people's DNA with such ease."

"Easy?" Professor Fournier shouted. "Did I give you the impression any of this was easy?" He looked like he was about to have a heart attack. "It was incredibly difficult. We're talking about some of the greatest scientific minds of their time. Not to mention they had the full resources of both the American and the British governments at their disposal. The team spent every waking hour of every day working on this project. And in the end, the only positive result they were able to obtain could pretty much be described as a fluke, one they were never able to reproduce. I assure you, young man, there was nothing *easy* about any of it."

Rock raised his hand in a calming gesture. "Chill out, pops! You look like you're about to check out on us."

While the others were watching the professor mumble to himself, Da Costa caught something from the corner of his eye. "Hey! Where are you going?"

Without anyone noticing, Ashrem had gone to the fireplace and had picked up a fire iron resting against the wall. It was an older type model, a heavy metallic rod.

The mercenaries immediately drew their weapons and took aim.

Professor Fournier was as surprised as they were. "What are you doing, son?"

Ashrem turned to the professor. "If they can't believe what you've told them up until now, how do you think they'll react to what you're about to say next?"

Fournier's gaze ran over the mercenaries' faces. "Ah, yes. I see your point."

"Ash is right," said Arianne. "It's faster to just show them." She turned to Kincade. "It's all right. You can put down your guns. He means you no harm."

The guns stayed up.

"I don't know what it is you want to show us," said Kincade, the barrel of his gun still locked in on the threat, "but why don't you start by putting down what you've got there, and we can talk about it?"

Arianne walked over to Ashrem and took the fire iron away from him. Then she held the bar in front of her, with one hand at each end.

She remained like this for a moment, like a magician allowing her audience time to prepare for a trick.

Then, tightening her grip and contracting the muscles in her arms, the young woman folded the metal bar in a steady, continuous motion.

Kincade's jaw dropped. It was one thing to hear words like *genetic engineering and DNA manipulation*, but quite another to witness the result in such an abrupt fashion.

From the very beginning, the mercenary leader had tried to remain open to the possibility Professor Fournier had been telling them the truth. All this talk about a secret scientific experiment sounded pretty far out there, but why not? The image of Mitsuki snapping her handcuffs certainly lent credence to the professor's claims. But what Arianne had just done breached the boundaries of what could reasonably be considered possible. She had bent an inch-thick steel bar into a near-perfect U-shape, and she had done it with moderate effort.

Kincade was having a tough time accepting what his eyes had just shown him. And his companions weren't faring any better. They all stared at Arianne with bulging eyeballs and gaping mouths. *How could this slender, gentle woman be so freakishly strong?*

Then, one after the other, the mercenaries' expressions began to change. Their initial shock gradually gave way to rising doubts. Surely this was a trick.

Rock walked up to Arianne and snatched the fire iron from her. "Let me see this thing." He inspected the object from every angle and tried to imitate her. Summoning every ounce of strength in his powerful muscles, the colossus attempted to restore the shape of the bent rod. He succeeded only in moving the tips a few inches. "Dammit!" he said, breathing heavily.

"Are you kidding me?" Sonar exclaimed. "That thing's real?"

Kincade took the bar from Rock and checked it for himself. Then it was Doc's turn. Even Da Costa looked more than a little rattled.

The bent metal bar was passed around until it landed back into Ashrem's hands. Just like Arianne had done earlier, he held the bar with both arms stretched out in front of him and returned it to its original shape.

This time the mercenaries could not deny the reality as it appeared before them.

Rock rubbed his hand over his shaved head. "Damn! I can't believe it!"

"Tell me about it," said Doc, equally stunned.

Suddenly the giant's expression changed. He snatched the bar from Ashrem and presented it to Lucielle. "Here you go."

138

The little girl looked up at him, confused.

What's he doing now? Kincade wondered.

"Your turn," Rock said, his eyes filled with eager anticipation. He was like a child waiting to see a repeat of the routine by some talented stage performer.

Lucielle tilted her head. "My turn?" But when at last she understood his meaning, she frowned at him, annoyed by the absurdity of his request. "Do I look like I can bend this thing?"

Rock looked disappointed. "Oh, you can't?"

Doc placed his hand over his eyes and whispered to himself, "This guy's unbelievable."

"Lucielle is different from the rest of us," Arianne declared.

"The rest?" Kincade noted. "Then all of you in the pictures are … genetically modified?" Even as he asked the question, he could not get over how crazy it sounded.

Arianne hesitated. "Hmm … yes, but … not in the way you think."

Her answer confused him further—if that was possible. "Meaning what?"

Fournier raised his index finger, like a teacher addressing his student. "If you recall, young man, I told you we were never able to successfully duplicate Professor Engel's experiment, which resulted in only four babies."

"What about you guys?" Kincade asked Arianne.

She took a long and slow breath, as if to brace herself for his reaction. "We're clones!"

"Ridiculous!" the woman on the screen shouted in a strident voice.

Jenkins winced due to the discomfort in his eardrums. "It's the logical conclusion," he replied.

"I must say, I too am skeptical, Mr. Jenkins." Leicester was seated at his desk, facing Jenkins and Carson.

"Why would they take the girl?" Schaffer asked over the screen.

"I never said they *took* her, Mr. Schaffer. I think she chose to go with them."

"Ridiculous!" Renard said again. "I want to see the security footage."

"There isn't any," Jenkins replied. "The security cameras were disabled. All except for one or two in the outer perimeter."

"meaning we don't know what happened?"

"We know for a fact the girl made it to the safe room," said Jenkins. "But for some reason, she decided to come out."

"Maybe they forced her out," Renard argued.

"I don't think so. Even if they found the safe room, they had no way of breaching it, not in that time frame. The girl had to have opened it herself. Besides, as I told Mr. Leicester, there was no sign of forced entry."

"What about the other two?" said Leicester. "Are you certain they didn't take her?"

"Darius and Mitsuki? No. One of the functioning cameras briefly caught them leaving the premises. It was just the two of them."

"Regardless," Schaffer said, "this new development changes everything."

"Indeed," Leicester nodded. "With the analyst gone, prudence is a luxury we can no longer afford. If we're exposed, so be it. We'll worry about that later. The important thing right now is to contain the situation before it spins further out of our control. Mr. Jenkins, you are now in charge of reacquiring the assets. Do what you must to find them."

Jenkins clenched his teeth to snuff out a smile of satisfaction. At last, he could act without having one hand tied behind his back. Leicester had come to his senses and put him in charge—as he should have done from the start. He exchanged a quick glance with Carson.

"It's fine with me," said Renard, "but how are we supposed to track the fugitives without the analyst? She was our best chance of finding them."

No one said a word. In two sentences, the French diplomat had laid out the conundrum they faced.

After a brief silence, Leicester pivoted in his chair and faced the screen. "Karl, have your people uncovered anything new regarding Karpov?"

"Perhaps," said the German. "We may have a lead on the recording. We think Karpov kept it close, somewhere within the city."

Renard was lost. "What recording?"

Leicester gave her a prolonged stare. It dawned on him that all discussions they had had about the recording had been with her predecessor, Charles Dumas, and never with her. "Apologies, my dear," he said. He then glanced at Carson and decided it was a good idea to clue him in as well. "Before he disappeared, Professor Karpov made a digital recording of his last telephone conversation with Adam."

Renard's glasses jumped on her nose. "He did what?"

"What's on this recording?" Carson asked.

Leicester opened his hands. "We're not sure."

"But there's good chance it contains a clue to the location of Adam's data card," Karl added.

Renard straightened up in her chair at the mention of the hidden memory card.

"It's probably what Damien was after," said Leicester. "It's imperative

141

we find the card before he does. Mr. Jenkins and Mr. Carson will go to Berlin at once. I think we can all agree this must be given top priority. The card might even lead our runaways back to us."

Renard did not hesitate. "Of course."

Schaffer grunted his approval.

"Good," said Leicester. "I believe that's all for now, Nathalie, Karl." He ended the video call with his two counterparts and spun around to face the room. "Gentlemen, you must recover the recording, by any means necessary."

"Understood," said Jenkins.

"Let me know when you arrive in Berlin."

The two men nodded and started on their way out. But as they were leaving, Leicester noticed a hesitation in Carson.

"What is it, Mr. Carson?" the Briton asked.

"It's nothing, sir. I was just wondering what Kincade and his men could want with the analyst."

"I'm afraid if Mr. Jenkins' assessment is correct, the real question is: what does *she* want with them?"

Chapter 16 – The Boy

A heavy silence had descended on Professor Jerome Fournier's home. A silence interrupted only by the clock hanging on the wall adjacent to the kitchen. The regular ticking of its needle echoed inside the living room as it inflexibly marked the passing of each second.

Five. Ten. Fifteen.

Over the past few hours, Kincade had been forced to re-examine his views on what he ought to consider possible. He had come to accept certain realities which, only a day before, he would have dismissed without a second thought. But of all the strange deeds he had witnessed, and of all the improbable claims he had heard, this one was by far the most preposterous. Always try to keep an open mind? Of course. Don't hesitate to question everything? Sure. But where do you draw the line? At what point do you put your foot down and say,

"This is insane!" Kincade exclaimed. "Did you say *clones*?"

Fournier nodded enthusiastically. "Yes."

Doc thought it necessary to clarify the term and avoid all possible misunderstandings. "Clones? As in … human … clones."

"Correct."

Sonar gave Ashrem a playful smile. "You guys are messing with us, right?"

Arianne stepped forward. "I understand it's difficult to believe but—"

"Difficult to believe? Hahaha" Rock laughed a forced laugh as he stepped inside the room. The inexplicable events and bizarre revelations had taken their toll. It was as though he had been on a roller-coaster ride for the past few hours and was now desperate to get off. "Difficult? I don't know what you mean, honestly." His tone was both nervous and sarcastic. "There's nothing difficult here at all. In fact, when I saw you, it's the first thing I said to myself. I thought, 'Hey, wait a minute! She looks like a clone.'"

"All right, you've made your point," Kincade said, himself shaken. "Take it easy."

But the giant showed no signs of calming down. "Come on, Nate! Tell me you're not buying this nonsense. I'm no scientist, but even I know there's no such thing as human clones. I don't care if they can bench-press a damned truck. There's no way those two are clones."

"Me too!" Lucielle's arm shot straight up in the air like a waffle popping out of a toaster. She had reacted instinctively, not wanting to be left out.

Rock stopped and stared at her. At first, he looked like he was going to say something. But he didn't. He went back to the doorway, folded his arms, and leaned against the frame. He had had enough and had decided he no longer cared.

The professor gently pushed Lucielle's arm back down. He wondered if it had been a mistake to reveal the truth about Arianne and the others so soon, without giving the mercenaries time to process everything else first. Having known the clones since birth, he had long stopped mulling over how they had come into existence. To him, they were children … special children, yes, but children all the same. And he couldn't have cared more for them if they had been his own. However, he realized it was not the kind of news a person could be expected to simply take in stride. "I'm sorry," he said. "I imagine it must be quite a shock."

Kincade looked Arianne straight in the eye. "You people are actually serious, aren't you?"

"Yes."

"Don't worry," said Fournier, "It'll make sense once I've told you the rest of the story." The old man resumed his tale. "With the experiment at a standstill, it was decided the four children would be taken back to the US for further observation. But there was one problem. Professor Engel still wouldn't go. And since he was the only one who stood a chance of figuring out what had happened, they offered him a compromise. Dr. Brainsworth would take three children back to the US and leave one with Professor Engel."

Fournier paused once again to examine his audience. This time, the faces staring back at him looked very different than before. There were no more skeptical frowns, no more dubious twitches, and no exchanges of furtive glances. The mercenaries no longer looked at him as they would a mad scientist who had sniffed too many fumes from the test tubes in his lab. Pleased with this change in attitude, Fournier continued.

"Professor Engel asked permission to select which child would remain with him in London. There was no particular reason to deny him, and his assistance was of vital importance to the project, so the higher-ups agreed. There was, however, some reluctance on Dr. Brainsworth's part when she heard of Professor Engel's choice. She tried to convince him to choose a different child, but he remained adamant. No one knows whether the professor's decision was based on a whim, or whether he knew exactly what he was doing, but his mind was made up."

"Why did Brainsworth object?" Kincade asked.

"The reason was simple. The child chosen by Engel had a strange, distinctive feature: he was born with silver-gray hair. It wasn't that Brainsworth believed the child's hair color held any scientific significance, but none of us had ever seen anything like it before. She—" Fournier stopped when he noticed his audience wasn't paying attention to him anymore. From the moment he had mentioned the child's abnormal hair color, the mercenaries' gazes had all converged on Lucielle. She had silver hair too, just like he had described.

Finding herself the focus of so many persistent stares, Lucielle started to feel uneasy. "Yes," she said in a belligerent tone. "It's the same as mine, Okay?"

During the course of her young life, Lucielle had not met a lot of people.

145

Unlike the other clones, she had been taken out of the facility at a very young age. But the truth about her identity had remained a closely guarded secret. In order to keep her existence hidden, she had been moved from place to place, forbidden from ever going outside, or from making contact with anyone other than her assigned caretakers and a select group of individuals, like Leicester and his assistant.

This isolation had not been easy, especially for a girl her age. And yet, there was something even worse than the constant feeling of loneliness. Something she'd first noticed when she was still living at the compound. Something that had followed her on the outside. It was the stares. Everywhere she went, people would stare at her like she was some kind of rare exotic animal. They would stare because of how she looked. And for those informed few, because of *what* she was.

Arianne knew how unnerving it was for Lucielle to be scrutinized in such a manner. "Please don't look at her like that," she told the group.

"Like what?" Sonar asked.

"Like I'm a freak," the young girl threw at him.

"Ah! You think *you're* a freak?" Sonar jabbed his thumb at Rock. "Trust me, this guy's the biggest freak of all."

"Hey!" the giant protested.

"What? You know it's true," Sonar continued. "What kind of name is Rock, anyway?"

"Like you can talk, *Sonar*. They got your name all wrong if you ask me. They should have called you *Radio* instead. Your mouth is a lot busier than your ears."

Lucielle giggled, amused by the pair's mutual banter.

Doc moved between his comrades. "If you two comics are done with your routine, maybe we can get back to the more serious discussion."

Kincade noticed a faint smile cross Ariane's lips as she stared at Rock and Sonar. "What is it?" he asked her.

She shook her head. "Nothing."

"Should I continue?" Fournier asked.

"Sure," said Doc.

"Dr. Brainsworth returned to America with three children, while Adam stayed in London with Professor Engel."

"Adam?" Doc noted.

"The boy, his name was Adam. Adam Cross." Professor Fournier glanced at Lucielle as he said the name. "During the first few years, everything was fine. The teams based in Virginia and in London worked well together despite the distance. They exchanged their findings on a regular basis and continued to evaluate the subjects' development. Everyone was pleased, but none more than the brass in the US and UK militaries. The physical aptitudes exhibited by the children defied belief, and those aptitudes continued to improve as they grew older. In light of those exceptional results, a decision was made to restart the project."

"Why am I not surprised?" said Sonar.

The old man ignored the comment. "Only this time, it would be run in the US, at the Virginia facility. Dr. Brainsworth agreed, on the condition they first find a way to guarantee the survival of the surrogate mothers. She knew the problem would be a difficult one to solve but, with Professor Engel's help, she felt confident they would come up with a solution. The greater challenge would be to convince Engel to make the trip across the Atlantic. She knew her best bet was to meet with him in person, so she went back to London. Unfortunately, it turned out to be a wasted trip. None of her assurances, promises, or concessions made a bit of difference. Professor Engel had no intention of going with her. She had expected some resistance, but she was surprised by his utter unwillingness to even entertain the idea."

"Didn't you say they had already tried everything?" Kincade remarked. "Maybe he didn't see the point."

"Even so, as a scientist, you always welcome the opportunity to test new ideas and to refine your procedures. In addition, they had been studying the children for years, and those studies had yielded lots of data. Professor Engel's complete lack of interest didn't make sense. It made Dr. Brainsworth curious enough to examine his private logs and reports. Her interest was casual at first, but the closer she looked, the more her suspicions grew. After a while, she became convinced Professor Engel was hiding something."

"Was he?" Doc asked.

"Yes. She found out Engel and his protégé had been keeping a big secret indeed."

Sonar rubbed his hands together. "Now we're getting to the good part."

"About time, too!" Rock grumbled.

Professor Fournier furrowed his brow, annoyed that the huge man kept trying to rush him. "Remember, from the very beginning, the goal had been to create a new breed of soldiers. And even though the research team had been left with only four candidates, they implemented every protocol to the letter."

"Meaning what?" Kincade asked.

"Meaning despite their young age, the children were already undergoing rigorous military training."

Doc raised an eyebrow. "How old were they?"

"By then they were around seven, I think, but the training had begun after their fourth birthday."

"Hmm. I suppose it makes sense from the Army's perspective," said Kincade. "If you're trying to create the perfect soldier, it's better to start at a young age."

"Yes, but when Dr. Brainsworth read through Professor Engel's private logs, she discovered Adam had undergone a separate set of sessions, in parallel with the military training. A series of tests and simulations aimed at

148

measuring his mental aptitudes. And even more surprising were the results of those tests. They were off the charts. Brainsworth thought the results had been entered incorrectly, or had been misinterpreted somehow."

"Did she confront Engel about it?" Kincade asked.

"She did."

"And what did he tell her?"

"He had no choice but to admit the truth. Needless to say, the four children couldn't go to school like normal kids, but their education was not neglected in the least. The ones in the US were tutored by scientists over there. As for Adam, Professor Engel personally took charge of his education, with only Alek … Professor Karpov, to assist him. He told Brainsworth that Adam had always exhibited an insatiable curiosity about a wide range of subjects. No matter how much the child learned during their sessions, it never seemed to be enough. At first, Professor Engel and Alek only answered the boy's incessant questions in order to keep him quiet long enough to run their tests. But over time, his questions became so complex they started to take notice. Fascinated by this, Engel decided to put Adam through a series of trials designed to evaluate characteristics like creative thinking, memory, reasoning etc. The results were nothing short of extraordinary. This is what Dr. Brainsworth had stumbled upon. When the professor shared the rest of those results with her, she could hardly contain her excitement. From that point on, the bilateral cooperation between the US and the UK on this project deteriorated rapidly."

"Why?" Sonar asked.

"Isn't it obvious? Brainsworth had no choice but to report what she had learned. Once her bosses understood the extent of Adam's potential, they insisted he be sent over to them without delay. They pressured the British into swapping him with one of the other subjects. Naturally, their request was denied. Engel convinced his side that Adam was far more valuable than the other three children combined. As a result, relations between the two sides became tense."

"I don't get it," said Sonar. "Why all the fuss over this kid? I mean, I understand he was some kind of genius and all, but—"

"Genius?" Fournier scoffed. "No, you don't understand."

Sonar looked confused. "What do you mean? You just said …"

Fournier opened his arms in dramatic fashion. "Professor Engel was a genius. Aleksandr Karpov was a genius. But Adam … he was something else entirely. The genetic manipulations did something to him, altered him in an unforeseen manner. His mind worked differently than ours. He understood things in a way the rest of us cannot. Engel couldn't have been more proud. But as I'm sure you're aware, nothing in life ever turns out completely good or completely bad. It was the same with Adam. There were signs … erm … questions about his mental stability."

Rock pushed off the wall and squinted. "Are you saying he was crazy?"

Fournier hesitated. "No, I … I mean there were certain psychological—"

"Sounds like you're saying he was crazy," the giant insisted.

"I wouldn't use the word crazy. There were concerns regarding his mental state, but nothing too alarming. Other perhaps than the fact he was becoming increasingly introverted, detached from the world around him. Then, tragedy struck. Not two weeks after Adam's seventeenth birthday, Professor Friedrich Engel died of a heart attack." Fournier paused and adjusted his glasses. "Needless to say, Adam did not take the news well. It triggered a psychotic episode. He shut everyone out and became completely non-responsive. It made the higher-ups pretty nervous."

"I bet," said Kincade.

"You see, at first Adam was only involved in projects with military applications: new detection systems, improved propulsion engines, decryption of intercepted coded transmissions, etc. But over time, his contributions extended far beyond this. They realized they could use him for just about anything: bio-medical research, geopolitical analysis … even stock market predictions. A lot of people were invested in his well-being. Fortunately, the episode didn't last too long. After a month or so, Adam recovered. However,

150

the whole incident had done little to ease the concerns over his mental stability, and—"

Clap! Clap!

Fed up with Fournier's protracted explanation, Rock gave two loud claps. "Hey, Pops! Get to the part about these guys being clones already."

Lucielle glared at him. "You're very rude, you know. The professor is only trying to give you all the facts."

"Nothing personal, kid, but this old geezer looks like he could go on babbling all the way to his grave. I wanna hear about this clone business."

"I'm actually more curious about that myself," said Doc.

"He was getting to it," the girl replied.

"Then he needs to get there faster," Rock retorted.

"I think we can leave out certain details for now Professor," said Arianne. "Let's tell them what they want to know."

"If you think it's best," Fournier sighed, a little disappointed to have to cut his explanation short. "To answer your question, young man, they're clones of Adam. He wanted to create others with the same gifts he had. The only way he could find to accomplish his goal was to use his own DNA."

Doc was stupefied. "He cloned himself?"

"Yes. He created nine clones in total. The three you see before you now, plus six others."

"Then the guys in the pictures are …"

"They're our brothers and sisters," Arianne replied.

Kincade's eyes narrowed to dubious slits. He gazed at her, Ashrem and Lucielle in turn. "Hold on a second! If you were all cloned from the same person, shouldn't you all look alike?"

"Yeah!" Rock exclaimed.

Professor Fournier had been waiting for the inevitable objection. "That would be reproductive cloning," he countered. But when he saw his argument had been received with blank expressions, the professor returned to his imaginary board. "There are different types of cloning methods. Reproductive cloning is used when you want to obtain an exact replica of the source material. Instead, Adam used a kind of transgenic cloning technique. In genetic engineering, transgenic organisms possess genes transferred from another species. For instance, maybe you've heard of fluorescent mice?"

"I'm no expert," Doc replied, "but yes, I've seen the pictures."

"Same here," said Kincade.

"The idea is similar. Only much, much more complicated. To be honest, we don't know how Adam did it. He only took on assignments he deemed interesting enough, and would always insist on working alone. It was a shame, because he was quite poor at leaving notes. Particularly in this case, he didn't leave a single bit of data related to Project Eritis."

"Project Eritis?" Kincade echoed.

"Yes," said Fournier. "It's the name Adam gave to the experiment he carried out to create the clones; his children, as he called them."

"Eritis? Funny name," said Rock.

"Yeah, what does it mean?" Sonar asked.

"It's Latin," the professor replied, "the future tense of the verb 'to be' in the second person plural."

"Then it translates to *you will be*?" Kincade concluded.

"Correct. I believe Adam chose that name because he hoped his children would represent what humans could become in the future. What we have the potential to become. It's only my personal opinion, though. Adam never told us. He was very secretive."

"I noticed you use the past tense when talking about him," said Doc.

"Yes. He died," Fournier said with a saddened expression, "many years ago."

Doc and the others waited for the old professor to elaborate on the circumstances of Adam's passing, but he didn't. And upon gazing at the faces of Arianne, Ashrem, and especially Lucielle, the mercenaries decided not to stretch the conversation on the topic of their *father*'s death.

Chapter 17 – Threat

This marked the end of Professor Fournier's explanation.

He gave a sweeping look around the room, expecting to be bombarded with questions. When none came, he wondered if the mercenaries still didn't believe him. But it was the opposite. They were silent because they did believe him. Each one was trying to digest this new surreal fact: human clones.

Arianne shot a timorous glance at Kincade and his team. Deep down, she had always worried about what people would think if they learned the truth about her and her siblings. "Now that you know," she said, "does it feel strange?"

"Hell yes!" Rock blurted out before anyone else could answer.

Sonar turned to him with a discouraged look on his face.

"Why don't you take a hint from Da Costa?" said Doc. "He knows when to keep quiet."

"Knows when to keep quiet?" Rock exclaimed. "The guy never says a word. I've had better conversations with corpses than I've had with him."

Da Costa was standing in a corner against the wall, half-hidden behind a tall bookshelf. Like his comrades, his head was still spinning from the professor's incredible revelations, but he had remained quiet the entire time.

Lucielle stretched her neck to see him better. Both she and the professor had almost forgotten he was there.

Arianne and Ashrem, on the other hand, had remained aware of Da Costa's movements. After everyone had settled down, he had ambled around the room for a while before stopping in a dark corner, which coincidentally happened to be in Ashrem's and Arianne's blind spots. And even though no one had a clear view of him, from where he was standing, Da Costa could keep an eye on all present—another coincidence.

"Your friend is very cautious," Ashrem remarked.

"Don't mind him," said Sonar. "He likes his space."

Kincade noticed Arianne intently staring at him, waiting for his answer to her earlier question. He hesitated and said, "Look, I'm not going to lie. This is freaking me out big time." Then his expression softened. "But there's nothing wrong with being different. You seem like a nice person. It's all that matters."

"He's right," said Doc, "It's a lot to take in all at once, but we'll get used to it ... I think."

Arianne smiled, relieved.

Sonar ruffled his reddish hair. "Wow! Clones, huh ...? Well, like Doc said, this one's gonna take some getting used to."

"I know, right?" said Rock.

"At least now we know why Leicester's hell-bent on getting you back," said Kincade. "It has nothing to do with any secrets you stole, does it? It's you he's after."

"Yes," Arianne replied. "They want to take us back to the Arc."

Kincade's eyebrows went up. "The Arc?"

"It's where we grew up. A secret compound near the French-German border. The official name is Genetics and Robotics Experiments in Alternative Technologies - Advanced Research Center."

"Quite a mouthful," Sonar chuckled.

"It is," Ashrem smiled. "We all refer to it as the *Great Arc*, or the *Arc* for short."

"What were you doing there?" Kincade asked.

It was Fournier who answered. "They were being used in the same way Adam was. Like him, each one of his children possesses a truly exceptional mind. It's what makes them so valuable. Leicester doesn't want them because they would make for fearsome soldiers or great spies."

"He wants the scientists," Kincade concluded.

The professor nodded.

"Ahem!" Out of the blue, Rock cleared his throat. But it had sounded too loud and too forced to be genuine—subtlety had never been one of his strong suits.

"What is it now?" Kincade asked in a jaded tone.

"Speaking of the English guy, what about the deal we made with him?"

Sonar scowled. "Haven't you been listening? It's a lot more complicated than we thought."

"Too damn complicated if you ask me. I say we don't get involved in this mess. Let's just bag'em and tag'em like we planned, and we're in the clear."

Lucielle jumped out of her seat. "You are so selfish! You mean as long as you're OK you don't care what happens to anyone else? You do understand we've basically been prisoners since the day we were born, right?"

Rock shrugged. "Sorry, kid. You seem like nice people and all, but if somebody's gotta go to prison, better you than us."

Sonar tilted his head back as he gazed up at him. "Whoa, that's cold, bro."

Lucielle dropped back in her seat and crossed her arms. "Humph, it doesn't matter anyway. If you try to take them on like this, without a plan, you'll only end up getting hurt … or worse."

An uneasy silence immediately filled the room.

Although it hadn't been her intention, the youngster's declaration had sounded very much like a threat, especially to a group of soldiers instilled with a healthy dose of paranoia.

Kincade gave Arianne a sharp look. "Why did you ask us to come here with you?"

"We need your help."

"With what?"

"To stop Damien and the others."

It was the last thing Kincade expected to hear. "The others? You mean the other fugitives?"

"Yes."

Rock frowned. "I thought they were your friends."

"They're not our friends, they're our family," Lucielle corrected. But her statement only added to the mercenaries' confusion.

"They are our siblings," said Arianne, "but we don't agree with what they're trying to do, with what they're planning to do. We need your help to stop them."

Kincade held the young woman in his gaze for a moment and said, "Look, what Rock said may have sounded harsh, but he did have a point. Our agreement with Leicester is the only thing keeping us out of prison. And you're asking us to renege on it."

Ashrem stepped forward. "Not necessarily. We have an idea on how you can help us, and still get a deal from Leicester."

"Do you?" Kincade said, sounding doubtful.

"Yes."

The mercenaries exchanged a long look.

"If that's true," Kincade said, "we'll need to hear this idea of yours. Then we'll think about it."

"I understand," said Arianne.

"Just remember!" Lucielle chimed in. "There isn't much time. The others won't wait around for us. And if they succeed … it'll be bad."

Sonar gave her a searching look. "How bad are we talking?"

Damien was walking back and forth in front of the window of a fifth-floor apartment in Berlin with his hands joined behind his back. He was deep in thought.

Lying on a sofa, Johann was watching the television, undisturbed by the sound of his brother's incessant footsteps.

The two carried on like this, ignoring each other, for a quarter of an hour, until the lock on the entrance door clicked.

A young red-haired woman walked in. She was wearing a burgundy faux suede skirt, black knee-high boots, a dark linen sweater, and a faux leather biker jacket.

Damien stopped. "You're early, Kadyna. Did you get all the information we need?"

She took off her jacket and tossed it on the sofa next to Johann. "I did."

Damien approached her. "And?"

"Security won't be a problem."

"Any sign of Jenkins?"

"No. I don't think he's found it yet."

"Good. We'll proceed as soon as Darius and Mitsuki are ready."

Kadyna's eyes narrowed as her gaze shifted towards Johann. "He could have helped them speed things up. Why is he still loitering around here?"

"Sorry, sister dear," Johann said without taking his eyes off the television, "something about staying under the radar. It would appear Damien doesn't trust me to behave."

"This is a crucial time," said Damien. "It wouldn't be wise to draw any unnecessary attention to ourselves."

"So true," Kadyna agreed. "This crazy fool would leave a trail of dead bodies leading straight to us. We should have left him at the Arc."

Johann chuckled, his eyes still riveted to the screen. "Crazy? Poor choice of word coming from you."

Kadyna rolled her eyes. "I don't even know why I'm wasting time talking to you." She turned to Damien. "You seem troubled. Is it about Luce? We all wanted to make sure Leicester and Jenkins couldn't use her against us. To think Arianne got to her first … do you think she intends to interfere with our plans?"

Johann burst out in laughter. "Of course Arianne's going to interfere. That's what she does. She and Ashrem have always been so self-righteous. Their first move after we escaped was to snatch Lucielle right out from under our noses. It's pretty clear they intend to get in our way."

"I know," said Damien, "but it's not what concerns me most."

Kadyna tilted her head. "What then?" Suddenly, her expression changed. "Wait … Soran?"

"If they're serious about opposing us, they'll need his help."

Johann put the remote down and sat up. He no longer looked amused. "He'll never help them."

"Won't he?" Damien sneered. "And just how much are you willing to gamble on this assumption?"

"Hmm … come to think of it," said Kadyna, "Arianne's the one person who might be able to convince him."

Johann stood and joined the other two. "Perhaps we should adjust our plans accordingly."

Kadyna nodded in agreement. "If Soran gets involved, not even you will be able to predict the outcome, Damien."

"Maybe not. Regardless, at this point, our best strategy is to act fast."

"What about the strangers?" Kadyna asked. "Mitsu thinks they might be soldiers. Knowing Arianne, she'll probably ask for their help too."

A malevolent grin formed on Johann's face. "I hope she does."

Kadyna eyed him with a look of contempt on her face. "You're sick."

"They're irrelevant," Damien said in a tone that demanded silence. He took out his phone and made a call.

"What's the status of your progress?

…

Good. We're moving up our timetable.

…

Fine, I'll leave it to you then."

Damien hung up and put the phone back in his pocket.

"What did Darius say?" Johann asked.

"Their preparations are almost complete. You and Kadyna will go meet up with them."

"You're not coming with us?" the young woman asked.

"No. As I said, we need to act fast. It's time to move the next piece on the board."

160

Johann cracked his knuckles. "Finally, some action."

Chapter 18 – Clue

The wheels squeaked as the cart raced through the hallways. Jordi could only afford to keep one hand on the handle. The other was needed to hold the precariously balanced heap of computer parts steady atop the wobbly vehicle.

Once a month, he made the rounds of all the departments to collect or replace computer and networking equipment. As he moved across the various floors, he liked to pretend he was a race car driver participating in a major Grand Prix.

"Hey! Be careful!" someone shouted.

Jordi's cart grazed one of the three men stepping out of the elevator as he rolled it inside the carriage.

"Sorry," Jordi called out from behind the closing doors.

He had finished his rounds. It was time to take his haul back to his underground lair, time for the final lap. He readied himself as the buttons counted down to the second basement. Those were the starting block lights. The chime when the elevator arrived at its destination floor signaled the start of the race. As soon as the doors slid open, Jordi rocketed out and traversed the narrow corridors at full speed, expertly negotiating each corner. This floor was reserved for the IT staff, and since most of them were out on their lunch break, the chances of him bumping into someone were slim. But they were by no means null. It was still possible for some unsuspecting bystander to find themselves an unwilling participant in the imaginary underground tournament. Then again, no one ever said car racing was safe.

Fortunately, this time around, Jordi made it to the finish line without incident.

He burst past the entrance to his office and crashed into his desk.

162

Ignoring the parts falling on the floor, Jordi quickly picked up his phone off the cart and pressed a button. "Oh noooo," he wailed, "so close."

This was his third-best time ever, less than a second away from his record.

He slumped in his chair, winded, and picked up the fallen computer parts.

"What's the matter?" a voice asked.

Jordi peered over his shoulder and saw Detective Heirtmeyer stride into the room and approach his desk. "Oh, it's you Marie."

"What happened?"

"Nothing, it's not important."

"If it's not important, why do you look so disappointed?" she asked, studying him. All of a sudden, a deep furrow formed on her brow. She spun him around in his chair. "Don't tell me you were running around the hallways like a madman again!"

He averted his eyes. "I don't know what you're talking about."

"Don't lie to me, Jordi. If the chief catches you one more time, you'll be in serious trouble."

He gave a worried look. "You're not going to tell on me, are you?"

"Of course not, but that's not the point."

He joined his hands together as if making his *mea culpa*. "You're right, you're right. I won't do it again."

"It's what you always say."

"More importantly," said Jordi, a gleam of eagerness in his eyes, "what about Lea from accounting?"

"What about her?"

163

"Did you ask her what she thinks about me?"

Marie looked hesitant. "Oh, yes, erm … she thinks you're … nice … and erm …"

Jordi had heard enough. "I knew it," he said, looking devastated. "She doesn't even remember my name, does she?"

"Sure she does," Marie said in a cheery voice. "She thinks you're a little strange, but … she did say you were the best at fixing computers."

Jordi closed his eyes and dropped his head on the desk. "It's a lost cause. I'm doomed to a life of solitude and unhappiness."

"Don't you think you're exaggerating a little?"

"She thinks I'm a nerd, Marie!"

"You are a nerd! But … in a good way."

His forehead still glued to the wooden surface, Jordi gazed up at her. "Are you trying to make me feel better, or worse? I can't tell."

"You should try talking to her."

He closed his eyes and pressed his face against the table again. "It's no use. I'm finished."

Marie gave him a good shake. "Oh, get a grip, will you?"

He exhaled deeply and sat back up, looking miserable. "Why did you come down here, anyway?"

Marie's expression turned serious. "I need a favor."

"Of course you do."

"It's important."

"Of course it is."

"And you can't tell anyone."

"Of course I … wait a minute, what?" He examined her with wary eyes. "This is for a case, right?"

She didn't answer, but her gaze grew more insistent.

"Are you kidding me?" Jordi exclaimed. "A minute ago you were yelling at me for breaking the rules, and now—"

"This is different. It's not some silly game. I told you, it's important."

He scratched the back of his head and made a complicated face. "Hmm … I don't know, Marie."

"Please, Jordi. I really need your help."

Despite her plea, Marie sensed a stubborn reluctance still clinging to him, so she decided to try a different approach: bribery.

"Next time the guys invite me out for a drink, I'll bring you along with me," she said.

He shrugged with indifference. "What do I care?"

A sly smile flickered across Marie's lips. "I'll make sure Lea is there too."

Jordi's eyes lit up.

Marie waited a moment and then pretended to walk away. "Fine, if you're not interested …"

"Hold on, hold on."

She stopped.

Jordi stared at her at length, and then finally agreed to help. "All right, what do you want me to do?"

She turned back and handed him a small piece of paper.

He unfolded it. "It's an email address."

"Yes. I need you to find out everything you can about it."

Earlier that morning, Marie had woken up to an unexpected revelation. In her sleep, she had re-lived the night she had surprised Professor Karpov at his apartment, and had subsequently learned the truth about his identity. She had recalled the picture he had shown her of his younger self, standing beside two other men, one of whom had just died in a car accident. Only, the professor had been convinced it was no accident. He had told her as much. Karpov had also considered sending a message to the third man in the picture. She had recalled the laptop on the coffee table, and the blank email. In the end, the professor had refrained from sending the message, but Marie had seen the email address. The moment she'd opened her eyes, she'd scrambled for a pen and paper and jotted it down. It was a clue. The only one she had to help her solve the professor's murder.

She hoped the email address would lead her to Karpov's friend. And maybe he, in turn, would lead her to the killer. She knew it was a long shot, but she had to try.

"By the way," said Jordi as he kept typing on his keyboard, "I heard you were going on holiday."

"Yes. I asked for some time off."

"I thought you and Hans had a case."

"I asked the chief if he could re-assign it. I haven't had a break in a while. I feel like I'm burning out."

"I know the feeling."

Marie knew she could not investigate the professor's murder via official channels. He had warned her that the people after him had connections high up in the police and the government. If she was going to have any chance of finding them, she would have to do it on her own, and in secret.

"Have you picked a destination for your holiday?" Jordi asked.

"We'll see," Marie replied in a mysterious tone.

A little intrigued by her cryptic answer, Jordi shot a quick glance at her. But it was nothing more than a passing thought. He was fixated on fulfilling his side of the bargain, and could already picture himself having drinks with Lea from accounting.

A few minutes later, Jordi stopped and leaned back in his chair. "Hmm … I see."

"Did you figure out whose address this is?" Marie pressed.

"Not quite. Usually, I'd be able to trace the IP address back to its source, but not this time."

"Why not?"

"It looks like whoever set up the account took measures to mask the real IP by re-routing it through a number of servers all over the world."

Marie sighed in disappointment. "It's a dead end."

Jordi looked up at her with a smile on his face. "Says who? There's a reason they keep me around, you know."

She slapped him on the back of the head. "I told you, this is serious."

"Ouch! No violence."

"What did you find out?"

"All I have for now is a country: France. If you can get the owner of the account to send you a message, I should be able to narrow it down."

Marie paused to think.

"I'm sorry," said Jordi, "I know it's not much to go on."

She gazed down at him. "It's more than I had ten minutes ago. Thank you, Jordi."

"No problem. Just don't forget our deal."

"I won't. Let me know if you find something else, OK?"

"Sure."

"And remember, no one can know about this."

"Yeah, yeah. I got it."

"Thanks again," she said. "I'll see you when I get back."

Jordi's gaze followed her as she walked out. The instant she disappeared into the hallway, he shouted, "Hey, wait!"

She popped her head back in the doorway.

"You still haven't told me where you're going for your holiday," he said.

"Looks like I'm going to France."

Chapter 19 – Games

"Do you like games?" Lucielle was lying on the living room sofa, brushing her doll's black hair.

Rock was seated at the dining table, cleaning his weapons. "You talking to me?"

"Yes."

"What do you want, kid?" he asked without looking at her.

"Do you like games?" she repeated in a measured voice.

"Look, I don't have time for this. Go find someone else to play dress up the doll."

"Don't be ridiculous! I wasn't talking about her." Lucielle held the doll close to her chest. "Like I'd let you touch her."

"Then what are you going on about now?" he asked in an irritated voice.

"She's talking about Soran." Arianne walked into the dining area, accompanied by Ashrem and Kincade. The two siblings had changed out of their black outfits into more casual attire.

"The guy you want to go look for?" Rock said. "Then why is the brat asking me about games?"

Lucielle glared at him. "Don't call me a brat, you ugly Neanderthal."

Ashrem went over to her. "What did we say about language, Luce?"

"But he started it!" the girl protested.

"No I didn't," Rock contested.

"Yes, you did."

"Did not!"

"Did too!"

Kincade moved closer to his comrade. "Are you kidding me right now? How old are you again?"

The giant turned away, a little embarrassed.

Arianne gave her sister a severe look. "The same goes for you too."

The young girl lowered her eyes and pouted her lips.

"Hmm … about Soran," Arianne said.

"What about him?" Kincade asked.

"Well … he can come off as … odd, at times."

"I wouldn't worry too much about it," Rock chuckled. "You all strike me as plenty odd already."

"What are you getting at?" Kincade asked, ignoring his comrade's comment.

"When we escaped from the Arc, Soran refused to join up with Damien, but he didn't want to come with us either."

"Yeah, you mentioned that already," said Kincade.

"I guess what I'm trying to say is … he tends to do things his own way."

"No need to explain," said Ashrem as he walked over to the dining table. "They're about to see for themselves." He sat down and unsheathed a gray laptop from its protective sleeve. "Before he went off on his own, Soran gave us a way to contact him. But knowing him, I doubt it'll be straightforward."

"Meaning what?" Kincade asked.

"This is what Luce meant," Arianne replied. "We'll probably have to solve some sort of game or puzzle in order to set up a meeting with him. And we'll only get one try."

Kincade gave an incredulous look. "You're joking, right?"

"I'm afraid not."

"Why would he do something like that?" Rock asked.

Ashrem logged onto the laptop. "No doubt he'll tell himself it's some sort of basic security check."

Kincade detected a trace of exasperation in the young man's voice.

"But the truth is," Ashrem continued, "he never takes anything seriously."

"I forgot to ask you guys," said Kincade, "how come Soran wasn't in the pictures Leicester gave us?"

A strange glance passed between the three siblings.

"There are a couple of reasons," said Arianne. "For one, Leicester knows Soran isn't trying to find Adam's data card."

"The card you say is hidden somewhere in Western Europe?" Kincade confirmed.

"Yes. Leicester and his people have been searching for it over the years with no success. Now that we're out, I'm sure they're worried we might find it. They'll do everything in their power to prevent that from happening. And since Leicester knows Soran isn't interested in the card, it makes sense for him to focus his resources on those of us he considers a more immediate threat."

Kincade studied her. "Is the card that important?"

"It is," said Lucielle as she joined the others at the large dining table. "We can't let Damien have it."

"What's on it?" Rock asked.

His query was met with an uncomfortable silence.

"We're not sure," said Arianne.

Kincade and Rock exchanged a puzzled look.

"You're not sure?" the giant exclaimed. "You mean you don't know?"

"We know it's important," Arianne told them, "and potentially dangerous. It's the last project our father completed. There's a recording of a phone conversation between Professor Karpov and Adam. The professor took the recording with him when he disappeared, but Leicester's men were able to intercept part of the call. Adam said the card contained the secret to '*his true legacy*'. He also mentioned something about a '*virus*' and '*consequences on a global scale*'."

A concerned frown appeared on Kincade's face. "A virus?"

Arianne nodded. "Whatever other secrets the card may hold, we have to assume it contains the formula for a virus. And if Adam did indeed create such a thing, I can assure you it will be both potent and resilient."

Rock threw his arms up in the air. "Great! It's just one piece of good news after the other with you people, isn't it?"

"Why on earth would he create a virus?" Kincade asked.

"Again," said Ashrem, "we're not sure."

"Now you understand why we have to find the card," said Arianne. "We are Adam's children. It's our responsibility to make sure it doesn't fall into the wrong hands."

"All right," said Kincade, "but if Soran chose to go his own way before, how do you know he'll agree to help you now?"

"We don't," she said. "But we have to try. We'll need his help to stop the others."

"How do you make contact?"

172

"A website," said Ashrem. "I'm loading up the page now."

Kincade and Rock conferred with a look.

The giant shrugged as if to say: *Don't ask me. I don't even care anymore.*

As the page finished loading, they all gathered around the laptop. The screen faded to black and a sequence of flashing digits started counting down from ten.

Kincade figured the point was to allow them time to get ready, because as Arianne had mentioned, there would be no do-overs.

"I wonder what nonsense he's come up with this time," said Lucielle. She sounded even more annoyed than Ashrem.

Kincade and Rock, on the other hand, were rather curious at this point.

The countdown was coming to an end.

Two, one, zero.

The screen's background brightened up and changed into a pair of red curtains. Then, the curtains pulled open to the sound of a clapping and cheering audience and revealed the virtual set of a daytime TV game show.

"What in the world!" Rock exclaimed.

A digitalized character wearing a tuxedo and a bow tie materialized in the middle of the stage. He held up a microphone and spoke into it in melodramatic fashion. "Welcome to our show! I would like to begin by welcoming today's contestants."

There was a round of cheers.

"Thank you, thank you. And now, allow me to introduce my beautiful co-hostess."

A digitized woman in a tight red dress appeared on the set and waved at the screen.

The virtual crowd whistled and cheered even louder.

The man in the tuxedo put on a large smile, revealing two rows of shining white teeth. "Ladies and gentlemen, it's time to explain the format of our game."

"This is the important part," said Arianne. "We need to pay attention."

Kincade glanced at her. He was still trying to decide whether this was really the way to make contact with Soran, or whether he and Rock had fallen victims to some elaborate prank.

"Dear contestants," the game show host continued, "you will be presented with three challenges. In order to win, you'll have to clear all three. If you succeed, you shall be granted a meeting with our gracious benefactor."

The crowd cheers again.

"Hah! Did you hear him?" Lucielle scoffed. "*Gracious benefactor,* he calls himself. What a Muppet!" She didn't look amused at all.

Kincade smiled. "Your brother does seem like quite a character."

"Thank you, thank you." The host quieted the virtual crowd. "Now, let's go over some rules: First, you can only give one answer per challenge, no more. Second, you have to give your answer within a specified time frame. Beyond this limit, your input will not be accepted. Third, each instruction will only be given once, so make sure you pay attention. And for all of you devious people out there, please don't try to fool the game in any way, like reloading the page in order to get another shot at answering a question. Such actions will result in immediate disqualification." He marked a short pause. "Ready? Let's begin."

A spotlight illuminated a table on the screen's foreground. Three small boxes, labeled A, B, and C, were aligned on top of it.

"One of these boxes contains two riddles," the host declared. "Those will constitute your second and third challenges. For now, your first challenge is to find the box which contains the riddles. You have fifteen seconds!"

174

The screen darkened and a countdown began. In the middle of the screen, below the flashing digits, was a small textbox with a blinking cursor for them to input their answer.

"How are we supposed to know which one to pick?" said Rock.

Kincade wondered the same thing as he turned to the three siblings.

They all looked uncertain.

"We don't know," Arianne admitted.

Rock frowned at her. "You don't know? I thought you guys were supposed to be like … super smart."

"Not now, Rock," Kincade told him.

"Strange," said Lucielle, "I don't see anything hinting at the correct choice." She sounded truly perplexed.

Meanwhile, the timer had counted down to seven.

"Maybe we should pick one at random," Kincade suggested.

"No," Arianne said categorically. "There has to be a clear answer."

"Hahaha!" The game show host burst into laughter. "I bet you were nervous for a moment there. I apologize. It was a little joke to lighten up the mood on our set."

The crowd laughed as well.

Lucielle glared at the screen. "When we find Soran, someone please punch him in the face for me."

"For once, kid, I agree with you," Rock snarled.

The presenter started again. "Very well, let's begin … for real this time. Please choose one of the boxes. Any of them will do."

Ashrem clicked on box A.

"Good!" The host extended his arm. "I'm going to ask my lovely co-hostess to walk over to the table."

The woman in red approached the table.

"Would you mind opening one of the other two boxes?" he asked her.

"But I don't know which one contains the riddles," she remarked.

"It's all right, dear, please go ahead."

She opened box C. It was empty.

"Oh, it's not this one," she said in a disappointed voice.

"Thank you," said the host. He then faced the screen. "Dear contestants, as you can see, box C was a miss. There are now two boxes remaining: A and B. Since you've been such good sport, we're giving you a chance to reconsider your answer. Would you like to change your mind and switch to box B, or would you like to stick with your initial choice of box A? You have ten seconds. Let's start the clock!"

"I know this one!" said Rock with great enthusiasm. "You're supposed to switch. Click on B, click on B." He was excited to know the answer.

Ashrem ignored him and clicked on box A without hesitation.

"What are you doing?" said the giant.

Arianne touched him on the arm. "Don't worry. It was a trick question."

After a lengthy theatrical drumroll, the presenter shouted, "Well done!"

The crowd congratulated them with a new round of cheers.

"You've cleared the first stage of our game," the host announced with an overdramatic gesture. "Let's move on to the next. Our benefactor will meet you at a certain place and at an appointed time. To find out where and when, you'll have to solve the two riddles you just uncovered. When you combine the two answers, you'll have the name of the place. As for the time, it is contained within one of the answers, but you'll have to guess which one.

You'll have thirty seconds to clear each challenge. Good luck!"

The woman in red took a piece of paper out of box A and unfolded it. The screen then zoomed in on the paper, making it easier to see the text.

She read the first riddle aloud.

I was swimming under the sea, on a clear sunny day, when it passed by me. It had come and gone in an instant, and had faded far off into the distance. Startled, I immediately rose to the surface. And to my surprise, there it was, passing by me once again.

A small counter started on the top-left of the screen. Thirty seconds.

Rock eyed the laptop like it was some strange object. "What the hell is that supposed to mean?"

Kincade shrugged. "Beats me."

"He told us already," said Lucielle. "It's a riddle."

Arianne glanced down at Ashrem.

"Yes, I know," he said as he typed his answer.

"Well done again!" said the host.

The crowd clapped and cheered.

"What did you type?" Rock asked.

But there was no time to explain. The final challenge was about to begin, and the thirty-second countdown about to reset one last time.

The hostess reached inside the box, pulled out another piece of paper, and unfolded it.

The screen zoomed in once again, and she read the second riddle aloud.

Sometimes fast, and other times slow,

Always together, around we go,

We tell you all you want to know,

Yet all we ever say is 'yes' or 'no'.

Ashrem thought about it for a brief moment and then typed his answer.

"Excellent!" said the host. "We have a winner!"

The crowd went into a frenzy. Vibrant music started playing in the background, and confetti rained down on the virtual set.

"I'm afraid we've come to the end of our show," the host announced. "I hope we'll have the pleasure of having you back with us again. Until then, I wish you all farewell."

The webpage went blank, and a '*Site Offline*' message appeared on the screen.

Chapter 20 – Answers

Lucielle crossed her arms over her chest. "Humph! I knew it! This was far too simple to provide any kind of real security check. He just wanted to fool around like always."

Ashrem started typing again.

Arianne arched over him. "Have you found it?"

"Not yet. Running the search now … OK, got it. It's in Paris. Here's the address."

Lucielle gazed up at the clock hanging above the kitchen door. "There's still time, but we'd better leave now."

"Yes," said Arianne, "but you're not coming. I should go alone."

Kincade and Rock exchanged a befuddled look.

"What's going on?" the giant asked.

"Not a clue," Kincade replied. He turned to Arianne. "You guys mind filling us in?"

"The meeting's in Paris," she said, "but it'll take place in a few hours. I need to hurry." She grabbed a set of keys from a tray on the table and headed for the door. "Luce, let the professor know I borrowed his car."

Kincade caught up with her. "Hold on a minute! Where do you think you're going?"

"To meet with Soran," she said, surprised by his question.

"Like hell you are! Look, I don't understand what just happened, but if you think we're letting you run off alone somewhere while the rest of us are sitting ducks here, you're out of your mind."

"You're right," she said. "We owe you an explanation. But if I don't leave right now, I might not make it in time. Ash can answer any questions you have."

"Fine," said Kincade, "then I'm going too."

Arianne looked uncertain. "Hmm ... I'm not sure that's a good idea."

Kincade locked eyes with her. "Here's the deal. Either I go with you, or you're not going anywhere."

Arianne held his gaze for a few seconds. Sensing he wouldn't budge, she realized she had no choice but to agree. "As you wish," she said. "We'll go together." She then rushed out the door.

As he followed after her, Kincade glanced back at Rock. "Bring Doc and Sonar up to speed when they get back from checking the area."

"Got it, chief," Rock replied.

Kincade stepped outside and slammed the door behind him.

The giant went to the window and watched the pair hurry to the shed and climb into the blue car.

As the vehicle pulled away from the house, Kincade motioned to the second floor. Rock knew Da Costa had stationed himself up there because it afforded a better view of the perimeter.

The giant waited by the window as the car drove past the gates and turned into the narrow road. He noticed that the vehicle jerked every time it slowed or stopped. *Car troubles?* he wondered.

Once the car was out of sight, Rock returned to the dining area. He got there just as Ashrem was opening the cellar door. "Where are you going?"

"Downstairs," Ashrem replied.

"I can see that. But the prisoner's down there."

180

"I know. I want to make sure he doesn't need anything."

Rock cocked his eyebrow. "Doesn't he work for the people who've been keeping you all locked up?"

"Yes, he does." Without further explanation, the young man proceeded down into the cellar.

Rock shook his head and turned to Lucielle. The young girl had returned to the sofa and was once again pampering her doll. "Your friend's a nice guy," he said.

"He's not my friend," she replied. "He's my brother. And, yes, a little too nice if you ask me."

"Hehe! You really do talk kind of funny for a kid."

"How many times do I have to tell you?" she said in a calm voice. "I'm not a kid."

"Yeah, yeah, whatever. All right then, lay it out for me."

Lucielle turned to him and tilted her head. "Huh?"

"You know … the riddles."

She stared at him for a good five seconds. "I'm not telling you."

He scowled. "Why not?"

"I don't want to."

"What the …" The giant marched towards her, a scary expression on his face.

Lucielle immediately shot up from the sofa and dashed towards the staircase.

Rock gave chase. He caught up with her at the base of the stairs, but when he reached down to grab her, she managed to slip past him even as the tips of his fingers brushed against her hair.

Carried by his momentum, the colossus tripped and hit his head against the railings.

"Ouch!"

Lucielle giggled as she ran up the steps. She stopped halfway up the staircase and turned around.

Rock brandished a menacing fist at her. "Why, you brat!"

She stuck her tongue out to taunt him.

"What are you two playing at?" Doc was standing in the doorway, staring at his comrade on the floor.

The giant stood up, grimacing as he rubbed his hand over his head.

"What happened to you?" Sonar asked, following in after Doc.

"Why don't you ask her?" Rock groaned, nodding to Lucielle.

Sonar gazed up at the eleven-year-old girl and then ran his eyes over the hulking figure from head to toe. "*She* hurt *you*? On the head? How exactly did she do that?"

"It's not … what I meant was …" Rock tried to come up with an explanation, but he couldn't think of any that didn't make him look foolish. He decided it was best to drop the subject and move on. "Argh! Never mind. Nate wanted me to tell you both that he left with Arianne. They've gone to meet up with that Soran guy."

"You've made contact?" Doc asked.

"Hmm … sort of."

Doc wasn't sure what to make of his comrade's strange answer, but he didn't linger on it. "Where are they meeting him?" he asked next.

"Don't know."

"You don't know?" Sonar echoed, surprised.

"Nope."

"Do you at least know when they'll be back?" Doc asked.

The giant shrugged. "No idea."

Rock's companions were starting to lose patience as they wondered why he wasn't being more forthcoming.

Sonar frowned. "Do you expect us to believe Nate just took off somewhere without telling you where he was going or when he was coming back? At a time like this?"

"There was no time to explain," said Lucielle. The young girl hadn't moved from her spot halfway up the staircase.

Doc glanced up at her. "Explain what?"

Rock took a deep breath and attempted to summarize what had happened. "All right, there was this website, OK? It was supposed to be the way to get in touch with Soran. The thing is, when we checked out the site, it was some kind of funky game with cartoon characters who gave us some riddles to solve in order to set up the meeting. It looks like the three weirdos figured out the solutions. Then they said someone had to leave right away, so Nate and the girl left in a hurry. And when you came in just now, I was trying to get the kid to tell me what she knows. There!" Rock had blurted out the confused explanation in one go.

His two comrades stared at him in silence for a long time.

"How hard did you hit your head again?" Sonar asked.

"What?" Rock said, almost shouting. "You don't believe me?"

"Fine," said Lucielle. "I'll explain."

But as she started down the steps, Professor Fournier appeared at the top of the stairs. "I heard a loud noise. What's going on down there?"

The young girl peered up at him. "Everything's fine, Professor, it was nothing. Oh, and Arianne said to tell you she borrowed your car."

"Good, good," Fournier replied, nodding absentmindedly.

He looked so distracted, Lucielle wondered if he had heard a word she had said. She had seen this look on the professor before. It was the look he had when he was lost in his research, working on some new theory. It also explained the long delay before he had come out to inquire about the noise caused by Rock's tumble.

The professor went back into his room without bothering to ask why Arianne had left or where she had gone.

Lucielle returned to the ground floor just as Ashrem emerged from the cellar. He turned the hallway corner and saw the small group gathered near the entrance.

"Everything cool down there?" Rock asked him.

"I suppose, though Stanwell's not too happy about his current situation."

"Yeah, I bet he isn't."

Doc turned to Lucielle. "You were about to tell us where Nate and Arianne went?"

"The meeting's at eight o'clock tonight," she replied. "At a place called *Sound Bite*." She looked at Ashrem. "You said it was in Paris? I'm guessing it's some kind of music bar?"

"Correct."

Rock gazed at them as though they were speaking in an unknown foreign language. "Where on earth did you get all this from?"

"You said it yourself," the young girl replied, "from the game."

Sonar was lost. "What game? What are you going on about?"

"I explained it to you a minute ago," Rock complained.

"Sure, like anyone could've understood your gibberish."

Ashrem joined them. "Soran had us solve a couple of riddles in order to set up the meeting with him. The location and time were contained within the answers."

"Why would he do that?" Doc asked.

"He can be a bit childish at times," Lucielle replied as she straightened her doll's dress.

The remark provoked half-smiles from the mercenaries, but all three refrained from commenting on it.

Lucielle gave them a quick summary of the game's instructions and recited the last two riddles verbatim.

"What the hell is this stuff supposed to mean?" Sonar exclaimed.

"I know, right?" said Rock. He was gratified to see someone else react the same way he had.

Doc's reaction was more restrained, but he was just as baffled. "How does this give you the time and place of the meeting?"

"Simple," said the analyst. "The first answer is *sound*."

"Sound?" Sonar echoed.

"Yes," she confirmed. "Sound is a vibration. It propagates via a medium. Meaning its speed will vary depending on the medium in question. Therefore—"

"Hey!" Rock interrupted. "Try in English!"

Vexed, Lucielle stopped talking and gave him a mean look.

Sensing the two were about to engage in yet another meaningless squabble, Ashrem decided to take over the elucidation. "In short, she's saying sound travels faster in water than it does in the air. Therefore, if you hear a sound while underwater, and you're far enough away from the source, it's possible to hear the same sound again by quickly rising to the surface."

185

"For real?" said Rock.

"Yes, so the answer to the first riddle is sound," Ashrem continued, "and as Lucielle mentioned, the second one is—"

"She said bite," Doc interrupted, "as in computer byte?"

"Good guess!" The silver-haired girl was impressed.

"How do you figure?" Sonar asked.

Once again, it was Ashrem who answered. "The line '*Sometimes fast and other times slow*', refers to an internet connection. It can be fast or slow depending on various factors. The part about telling us all we want to know also refers to the internet. People go online to find information on pretty much anything."

"OK, then what about the *yes* or *no* thing?" Sonar asked.

"Today's computers exchange information in digital form, meaning it's made up of bits, series of ones and zeroes. Those ones and zeroes are sometimes called *true* and *false*, or *yes* and *no*."

"But you said byte, not bits," Rock disputed.

"Again," Ashrem replied, "think about the wording of the riddle. *Always together*. Bits are combined in groups of eight, called bytes. Digital computers process information in bytes, not in individual bits, hence the terms megabyte, gigabyte, etc."

"It's also where we got the time from," Lucielle added. "Eight bits for one byte: eight o'clock."

"I meant to ask you about that," said Doc. "How can you be sure? Couldn't the time be in the other riddle? Like the speed of sound, for example?"

"No," she said. "The speed of sound is not a constant. We wouldn't know which value to use, whereas the number of bits in one byte is always eight. That's why we knew it had to be the time."

"Damn!" Rock exclaimed. "And you guys figured out all of this in what … five seconds?"

Sonar was amazed. "They did?"

"It's no big deal," said Ashrem. "Anyway, I combined the two words and ran a search on the internet for a place called *'sound bite,'* which is phonetically identical to 'sound byte.' From the name, I assumed it was the kind of place where you can eat and listen to music, like a piano bar or a restaurant."

Lucielle smiled. "It's a play on words. *Sound bite*, as in a piece of music, combined with grabbing a *bite* to eat. I think it's kind of funny."

Rock shook his head. "Man, this Soran's got way too much time on his hands."

"How do you know the meeting's today?" Doc asked. "Why not tomorrow? Or the day after?"

"Good point," said Ashrem. "It's because, even though no one else should know about this website, the fact it's on the internet presents a risk in itself. It's safe to assume Soran would start the clock from the moment the site was accessed. And it would be counting in hours, not days, in case Leicester's men, or even Damien, somehow found out about it. He wouldn't want to leave anyone time to set a trap for him. That's why I started my search with Paris. It's the nearest major city."

"What if you guys were too far away to make it to Paris within hours?" Sonar challenged.

Ashrem smiled. "We might not know where Soran is, but you can be sure he knows where we are."

"How?" Rock asked.

"All of us have always had some idea where Professors Karpov and Fournier had been hiding. We just never told Leicester. Soran knows in which direction Arianne and I traveled after we escaped. It would have been easy for him to guess we'd contact Professor Fournier. He knows we're here."

187

At that moment, the professor showed up at the top of the stairs once again. "Luce! Luce! Could you get Ash and come up here for a minute? I need your help with something."

"Did you have more questions?" Ashrem asked Doc.

"No, go ahead."

"We're on our way," the girl shouted back at the old man.

The two siblings left the mercenaries and went up to the second floor.

Doc checked the time on his phone. "Sonar, you should get up there too. Da Costa's been keeping watch for over three hours now. It's your turn to take over."

"All right," said Sonar. He started on his way, but after climbing a few steps, he stopped and leaned over the railings. "Hey, guys, I just thought of something. The meeting … Nate will be alone with two of them. I mean, we've seen what they can do. Is that a good idea?"

He had asked the question in a casual manner, and the point he had made was simple, even obvious. But it also highlighted the prospect of real danger.

Doc and Rock suddenly looked worried.

"Dammit!" Rock exclaimed. "I knew I should've gone with him." He took out his cell phone and dialed.

"What are you doing?" Sonar asked.

"What do you think I'm doing? I'm telling Nate to get back here. They've only been gone a few minutes. They can't be far yet."

Chapter 21 – Driving

Inside the professor's car, the theme music of a famous evil galactic empire started playing.

"What's that?" Arianne asked, her eyes fixed on the road.

Kincade smiled. "It's the ring I set for Rock's number. It's a private joke, because he always calls me with bad news."

"Interesting tune," she said.

Kincade shot a quick glance at her as he answered his phone. "What's up?

…

"How do you mean?"

Kincade shot another glance at Arianne.

"I don't think it'll be a problem."

…

Noted."

He hung up.

"Something wrong?" Arianne inquired.

"No. He was just letting me know Doc was about to interrogate Stanwell."

She smiled. "There's no need for deception. Your friends are worried about you, aren't they? After all, we're off to meet my brother. If our intentions are not what we said, or if the meeting goes wrong, you could end

189

up being outnumbered two to one."

Kincade froze for a second. Her insight and perception had caught him off guard. "You're right," he confessed. "Sorry, I should've been upfront with you."

"Would you like me to turn back?" she asked. "To be frank, I'd rather not, but if you'd feel more comfortable—"

"It's fine," said Kincade, "keep going." Embarrassed to have been caught in a lie, he felt the need to justify himself. "We're wound up a bit tight at the moment. And you understand we can only afford to trust you up to a certain point."

"I understand," Arianne assured him. "Don't worry about it. You've already taken a big chance trusting us this far. We're all aware of it, and we're grateful."

They spent the next few minutes in awkward silence, until Kincade decided to try to lighten the mood. "Hey, you were pulling my leg earlier, right? About my ringtone."

She didn't answer.

"Come on," he insisted, "you must have recognized it."

Arianne glanced at him and shook her head. This time, it was she who looked embarrassed.

Kincade realized she wasn't pretending. She honestly didn't know it, and he sensed it made her uneasy. "Hey, it's no big deal. A lot of people aren't into sci-fi."

"It's not that," she said. "It's, erm … we've been isolated from the outside world our entire lives. There're many things we've never experienced, things regular people take for granted. Like swimming in the sea … going to the movies … traveling to different countries … or even driving a car."

Listening to her, Kincade tried to imagine what it had been like for her and her siblings growing up in a secured facility, surrounded by guards and

190

scientists who were watching their every move.

They hadn't done anything wrong, and yet they had been handed down a life sentence in prison. It was a terrible injustice, one which they had had to suffer since birth. And as Kincade pondered on it, he began to see Arianne through a different lens. The sympathy he had been feeling for her from the moment they had met was now laced with a measure of admiration. He wondered how, having grown up in these conditions, she had turned out to be such a balanced and gentle person.

"Can I help you with something?" she asked, unsettled by his prolonged stare.

"What …? Huh, no," he replied, turning away, "I was just lost in my own thoughts."

Then came another long moment of silence.

Kincade spent it gazing out at the green countryside streaming past as the car sped along the highway. At times, he would cast a quick glance at Arianne. She seemed to be smiling at the road. He had never seen anyone look this happy to be behind the wheel of a vehicle. She was like a child on a merry-go-round.

He smiled in turn.

Then, all of a sudden, his smile vanished and was replaced by a deep frown. "Wait a minute, what did you say?" he asked in a loud and nervous voice.

"I didn't say anything," she replied, startled by the abruptness of his tone.

"No, earlier," Kincade pressed. "Did you say you've never driven a car before?"

"Yes, this is my first time."

The blood instantly drained from Kincade's face. "What?"

"I wanted to drive the van," she said. "Ash and I flipped a coin for it. I lost."

"Stop the car!" he commanded. "I'm driving."

She clutched the wheel even tighter. "No way, it's my turn."

"Your turn? This isn't a game, you know. You could get us killed."

"It's OK. We've all practiced on simulators many times."

As she offered the less-than-convincing argument, Kincade saw a glimmer of excitement in her eyes. It worried him even more. "Simulators! Are you kidding me?"

For a moment, he seriously considered drawing his gun on her to force her to pull over.

She did her best to reassure him. "I realize it's not the same as the real thing, but Ash did all right, didn't he? I admit I had some trouble at first, but I think I'm getting the hang of it now."

"Hold on ... you mean that stop-and-go dance back when we left the house? I thought it was because the car was old or something."

"Nah, the car's fine. It was me. But we're good now."

Kincade was dumbfounded. This facet of her personality was nothing like the serious and poised woman he had seen thus far. She seemed more like a child now. In fact, she reminded him of Lucielle, which was how he knew he wouldn't win this particular argument. He could tell she was determined not to let him spoil her *fun*.

"Will you at least slow down?" he said. "You're going kind of fast for a first-time driver."

"You think so?" She checked the speed gauge. "We're right around the speed limit."

"Exactly!" he barked.

"Come on, don't be such a bore," she said with a playful smile. "We're in a hurry, remember?"

Another period of awkward silence ensued.

After a while, Arianne attempted to restart the conversation. "So, how long have you been in this line of—"

Kincade cut her off with a hand gesture. "Don't! Don't talk to me right now. Just … focus on the road."

"OK, OK. There's no need to be so tense, you know."

Kincade disagreed. He was wriggling nervously in his seat. He started to notice every bit of wear and tear inside the vehicle, and to pay attention to every creaking and squeaking sound. He reached underneath his seat to adjust it and give himself more leg room, but his hands were moist with sweat. The handle slipped through his fingers. "For crying out loud," he muttered.

He adjusted it on the second try and sat back up. Then, it occurred to him he shouldn't have been able to move so freely. He looked at Arianne and, for the first time, noticed she had on her seat belt. He quickly fastened his.

She winked at him. "That's right, safety first."

Chapter 22 – Friends

The music bar was fairly crowded despite the early hour of the night. The main area consisted of a large open space with a modern décor, illuminated by soft strobe lights hanging from the ceiling. To the right of the entrance, seated at small cubic tables with alternating-colored lights glowing at their centers, groups of customers were enjoying drinks and simple dishes ordered from a triple-folded menu. To the left, a live band was playing on a small stage. The lead singer, a woman wearing a flowing green dress adorned with fluorescent butterflies, crooned a melancholy tune. Gathered on the dance floor in front of her, a small crowd swayed to the melody, as if mesmerized by the singer's soft and soothing voice. The remaining patrons were scattered around the bar on the opposite side of the room.

"Interesting place," said Arianne. "Not at all like I imagined."

Kincade smiled. "Actually, most bars I know are very different from this."

"Are they?"

"Yeah. So, how do we find our guy?"

"I'm not sure," she replied, casting an eye over the crowd. "I guess I'll have to look around."

"All right, let's go."

She placed her hand on his chest. "Wait. I don't know how Soran will react if he sees someone he doesn't recognize. He might not show himself. Please, let me try to find him first."

Kincade hesitated briefly. "Fine, I'll go have a drink. Just make sure you check back inside of five minutes."

"I will."

Kincade watched her disappear into the crowd.

Then, he headed over to the bar. He found a narrow space and leaned over the counter to order a cold beer. After the bartender had handed him his bottle, he turned around and pretended to listen to the band as he scanned the faces around him.

The first thing Kincade noticed was that, unlike most bars, the patrons of this establishment genuinely seemed more interested in the music than in their drinks.

There were, however, a few exceptions. The young man to Kincade's right, for instance, clearly had no interest in the band's performance. He was far too busy trying his luck with a couple of pretty girls dressed in provocative outfits.

Kincade hardly knew any French, but from the looks of it, the young man's pick-up lines were in need of serious improvement, as was their delivery.

Kincade couldn't help but feel bad as he watched the clumsy attempt at flirting. And although he was curious to see what would come of it, he directed his attention away from the trio. He was far more intrigued by the brawny figure standing in the shadows at the end of the counter. Kincade couldn't make out the man's face, but he sensed the shadowy character had been surveilling him ever since he had shown up at the bar. He considered going over to confront him directly, but in the end, he decided against it. *Best to keep a low profile,* he told himself. *At least until Arianne returns.*

But, unfortunately for Kincade, keeping a low profile would turn out to be a much less straightforward proposition than he had hoped. While he was still focused on the man in the shadows, from the corner of his eye, he caught a glimpse of someone closing in on him from the right. He tried to move out of the way but wasn't able to react fast enough.

"Hey!" Kincade yelled as a half-drunken idiot bumped into him, causing him to spill his drink.

195

"Sorry, mate. Je su-is … dé-so-lé," the man struggled to apologize in crooked French with a strong British accent. He reeked of alcohol.

"Don't worry about it," said Kincade.

"Ah, English!" the man exclaimed with relief. "Good. Then again, I don't think you can find ten French people in here. It's all tourists and expats."

"Good to know," Kincade replied. He then promptly turned away to indicate he had no interest in engaging in a conversation.

But the man had other ideas. He matched Kincade's movement so as to remain in his line of sight. "My name's Gavin. What's yours, friend?"

"Nate."

"Look, I'm really sorry about your beer. Here, let me buy you another one." He motioned the bartender to bring two more bottles.

"There's no need."

"No, no, I insist. It's the least I can do, right? Besides, I'm running on empty. I was coming to get a refill."

Before Kincade could voice another objection, the bartender showed up with their drinks.

Gavin traded a bill for the bottles. He handed one to Kincade, and he raised his. "Cheers, mate."

Kincade acknowledged him with a faint nod and then turned away, hoping the pestering Brit would take the hint.

He didn't need the distraction.

Since his unfortunate encounter with Gavin, Kincade had been feeling a stubborn stare burning a hole in the back of his head. No doubt it was the man in the shadows taking advantage of the incident to scrutinize him more overtly. He placed his bottle on the counter and adjusted it to catch his stalker's reflection. The man hadn't moved from his spot.

196

"So, what brings you here? Did you come for the band?"

Kincade closed his eyes and let out a weary sigh. Apparently, he had underestimated Gavin's determination to hang around. "I'm waiting for someone," he said, checking the reflection one more time.

"Girlfriend?" Gavin pried.

"No."

Gavin nudged Kincade on the arm. "Ooh, I see. Trying to score, eh? I'm waiting for this chick myself … ah, speaking of which," he discreetly pointed with his bottle, "crash and burn at three o'clock."

Kincade glanced to his right.

The two girls from earlier were walking away from the bar under the gloomy gaze of the young man who had been chatting them up. As the man followed the girls with his eyes, he noticed that Kincade and his drinking buddy had been observing the scene. He shrugged at them. "I guess I need to work on my game."

Gavin waved his hand. "No worries, mate, we've all been there. Why don't you come and join us?"

Kincade frowned and turned towards Gavin in slow motion. *Join us?* Not only did this clueless idiot not seem to have any qualms about imposing on a total stranger, now, despite the not-so-subtle signals he was being a nuisance, he wanted to recruit a new member into his merry band.

Kincade decided he had had enough. It was time to borrow a page from Rock's book on how to deal with troublesome individuals.

Just as he was about to convert intent into action, he heard Arianne's voice call out to him.

"Making friends?"

Kincade turned around and sighed. "You have no idea. Any luck?"

A tinge of surprise flashed across Arianne's face as she approached. "No, but I see you have."

It took Kincade a second to get her meaning. But when he did, he spun around and clamped his hand around Gavin's arm. "What's with the act? Why not tell me it was you?"

Gavin wailed in pain. "What are you talking about? Let go! You're hurting me."

"Hi, sis!" a voice said.

"Hello, brother," Arianne replied.

Kincade whipped his head around.

He was so stunned that he involuntarily released his grip on the poor Gavin.

The Brit walked away, nursing his arm. "Crazy American!"

But Kincade wasn't paying him any mind. All his attention was directed at the young man who had been ditched by the two girls. He stared at the cheerful face smiling at him and then turned to Arianne. "Is this him?"

It was clear from Kincade's tone and expression that his first impression of Soran was far from awe-inspiring. A thought occurred to him, and he shot a glance at the figure in the shadows.

"He works here," said Soran. "He's security. I noticed you've been checking up on him, wondering why he's been keeping an eye on you this whole time. Hey, let's face it! You don't exactly blend into this crowd. I guess he wanted to make sure you weren't going to start any trouble or anything."

Kincade raised an eyebrow at the young man, impressed by his sharp sense of observation.

"Can we talk?" said Arianne.

"Sure," Soran replied. He guided them to one of the quieter corners of the bar, and the three of them sat around a glowing cube.

Arianne got straight to the point. "We need your help, Soran."

"Well, duh … it's only been a few days. I didn't think you missed me already. But first things first, who are you?" he asked, turning to his sister's companion.

"The name's Nate Kincade."

"It's all right," said Arianne, "you can trust him."

"Come on, sis. You've obviously just met the guy. You have to be more careful with the people on the outside, you know. Most of them are different than we imagined. And I don't mean that in a good way."

"I know," she said. Her eyes then shifted to Kincade. "Most … but not all."

Soran gave the mercenary a big tap on the back. "That's quite an endorsement, my good fellow. You should be flattered."

"I'm thrilled," Kincade quipped. "How about we talk about why we're here?"

"Sure thing," the young man replied. "So, what do you need, sis? Plane tickets? Fake passports? A place to crash?"

Arianne wasn't amused. "Stop being silly, Soran. You know it's about Damien."

"And you know I don't want to get involved."

"He's searching for Adam's data card."

"Not my problem."

"Of course it is!" she said, raising her voice.

Kincade's brow twitched in surprise. In the short time he had known her, Arianne had shown herself to be such a composed and level-headed person, it felt strange seeing her get so worked up this early in the conversation. *I guess it's the kind of effect siblings can have on one another.*

"I know how much harder it was for you at the Arc," Arianne continued in a calmer tone. "I can understand why you'd want to forget all about it. But you can't go on pretending like none of this has anything to do with you."

"Maybe not ... but I can try."

"They killed Professor Karpov," she bellowed in frustration.

Soran's cheerfulness faded. "Professor K. is dead?"

She nodded.

"Johann?"

"Most likely."

"Did you find Professor J.?"

"We did. He's fine. Ash and I are staying with him. Luce is with us too."

Soran paused for a moment before turning to Kincade. "And where do you fit in all of this?"

"I suppose I'm like you," Kincade replied.

"Oh! How so?"

"I'm still not quite sure where I stand. For now, let's just say I made a deal with Arianne and agreed to hear her out."

"You're military, aren't you?"

"Ex."

"Think you know what you're getting yourself into Mr. Ex-Military?"

"I think I'm starting to."

"Do you? And you, sis, do *you* know what you're getting yourself into?"

"What do you mean?" Arianne asked, a little taken aback by the question.

Soran leaned forward, his eyes glistening with a solemn foreboding. "You won't be able to *talk* Damien out of this. If you're serious about stopping him, sooner or later he will come after you. You know how he is. I guess what I'm asking is: what are you prepared to do?"

Arianne knew her brother was right. This was an all-or-nothing proposition. There would be no room for half-measures or compromises. She locked eyes with him. "Whatever it takes."

After a long silence, Soran leaned back in his seat. He looked cheerful again. "Fine, I don't know how much help I'll be, but I'll tag along if you think it's wise."

She smiled. "Thank you."

"Don't mention it."

If you think it's wise? Kincade wondered about the passing comment. He thought it was a strange thing to say. Normally he would have reacted to it, but he didn't want to waste any more time. He didn't think it was a good idea for fugitives to hang around in such a public place.

"If it's all settled, how about we get out of here?" he asked them. He then turned to Soran. "Next time you pick a meeting place, try not to make it a dark and crowded room with only one exit."

"Sorry, Mr. Ex-Military. We know a lot when it comes to theory, but I guess we're still lacking in the 'practical experience' department."

"Yeah, I'm starting to get that too." Kincade shot an accusatory glance at Arianne to remind her of his unwilling participation in her first experience behind the wheel of a car.

She turned away with an innocent expression and pretended not to notice.

On their way back to the car, the trio strode past various groups of people out to enjoy the nightlife. They were scattered around the many bars lining the streets and engaging in loud drunken conversations.

When they arrived at the vehicle, Kincade reached into his pocket and took out the car keys. He had confiscated them from Arianne as soon as she had turned off the engine. He had no intention of spending the return trip sweating it out in the passenger seat again.

With one quick look, Arianne knew not to raise any objections when she saw Kincade circling over to the driver's side. But by the time she noticed Soran going around as well, it was too late to warn him.

The young man walked up to Kincade all excited. "Hey, mind if I drive?"

"Yeah, I mind!" Kincade snapped.

"What did I say?" Soran asked, confused.

"Just get in the car!" Kincade told him.

"All right, all right." Soran sank into the backseat, muttering to himself. "What's his problem?"

Arianne climbed into the passenger seat and eyed her brother in the rearview mirror. "Don't take it personally. He doesn't like to let other people drive. I think he has trust issues."

Kincade, who had taken his place behind the wheel, turned to her in disbelief. "Trust issues? Seriously?"

Arianne looked away and faced the window in order to conceal a mischievous smile.

Realizing she was only teasing him, Kincade smiled too. *So, she does have a sense of humor after all.*

All the while, Soran gawked at the pair from the backseat, unhappy about being excluded from the private joke.

"Buckle up!" said Kincade as the engine roared.

The car pulled away and disappeared into the night.

202

Chapter 23 – Bloody Knives

The tires screeched as they ground against the asphalt, leaving black swerving skid marks on the road. Before the dark SUV came to a complete stop, Jenkins jumped out of the front passenger side and rushed over to a white brick building.

Seconds later, an identical SUV turned the corner, followed by three police cars. The four vehicles sped down the road and parked alongside the first one under the curious gazes of passers-by in the Berlin business district.

Carson emerged from the second SUV along with two other men in black suits, and the three of them ran up to Jenkins, who was waiting in front the building.

A police inspector and a dozen plain clothes officers exited the other vehicles and caught up with them.

"Is this the bank, Mr. Jenkins?" the inspector asked.

Jenkins nodded without taking his eyes off the structure.

Carson checked the time on his phone. "The rest of our men should be here in less than six minutes."

"We're not waiting for them." Jenkins raised his two-way radio. "Sniper teams report!"

"Team One in position, over"

"Team Two in position, over"

"Team Three in position, over"

Jenkins was pleased. His men had been quick to deploy to their designated positions.

203

Carson glanced at the crowd of onlookers gathered on the other side of the road. "What about these people?"

Jenkins eyed the inspector. "We'll let the police handle them."

The inspector ordered three of his men to keep the crowd away until uniformed police arrived.

"It won't be long before the press shows up as well," Carson pointed out.

"True," said Jenkins. "Let's hurry."

All but the three officers on crowd management duty went inside the bank.

As soon as the group barged in, four security guards came rushing with their guns raised.

The inspector stepped forward and held up his badge. "We're from the Berlin police. We're here on official business."

"No one told us you were coming," said the head guard as he cast a suspicious eye over the trespassers. "I'm going to have to contact my superiors."

"Feel free to do so." Jenkins walked past him, shadowed by Carson and the two men in suits.

"Hey, where are you going?" The head guard wanted to go after them, but the inspector stood in his way.

"I'm sorry," said the inspector, "but I need you and your men to wait here."

The head guard became incensed. "Wait here? The security of this bank is my responsibility. You don't have the authority to—"

"Actually, I do. The bank manager will get in touch with you shortly. In the meantime, by all means, contact your superiors."

Leaving the inspector and his men to deal with the security guards, Jenkins' group proceeded inside the bank all the way to the strong room. Once there, Jenkins took out his phone and dialed. "We're at the vault. Do you have the code?"

He paused with the phone pressed against his ear.

After a brief wait, he approached the electronic panel on the door and keyed in a combination. It triggered a long beeping sound, and the red light on the panel turned green.

Jenkins then rotated the wheel at the center of the vault door, spinning it alternately clockwise and counterclockwise several times until he heard a loud click. Without a word, he hung up the phone and pulled the heavy metallic door towards him.

"Looks like Mr. Schaffer's contact came through," said Carson.

The four men entered the vault.

It was a plain room with safe deposit boxes embedded in the walls and a rectangular metallic table at its center.

"Number 02997," said Jenkins as he began to inspect the numbered labels on the walls. He saw that the safe deposit boxes were arranged in numerical order, and he soon realized he was on the wrong side of the room.

"Over here, Patrick!" Carson called, pointing to one of the lower boxes on his side.

Jenkins circled the table and checked the number on the label: 02997. *This is it.* He ordered his men to leave the room.

Only he and Carson remained.

They lined the edge of the safe deposit box with minute amounts of plastic explosive and blew the lid open.

There was a smaller box inside. Jenkins pulled it out and placed it on the table. It didn't look like anyone had tampered with it. He carefully lifted the top.

The box contained a cell phone and other electronic devices linked together by a bunch of mingled wires. The phone turned on by itself, and one of the devices started blinking.

"What the hell is this thing?" Carson exclaimed.

Jenkins studied the contraption.

All of a sudden, he picked up the box and smashed its contents on the floor. "It's a decoy. The recording isn't here."

"You sure? What about all this equipment?"

"There's a motion sensor, and another gadget I don't recognize. My guess is Karpov rigged the phone to send him a message if the box was ever moved. It's probably why our people were able to find this place so easily. He left the trail on purpose to make sure anyone looking for him would end up here. The whole thing is nothing more than an early warning system. Crafty old bastard!"

"For all the good it did him," Carson remarked.

Jenkins' phone rang. He answered it. "What?"

"Sir, we're receiving reports of alarms going off."

"I thought I told you to kill the alarm," said Jenkins in an irritated tone.

"We did, sir. This isn't happening at your location."

Jenkins was getting impatient. "Then where?"

"Everywhere else. Alarm signals are going off at banks and security offices all over Berlin."

"Dammit!" Jenkins was livid. "Deploy the men. Check out every single location. Use the police if you have to. Report in when you have a visual on the suspects."

"Understood, sir."

Jenkins hung up, cursing to himself.

Carson gave him an interrogative look.

"Alarms are being set off at several sites around the city," Jenkins told him.

"Several sites? Why?"

"This is Darius' doing," Jenkins replied through grinding teeth.

"They've found the recording, haven't they?" said Carson. "They set off the alarms to cover their tracks, so we won't know where they are."

Jenkins' jaw tightened even harder.

Meanwhile, across the city …

The security guard froze.

He was in the middle of his rounds when the alarm went off. In all his years working the night shift at the bank, he had never heard this sound outside of the weekly systems checks. He fumbled for his two-way radio. "Thomas! Come in, Thomas!"

"I read you, Matts," a voice replied.

"Where are you right now?"

"I'm in the main lobby, with the new guy."

"What's going on down there?"

"I don't know," said Thomas. "We were about to go check it out."

"And Sebastian?"

"He went to have a look at the back."

"Anything on the monitors?"

"No, nothing."

"OK. I'll contact the main office and—"

"Please repeat," said Thomas. "I didn't catch that last part."

"Hold on!" said Matts, his voice dropping to a whisper. "I hear footsteps … I think there's someone up here."

Matts drew his sidearm and pressed his back against the wall. He could hear it clearly now. Not only were the footsteps getting louder as they grew closer to him, they also seemed to be getting faster.

Rather than charge into an unknown situation, he decided to lie in wait and listen.

As soon as the intruder turned the corner at the other end of the corridor, the footsteps accelerated to a sprint. Matts clenched his pistol and stood at the ready. He didn't want to let the intruder get too close to him, but close enough they wouldn't be able to get away.

He waited a bit longer.

When he judged the timing was right, he sprang from behind the wall and aimed his gun down the corridor with both arms outstretched.

Unfortunately, Matts had underestimated the speed at which the intruder had been charging towards his position. He had expected to be at least eight or nine feet away from them. Instead, he saw a pair of hazel eyes surrounded by a thatch of red hair floating less than three feet away from his face. It was a woman.

Surprised to find her this close, Matts instinctively fired twice.

But even from such a short distance, both shots inexplicably missed their target. The bullets flew unimpeded along the corridor and lodged themselves into the far wall.

Before Matts knew what was happening, his head was sandwiched

208

between a pair of hands. The woman had performed a twisting somersault and was staring at him with her body upside-down in the air.

Matts suddenly understood what she was doing. But it was too late to do anything about it. She completed her jump over him while keeping his head firmly secured between her hands. The security guard's neck snapped instantly.

The woman landed on her feet as Matts' lifeless body crumpled onto the floor.

"Matts! Matts!" Thomas called out over the radio. "I heard gunshots, what's going on?"

The woman knelt down and picked up the two-way. "Your friend is dead."

"Damn you!" Thomas cursed as he fired at the elusive figure. But his target was moving too fast, slithering in and out of the shadows across the room. And there was that laugh, that sickening laugh, taunting him.

Thomas was shaking with rage as he discharged his weapon. Until, finally … *click, click* … his clip was empty. "Shoot him!" he shouted at his colleague while he reloaded.

The new guy obliged but fared no better.

The hall was vast. There was a large circular counter near the entrance and several desks spread between two rows of wide pillars running down on either side of the room.

Eventually, the two security guards managed to pin the intruder behind one of the farthermost pillars.

Seeing a chance to outflank him, they cautiously approached from opposite sides. They were almost in view of their target when, suddenly, two large knives closed in on them from the sides like a pincer.

In a defensive reflex, Thomas took a quick step back and folded his arms. He cried out in pain as one of the blades slashed his forearm, causing him to loosen his grip on his gun and drop it.

The new guy had been far less fortunate.

Thomas stared in horror at the bloodied corpse lying on the floor with a knife planted in his flank.

But there was no time to lament the loss of his colleague. Thomas' own life was still in danger. He bent down to pick up his firearm.

But then the impossible happened.

The knife that had injured him began to slide on the floor, dragging his gun along with it until it took off and swiftly retreated back behind the pillar.

The same happened with the other knife. It left the guard's body and flew into the shadows. It was like they had a will of their own.

Thomas was petrified with fear. He tried to understand how he could be both awake and inside a nightmare at the same time.

He stood in the open space, helplessly staring at the darkness. He knew the knives were coming back for him. It was only a matter of time. He shut his eyes and waited for the end.

A second passed.

Two seconds.

It wouldn't be long now.

Five seconds.

Still, nothing happened.

Thomas willed his eyes to open again.

He couldn't see anyone, nor hear anything other than the sound of his own blood dripping on the floor. *Had the assailant left? Why would he leave?*

He glanced down at his firearm. It was only a few feet away. He was about to go for it when he sensed a chilling presence. Someone was still nearby. He was certain of it. *The assailant?* It had to be. He was still there, hiding in the shadows, watching … waiting. *What's he waiting for?*

Thomas decided to dive for his gun. With luck, he would reach it in time. What did he have to lose? But as he tried to move, he found he couldn't. His legs wouldn't respond. They felt heavy, weighed down by dread and a quiet panic.

"Aren't you going to pick it up?" a voice asked.

Thomas looked up.

A young man was slowly advancing towards him, his face covered by strands of blond hair.

As the man approached, Thomas' gaze was drawn to the bloody knives he was holding in each hand.

"Who … who are you?" Thomas stammered.

The blond man stopped about twelve feet away and glanced at the guard's wounded arm. "You've got good reflexes. I'm impressed."

"Wh … what do you want?"

"I want you to pick up your gun," the man calmly replied.

"My gun? … Why?"

"So we may finish our little game."

Thomas' eyes widened in horror. He pointed at the body of his dead colleague. "You call this a game?"

The blond man lowered his eyes toward the corpse and tilted his head. "To be fair, you guys did shoot first."

"You killed Matts!" Thomas shouted, a surge of anger driving back his fear.

The man shrugged. "That wasn't me."

"What … what are you saying?" Thomas' heart skipped a beat. It was true. He was the one who had opened fire on the intruder after hearing about Matts. Could the blond man only have been defending himself? As Thomas stared at the new guard's body once again, a terrible thought occurred to him. What if this was his fault? What if he was to blame for the death of his colleague?

The blond man burst into laughter. "Don't look so distressed. I would have killed him anyway."

"Johann, what's taking you so long?" a voice interrupted.

Thomas turned around. A tall, muscular man appeared. He was carrying someone on his shoulder.

Johann rolled his eyes. "Pfft, Darius."

Thomas looked on as the big man walked up to him and dropped his charge on the floor. "Sebastian! Did you kill him too?"

Darius examined the injured guard from top to bottom before answering. "No."

"No?" Johann echoed in surprise. "Why not?"

"There was no need."

Thomas breathed a sigh of relief. "Oh, thank you."

Darius stared at the guard once again.

Then, out of nowhere, he struck the side of Thomas' head with the palm of his hand in a downward diagonal motion.

It was a violent blow.

Thomas slammed into the ground with such force it knocked him out cold.

Johann frowned with irritation. "You spoiled my fun."

"Your *fun* is of no concern to me," Darius replied with a placid expression.

"Couldn't agree more!" a woman's voice said. Matts' killer emerged from the staircase door and walked over to her brothers. "We're here for Professor Karpov's recording. We don't have time for your sick games. Besides, how long does it take to get rid of two guys?"

Johann shrugged. "Couldn't be helped, Kadyna. He wouldn't pick up his weapon."

"Oh, I almost forgot. You don't attack people who are unarmed."

"It's beneath me," said Johann. "It's beneath all of us."

"You mean you don't get a kick out of it," Kadyna corrected.

"Maybe," Johann admitted. "Still, the fact remains. We're superior to those … people in every way. It's bad enough we have to lower ourselves to deal with them personally. The least I can do is give them half a chance." A malicious grin appeared on his face. "Well, I suppose it's nowhere near half, but … you get my meaning."

"Hey, don't blame us for not going along with your warped logic," Kadyna told him.

"You know I'm right."

She frowned. "Oh yeah? What about Professor Karpov? Was he armed?"

Johann's expression turned severe. "That was different. The old man had it coming. He worked with the people who kept us prisoner and experimented on us during all those years."

"Aside from our father, Professor Karpov and Professor Fournier were the only ones who ever cared about us," Kadyna argued.

Now Johann was getting upset. "Don't be naïve, sister. They only pretended to care in order to run their tests. They were using us, just like the others."

"Believe me, Johann. No one can *pretend* to care about a psycho like you for such a long time."

"Enough!" Darius interjected. "The alarms may have provided some cover, but after all those gunshots, we can expect the police to be on their way."

"Quite right," said Johann. He spun around and headed towards the entrance.

"Where do you think you're going?" Kadyna asked.

"Outside."

"Are you stupid?" she shouted. "What if someone sees you?"

"That is the point," Johann replied as he kept walking. "With any luck, Jenkins' men will make it here before we leave. If they do, I want to make sure they don't overlook us in their haste."

"You could end up leading Jenkins straight to us," said Darius.

"So what? There are four of us here," Johann countered. "And like I said, you spoiled my fun. I'm only trying to find some other way to pass the time." He opened the door and exited the bank.

Kadyna turned and glowered at Darius.

"What is it?" he asked her.

"Don't play dumb. You know what. Are you going to let this fool jeopardize the plan for such a childish reason?"

Darius stared at the door for a while. Then, he turned away and headed to the vault. "I'm going to check on Mitsuki. She should be almost done."

Kadyna was annoyed, but she didn't voice her discontent. She knew trying to argue with Darius was about as useful as trying to argue with a wall.

He and Mitsuki truly were a matching pair. She stood with her arms crossed and silently watched him walk away.

"Shouldn't we get out there too?" Carson asked.

"There's no need," said Jenkins. "It won't make any difference."

Carson looked surprised. "I know it's unlikely we'll find them in time, but with any luck—"

"Luck has nothing to do with it. Our guys are spread too thin right now. Even if one of the teams stumbled upon the right place, they wouldn't have enough men to hold out until we arrive."

"Even so," Carson insisted. "It's still our best chance to get them before they disappear again."

Jenkins wore a pensive frown. "As long as we keep chasing after them, we'll always be one or two steps behind. We need to think ahead."

"Did you have something specific in mind?"

"Maybe … we'll see. For now, we go back to Paris."

At 10:20 p.m., a non-stop flight from Berlin landed at Charles de Gaulle Airport in Paris. The passengers breezed past customs and only had to bear a short wait at the conveyor belt before collecting their luggage.

Half an hour after setting foot on French soil, Detective Marie Heirtmeyer was in a cab on her way to her hotel. It was her first time in Paris. She had always wanted to visit the French Capital, but now that she was here, she wished it had been under different circumstances. Once, Professor Karpov had told her about his time in France. They had even made plans to visit the city together at some point in the future but they had never gotten around to it.

Sitting in the backseat of the cab, her head resting against the window,

Marie was absent-mindedly gazing at the bustling city when her phone rang.

She dug into her bag and answered it with eager anticipation. "Jordi, did you find out something else?"

"Not yet. That's not why I'm calling."

"What is it?" Marie asked, feeling deflated.

"It's about your partner, Hans. He's been sniffing around here a lot. I think he knows there's more to your holiday than you let on, and he probably also suspects I'm helping you."

"You didn't tell him about the email, did you?"

"Of course not!"

"Then why would he suspect you?"

"I don't know, Marie. He's a detective. And he's your partner. Look, you don't want to tell me what's going on, fine, but you should talk to him at least. Maybe he can help with … whatever it is you're doing."

"No. I don't want to involve Hans in this. You can't tell him anything."

"What am I going to tell him? I don't know anything."

"I mean it, Jordi!"

"OK, OK. I'm just worried about you."

"I know. I'll be fine. Let me know when you have more on the email."

"I will."

"Thanks."

She hung up.

Marie was well aware of the fact that her impromptu holiday was not without its dangers. She knew her search for answers could earn her the attention of the people behind Professor Karpov's murder. And according to

216

the professor, those same people had also been responsible for the death of a French diplomat. If true, it was safe to assume they wouldn't be too bothered about getting rid of one police detective.

Marie understood the risks. But she had to go through with it. For her friend. For herself. However, she refused to see others embroiled in this perilous enterprise. Not even her trusted partner.

Chapter 24 – Different

The digital clock on the coffee table displayed 1:24 a.m. when Kincade entered Professor Fournier's house, followed by Arianne and Soran. He halted in surprise when he saw everyone gathered in the living room waiting for them.

Arianne was surprised too, especially when she spotted Lucielle sitting on the sofa between Ashrem and the professor. "What are you still doing up? It's well after 1 a.m. You were supposed to be in bed hours ago."

But the young girl wasn't listening. She jumped to her feet and ran past Arianne and Kincade, straight into Soran's arms.

He lifted her off the ground and hugged her tightly.

Then, he extended his arms and held her up in the air. "Wow! You've gotten so big."

"Yeah, I'm not a kid anymore," Lucielle replied in a serious voice.

"I know. You're eleven now."

She was about to correct him, but Rock pre-empted her. "Don't you start this again," he threatened, pointing a menacing finger.

"What's his problem?" Soran asked a little startled.

Perched on Soran's shoulder, like a koala hugging a tree branch, Lucielle shot a sneering look at the colossus. "He's a big bully. He's mean and nobody likes him."

"I don't care!" Rock threw back at her.

"Hello, son." Professor Fournier had gotten up as well and was smiling at Soran. "You look well," he added, his voice quivering with emotion.

Soran smiled back. "As do you, Professor."

Ashrem stood up in turn. "Hey, troublemaker."

"Didn't expect to see me again so soon, did you, Ash?"

"To be honest, no. But I'm glad I was wrong."

After the brief family reunion, the entire group assembled around the fireplace.

Kincade glanced at Da Costa, who was leaning against the wall at the far end of the room—in the exact same spot as last time. "Where's Doc?" he asked.

It was Rock who answered. "He's upstairs. It was his turn to keep watch." The giant then leaned towards Kincade and spoke in a low voice. "So, this is the guy?" he said, casting an eye over Soran.

"Yep."

"He doesn't look like much to me. Then again, I guess none of them do."

It occurred to Kincade he hadn't really had a good look at Soran up until now, given that his photograph wasn't among those handed over by Leicester.

The first time he had laid eyes on the young man was inside the music bar, which was dark and flashing with strobe lights. The streets outside the bar were dark as well, and Kincade had kept a watchful eye out for Jenkins and his men during their walk back to the car. And finally, Soran had been sitting alone in the backseat on the return drive. All of this added up to the fact it was Kincade's first clear look at their new companion.

Soran was a mixed race—Afro-Caucasian—man who, like his other siblings, appeared to be in his early twenties. Far from being physically impressive, he was roughly the same height as Arianne, with an average build. He did, however, have two notable features. The first was his salt-and-pepper hair, a mix of black and gray which was typically seen in middle-aged and

219

older men. The second was his different-colored eyes, one brown and the other green—a condition known as heterochromia iridum.

As Kincade and Rock stared at the young man, Sonar moved closer to them, looking perplexed.

"What's up?" Kincade asked.

Sonar hesitated. "The new guy … he seems familiar somehow."

On close inspection, Kincade had the same impression. "Now that you mention it …"

While he was still carrying Lucielle, Soran went into the dining area. He grabbed one of the chairs around the table and brought it back into the living room because they had run out of seating space.

Seeing the faces of the two siblings so close to each other, Kincade understood where this sense of familiarity came from. The silver-gray bits of Soran's hair and his green eye exactly matched Lucielle's hair and eye color. There was also a striking similitude to them beyond those two traits. With the exception of Damien, to whom Lucielle bore an uncanny likeness, Soran was the only one who shared this subtle, yet undeniable resemblance to the young girl.

Soran put his young sister down on the sofa and took a sweeping look around the room. "So, you guys are the mercs, eh? Arianne filled me in on the way here. I gotta say, I expected a scarier-looking bunch."

Rock and Sonar were taken off guard by the young man's demeanor. He was nothing like what they had expected. With Arianne and Ashrem being so composed and courteous, and with Mitsuki having been little more than a moving statue, the mercenaries had come to expect all the clones, with the exception of Lucielle, to behave in the same restrained manner. But Soran came off as much more outgoing and carefree.

"Hmm, I thought there'd more of you," Soran said, frowning.

"There is." Rock nodded to Doc, who was emerging from the hallway.

"Spot anything?" Kincade asked.

"No," Doc replied. "It doesn't look like you were followed." He sized up the newcomer as he joined the others in the living room and gave Kincade a questioning glance.

Kincade nodded.

All the while, Soran kept staring at the doorway, waiting. When he realized no one else was going to show up, he turned to the group. "Just one guy? Yeah, that'll make all the difference."

Sonar grinned. "Our motto is 'Quality over quantity.'"

"It's all right," said Lucielle, "I checked them out before recommending them to Andrew. They're really good at what they do."

But Soran was unimpressed. "Good? We're up against five of our siblings, Jenkins and his goons, and let's not forget about our buddies from *vice*. And you're telling me they're *good*. They'd better be freaking magicians."

That last comment got Rock fuming. He marched up to Soran and poked him in the chest. "Now hold on a minute! I thought *you* were some kind of big shot who was going to tip the scales in our favor."

The young man's eyebrows jumped. "Me? Where did you get that idea?"

"Then why the hell did we go through all that trouble to bring you here?" the giant shouted.

"How the hell should I know?" Soran shouted back.

"Please calm down," Ashrem pleaded, "both of you." He turned to the group and added, "Don't worry about Soran. He's quite capable when he wants to be."

The giant shrugged and walked away. "If you say so."

Kincade suddenly looked perplexed. "Hey, Soran, what did you mean when you said '*our buddies from vice*'?"

221

The young man gave Kincade a long incredulous stare. Then his eyes rolled over to Arianne. "You haven't told them?"

"We haven't gotten around to it yet," she answered, looking uneasy.

The mercenaries immediately flashed suspicious frowns.

"Told us what?" Kincade asked.

"There's another party involved in all of this," said Arianne. "An organization known by the acronym W-I-A-S, but it's pronounced *vice*."

"Adam was the one who first found out about them," Fournier continued. "He discovered the group had infiltrated the highest levels of military and government of some of the world's most powerful countries. He believed they had somehow learned of the Eritis project and were coming after him and his children. But he didn't know how far WIAS's influence had spread. He didn't know who to trust. Realizing he wouldn't be able to protect himself, or his children, from within the confines of the Arc facility, he destroyed all data pertaining to his research, save for one flash card, and escaped."

"Why destroy everything?" Kincade asked.

"Adam's research was very sensitive, and often very dangerous. He didn't want it to fall into WIAS's hands."

"I'm curious," said Doc. "What does the acronym stand for?"

"It stands for 'Weakness Is A Sin,'" Ashrem replied.

"Charming," Sonar joked.

"They're not nice people," Lucielle added.

"You don't say," Rock remarked in a sarcastic tone. "With a name like that, I assure you no one here thought they were a charity."

Kincade gave Arianne a sharp look. "How come this is the first we're hearing of this?"

Lucielle immediately pointed an accusatory finger at Rock. "It's his fault!"

"Me? How is it *my* fault?" the giant protested.

"When the professor tried to explain everything, you were the one who told him to skip to the end."

Sonar nudged his comrade and said with a teasing smile, "She's got a point there, big fella."

"I'm sorry," said Arianne. "We should have mentioned it sooner."

"The truth is," Ashrem said, "we felt it was better to wait a bit and give you time to process everything else. We didn't want to burden you further."

"Oh no," Rock said, acting as though he was touched by Ashrem's sentiment, "by all means, burden us. What else haven't you told us?"

"You know most of it already," said Fournier. "I'll tell you the rest now if you wish."

"Fine," said Kincade, "but just so we're clear. We've agreed to play ball up until now, but my primary concern is keeping my team out of prison. If that plan of yours doesn't work, we'll be right back where we started. So, after everything is said and done, I can't guarantee we won't grab all of you and deliver you to Leicester like we planned on doing from the start. And fair warning: we're the ones with the guns. Now that we know how dangerous you guys are, we won't take any chances."

Rock raised his hand. "Again, I vote we skip the storytelling and go straight to that."

"Come on," said Sonar, "we've been through this already."

A thought occurred to Soran, and a concerned frown formed on his face. "Hey, it's Nate, right? When you said '*all of you,*' you weren't including me, were you?"

"Technically you're not part of our original assignment, so we had no reason to go looking for you. But since you're here …"

Rock dropped a firm hand on Soran's shoulder and presented him with a large smile. "Hehehe!"

"You've gotta be kidding me," said Soran. And as he gazed uncomfortably around the room, he saw a strange gleam in the mercenaries' eyes. He understood right away that, as far as they were concerned, his fate would be bound to that of his siblings. He looked at Arianne sideways. "Thanks, sis! You could have straightened all this out *before* you brought me in, you know."

She gave a crooked smile. "Oops!"

"Let's not get ahead of ourselves," said Kincade. "We haven't decided not to help you either. Considering everything Leicester failed to mention before sending us on this mission, I'm beginning to wonder if he can be trusted to hold up his end of the deal." He cast a glance over his comrades. "I think we should keep all our options open for now."

The room filled with an awkward silence as the mercenaries conferred with their eyes.

When no objections came, Professor Fournier cleared his throat. "Ahem! Then I'll continue. Sometime after he escaped, Adam got in touch with us, Alek and me, and explained everything."

The old man paused as he delved inside his memory.

"Even though we were speaking over the phone, I remember sensing Adam was troubled. No doubt he believed it was only a matter of time before WIAS succeeded in planting an operative inside the Arc. He was worried about the children. He asked us to keep a close eye on them for as long as we could. But he warned the day might come when we too would need to disappear."

"Why?" Doc asked. "Did he think the same organization would target you as well?"

Fournier nodded. "With Adam on the run, Alek and I became the de facto specialists on the Eritis project."

"Which, sooner or later, would have put a big flashing bullseye on your backs," Kincade concluded.

"In a manner of speaking," said the old man. "In preparation for this eventuality, Adam helped us acquire safe houses and set up untraceable bank accounts with enough money for both of us."

"What about the clones?" Doc asked.

"After Adam's disappearance, security around them was tightened. Even Alek and myself were granted less and less access." Fournier glanced at Arianne and her siblings. "Eventually, we were forced to accept there was little more we could do for them. There was, however, a silver lining. The increased security made it harder for WIAS to get to them. It kept the children safe. Meanwhile, Alek and I had become more of a liability than anything else because of all we knew about Adam, about the children, and about the project in general. One day, Alek told me he thought someone had been following him. Fearing it could be WIAS making their move, we decided it was time to follow Adam's advice. We went into hiding, leaving everything and everyone behind."

"After all this time, you believe this organization is still trying to get their hands on the clones?" Doc asked.

"I'm certain of it," Fournier said without hesitation. "If just one of them decided to cooperate with such a group … I don't even want to think about what could happen. WIAS understands this. It's why they'll keep trying. The clones are too valuable."

"Well, some of us more than others," Soran remarked.

"What do you mean?" Kincade asked.

"Take those two, for example." Soran nodded to Arianne and Ashrem. "The military considered them failures because they made for the lousiest of soldiers. You see, Ash is wired to be about as violent as a baby panda. And Arianne … because she can feel what the people around her feel, it makes her

225

want to save the entire planet. In fact, her empathetic abilities are so abnormally high, the scientists at the Arc kept arguing over whether or not she should be considered psychic."

Rock suddenly backed away from Arianne with a worried look on his face. "Really? You're a psychic?"

"Of course not," she reassured him. "Soran, you know I don't like it when you say such things."

"Why not? It's true, isn't it? But you turned out OK if you ask me." He glanced at the mercenaries. "Johann and Kadyna, on the other hand … now those two you need to worry about, especially the blond psycho."

"He's right," Lucielle agreed emphatically. "Johann's mind is more twisted than a roller coaster."

"Wow, you guys really don't like him, do you?" said Sonar.

"Arianne doesn't want to believe it," said Ashrem, "but I'm afraid our brother is beyond help."

"That's precisely what's wrong with her, isn't it?" Soran grinned at his sister. "You probably think even tigers could be persuaded to go on a vegetarian diet, don't you?"

"They're right," said Arianne, ignoring her brother's taunt. "I haven't given up on Johann, in spite of all he's done. I am, however, very much aware of his psychological issues. We all have them, although the symptoms are more pronounced in some of us than in others."

Rock glanced at Lucielle. "I guess that explains a few things."

"What are you talking about?" the young girl protested. "I'm perfectly fine."

"You are?"

"We told you before," said Fournier. "Lucielle is different. And not just because she's younger."

226

"Different how?" Doc asked.

"Although she is every bit as brilliant, Lucielle doesn't have the same physical abilities as the others. She's not as strong as they are. But she also avoided the psychological side-effects that came with those enhancements."

"I see ..."

"There's one other thing," said the old man. "I told you Adam created the clones using a transgenic technique, yes?"

"What about it?" said Doc.

"Well, I should have said *most* of the clones. Damien was created using a reproductive cloning method. He's an actual replica of Adam." Fournier directed his gaze at Lucielle. "And so is she."

Once again, all eyes converged on the young analyst.

Then, all of a sudden, Kincade's expression changed and he turned to the professor. "Hold on, that doesn't make sense."

"Nate's right," said Doc. "She's a girl, isn't she?"

Lucielle scowled at him. "Of course I'm a girl! What are you implying?"

"I'm sorry," said Doc. "I was just trying to point out that, being a girl, I don't see how you can be a direct clone of Adam."

Fournier smiled. "It's a perfectly logical objection. In fact, it's the same one I made when I first saw her. But then I remembered AIS."

"AIS?" Doc and Kincade echoed in unison.

"Yes, Androgen Insensitivity Syndrome. Without getting too technical, it can be described as a condition in which people having XY chromosomes, are born with a female phenotype because their cells do not respond to male hormones, called androgens. In cases of complete AIS, the women will have all of the normal external female characteristics, but they won't possess a uterus. They cannot have children."

The professor marked a pause.

"Adam artificially recreated the condition. When I asked him why, he said it felt right for the baby to be a girl. In truth, I had never seen him look so happy." The old man stroked his chin. "Maybe he had anticipated Lucielle would be granted more freedom since she didn't pose the same threat as her siblings."

"Is that why you weren't kept locked up with the others?" Kincade asked the youngster.

"Yes," she said, "and because Andrew wanted me to work for him."

"What is it you do for him exactly?"

"Luce inherited something very special from our father," Arianne declared.

"Yes," said Fournier, sounding excited. "A unique talent indeed, a kind of high-level pattern recognition. It's the reason Leicester assigned her to head his team of analysts."

Rock raised his eyebrows at the old man. "High-level what now?"

Fournier scratched his head as he tried to come up with a simpler way to explain it. He shot a sweeping look at the mercenaries and then focused on their leader. "You've known your friends for a long time, correct?"

"Yeah," Kincade replied, not sure what the professor was getting at.

"Given everything you know about them, could you anticipate how they will react, or even what they might say, in certain situations?"

"Sure," Kincade replied.

"Good!" said Fournier. "It's basically what Lucielle does. Only, she can do this with people she's never met, provided she has enough data to work with."

The professor paused to check the faces around him and saw he had some ways to go before all the dots connected inside the mercenaries' heads.

He decided to try a different approach. "What benefits come from being able to identify patterns?" he asked. But it was a rhetorical question, one that he answered right away. "It allows us to extract meaning from seemingly random information. And in some cases, to make predictions, correct?" Another rhetorical question. "That, in a nutshell, is Lucielle's gift. She is able to extrapolate patterns from behaviors or events, and to make predictions based on those extrapolations."

Kincade was beginning to understand. "Are you telling us she can predict what will happen?"

"Yes, to a certain extent."

Just as he had done with Arianne earlier, Rock abruptly pulled away from Lucielle. "Wow, you can see the future?"

She sighed. "Oh, don't be ridiculous. I only guess the outcomes with the highest degree of probability based on certain key indications and interrelated factors."

The giant froze. "I have no idea what you just said."

"Think of it as a form of deduction," Fournier said, "like a detective. Only, instead of bloodstains and fingerprints, her clues are things like a company's business acquisition, a government's foreign policy decision, or even a speech from a prominent individual. Imagine knowing before everyone else what influential people, major companies, or governments will do in the near future."

"This kind of insight would prove an enormous advantage," Doc concluded.

Fournier raised his index finger. "Exactly! You can see how someone like Leicester would benefit from such an advantage, in both his business and political dealings."

Rock moved close to Lucielle and ruffled her hair with his massive hand. "Damn, kid! You're not just an annoying brat after all, huh?"

The spontaneity of the giant's action had taken everyone by surprise. No one had reacted in time to stop him. And now, they all expected Lucielle to literally blow a fuse.

Kincade was already moving to pull his companion away from the young girl, while Arianne poised herself to contain the forthcoming explosion of anger from her sister.

But to everyone's utter stupefaction, Lucielle simply gave an annoyed grunt as she slapped the giant's hand away. There was no shouting, no insults, and no indignation. Only a moderate display of discontent.

Kincade watched in stunned silence.

He thought Lucielle's lack of reaction was as shocking as anything he had seen or heard in the past couple of days. And from the dumbfounded looks on Arianne's and Ashrem's faces, it was clear he wasn't the only who felt that way.

Eager to move on in case the young girl decided to throw a fit after all, Kincade asked Arianne, "Can you do it too? Predict things?"

She shook her head. "No. Only Luce can … and Damien."

"Damien?"

Arianne nodded. "I'm afraid so."

"He's actually better at it than I am," Lucielle declared.

Kincade and Doc exchanged a sharp look. Even though they didn't fully comprehend this so-called predictive ability, they could hear the concern in Arianne's voice.

Sensing their worry, Arianne offered an argument to alleviate it. "It's not a magic trick," she said. "To do it requires information. In other words, Damien would still need to know you, or at least to know things about you, in order to predict your actions. But he doesn't, which is why I believe, with your help, we *can* stop him."

Kincade still looked uncertain. "There are plenty of people he doesn't know. Why ask us?"

"We already told you," said Lucielle. "After searching through Andrew's databases, I determined you were the most qualified. And you may be mercenaries, but deep down, I believe you're not bad people."

"We're not exactly good guys either," said Kincade.

"I know," the young analyst replied. "That's fine."

Kincade smiled. Having a conversation with Lucielle was often a strange experience. One minute you were talking to a capricious kid, and the next, it was like you were talking to a wise old woman. There were times when it was hard to tell which one you were dealing with at a given moment. And the silver-gray hair didn't exactly help either.

"Why didn't Leicester enlist Damien to work as an analyst too?" Doc asked.

"Too risky!" said Fournier. "He couldn't take the chance."

"They could have simply beefed up security around him," Sonar suggested.

Arianne stepped towards the center of the room. Her expression was grave, almost solemn. "Listen to me very carefully. Whatever you may think about the rest of us, do not underestimate Damien."

"She's right." Ashrem stood up and cast a sweeping look around to make sure every mercenary was paying attention, including Da Costa. "Darius is quite strong, and Johann is a vicious killer. But Damien is undoubtedly the most dangerous among us."

Chapter 25 – Uninvited Guest

The padded door opened with a squeak, interrupting the vibrant exchange of banter and laughter. Startled, the two men standing guard at the entrance quickly drew their firearms out of their jacket holsters.

Everyone else looked on and froze.

A sharply dressed man emerged from the doorway and walked past the two sentries. Unfazed by the gun barrels locked in on him, he moved at a leisurely pace, his footsteps echoing off the floor.

When he was well inside the room, the stranger stopped and gave a deliberate look around.

There were no windows, the only light came from three bowl-shaped lamps hanging from the ceiling. And the air was stale, and heavy with the scent of strong liquor. He counted eight men—including the two behind him—standing at the four corners of the room. Seven more were seated at an elongated oval table, engaged in a game of no-limit Texas Hold'em poker— six players and a dealer.

The man sitting at the far end of the table calmly put down his glass next to the imposing stack of chips piled up in front of him. "Who are you? How did you get past my men outside?"

"My name is Damien Cross," the stranger replied.

"Is that supposed to mean something to me?"

"No, you don't know me. But I know you."

"Is that so?"

"You're Jonas Fergusson, head of one of the largest criminal organizations operating on this side of the Atlantic."

Fergusson leaned back in his chair. "You've been misinformed. I'm a reputable businessman. What are you anyway, a cop?"

"No."

Fergusson frowned. The trespasser's aloof demeanor was starting to annoy him. "I don't know who you are, but this is a private game, and you, weren't invited." He motioned to the man standing to his left. "Ruben, escort the stranger out. And bring Boris back with you. I want to know why he's letting people walk in here like it's a casino."

Fergusson's dismissive tone dispelled much of the tension in the room. Put at ease by their boss' confident attitude, the guards relaxed a little. Damien watched impassively as two of them circled the table and approached him from both sides. The two by the door also closed in to within arm's reach.

The one called Ruben walked up to Damien and tugged him by the sleeve. "Come on, friend, let's go."

Damien didn't budge. He flashed an intense glare and clamped his right hand around Ruben's throat. Even sitting a good twenty feet away, Fergusson heard a faint croak, followed by the chilling crack of bones breaking as Damien tightened his grip.

While still holding on to his victim's neck, Damien's left hand shot towards the other man standing in front of him. He palmed the side of the bodyguard's face and crushed his head against the wooden frame of the table.

The combined actions had taken little more than a second. Which was more or less the amount of time Fergusson and the others needed to shake their surprise.

"Shoot him!" Fergusson yelled.

But Damien was quick to act. Without turning around, he reached back and grabbed the two sentries by their wrists.

Meanwhile, the rest of Fergusson's henchmen wasted no time executing their boss's order. All four took aim and discharged their weapons at their

233

target. But they ended up hitting their two colleagues instead.

Damien had swung his arms in front of him while still clinging on to the sentries. Like fishes on a hook helplessly pulled out of the water, the pair had been flapped through the air and had crashed into each other just in time to stop the hail of bullets converging on the intruder.

Now sheltered behind his gory human shield, Damien snatched the guns from the dangling arms of the corpses leaning against him and waited.

Fergusson thumped his fist on the table. "What are you all doing? I said shoot him!"

Unable to see the intruder behind the two standing bodies, Fergusson's men began circling the table in order to get him back into their line of sight.

But once the guards were exactly where he wanted them, Damien sprang out like a jack-in-the-box. Pushing with his forearms in a sudden outward motion, he propelled the two bodies through the air.

His human projectiles took out the two men closest to him on either side of the table by knocking them over like bowling pins.

In the same continuous motion, Damien's arms extended until his guns were aimed at the last two guards still standing.

A quick-fire exchange ensued. But in a contest of quickness and accuracy, the guards never stood a chance.

Fergusson gaped in stupefaction as his last two men collapsed on the floor. When his gaze slowly returned to the silver-haired stranger, he felt his blood run cold as he stared at the green pupils locked onto him. *Who is this man?*

His eyes still on Fergusson, Damien mercilessly finished off the two men who were just recovering from getting knocked down by the flying bodies of their colleagues.

During that time, the men seated around the table had remained glued to their chairs as they had watched the incredible scene unfold. All they could do was wait and see what the deadly visitor would do next.

To their amazement, Damien pulled out a chair and sat at the end of the oval table, opposite Fergusson. Then, even more surprising, he placed his two guns in front of him and folded his arms over his chest.

That was when the dealer chose to make his move. He began sliding his hand under the table in a barely perceptible motion.

Having caught sight of the sneaky maneuver from the corner of his eye, Fergusson attempted to draw the stranger's attention. "What now?" he asked.

The only response from Damien was a long, menacing stare directed at the dealer.

Realizing the danger, the dealer raised one hand in the air as a sign of surrender, and with the other, he slowly retrieved a shotgun from under the table and tossed it away.

Fergusson's jaw tightened as he tried to contain his frustration at the aborted attempt. But he found solace in knowing there was still a way out of the perilous situation. He shot a quick glance at the door. Surely his men outside would have heard the gunshots and would be rushing in at any moment. A few seconds passed. *What the hell are they doing?*

"No one's coming," said Damien.

Fergusson's heart skipped a beat. But once again, he managed to contain his emotions and limit his reaction to a slight twitch of his left eye.

Damien looked around at the anxious faces around him and said, "I have a proposition."

"I'm not interested in your propositions," Fergusson retorted defiantly.

"I wasn't talking to you," said Damien. He turned to the man sitting to Fergusson's right. "You're Craig Thompson. You're technically number two in your organization, but in fact, you've been overseeing most of its illegal activities for the past year and a half, which makes you the de facto number one. Recently, you've been trying to find a way to … formalize this position

235

and take over as leader."

Thompson straightened up in his chair and shot a nervous glance at his boss. "I have no idea what he's talking about."

Fergusson gave his associate a long, distrustful look.

Damien pulled a USB drive out of his jacket pocket and slid it over to Thompson. "This contains recordings of phone conversations between you and two of the people sitting here tonight. Those recordings prove you've been plotting to get rid of 'the old man,' as you call him. I also have proof of other little side schemes you've set up in preparation for your coup, so let's dispense with the silly games. Here is my proposition: I get rid of Fergusson for you, right here, right now. In exchange, I get to use the full resources of your organization to help me pull three jobs, from which we'll split the profits fifty-fifty. I would have made this offer to Fergusson himself, but he would have agreed, only to betray me at the first opportunity."

"This is absurd!" Fergusson shouted. "Don't listen to him, Craig. Who is this guy anyway?"

Thompson looked back at his boss with a strange expression but said nothing.

Sensing his right-hand man's hesitation, Fergusson recoiled in his seat. "Craig … you can't seriously be thinking about this …"

"Time's up, Thompson!" Damien stood up and grabbed the guns. "If you turn down my offer, I will walk out of here right now and you'll never hear from me again. Incidentally, it would leave you, and your co-conspirators, to explain those troublesome phone conversations to your boss. Or, *you* can be the new boss. You were waiting for the right moment. Well, that moment has arrived. Decide."

Thompson peered into the soulless eyes staring down at him, trying to get a sense of what was going on behind them.

It was a wasted exercise.

All he saw was indifference. He truly believed the stranger was prepared to peacefully walk away from a room filled with witnesses to the murders he had just committed.

"Let him leave," said Fergusson. "I know he's lying about this conspiracy nonsense." He tried his best to keep his poker face, but cracks were starting to show. His fretful tone and heavy perspiration belied his growing distress.

All eyes were now turned to Thompson. Two men in particular, one sitting next to him and the other on the opposite side of the table, stared at him with anxious anticipation.

"I'll take your silence as a no," said Damien. He turned around and headed for the exit.

Relieved to see the back of the cold-blooded killer, Fergusson sank into his chair and exhaled.

But Fergusson's reprieve would be short-lived.

As Damien neared the door, Thompson called out tentatively, "All right, it's a deal!"

He had made his choice.

Damien's reaction was swift and definitive. He fired two bullets into Fergusson's chest before the crime boss had time to utter a single word.

Fergusson fell back off his chair, dead.

"Congratulations, Thompson! You're in charge," Damien declared. "Now, once you've had a chance to look back on tonight's events, you'll be tempted to renege on our agreement. You'll consider setting up a meeting under some false pretense to try to eliminate me. I'll give you two reasons why you should try very hard to resist that temptation. One, with Fergusson out of the picture, your rivals will smell blood. They'll no doubt take advantage of the ensuing period of … adjustment to attempt a power grab on your territory. They might even come after you directly. It's in your best interest to help me with the three jobs I mentioned. If everything goes according to plan, your organization will receive a big infusion of cash. This will help you buy some much-needed endorsements to secure your new position of leader. And it will send a message to the other groups. They'll see that losing Fergusson in no way diminished your operational capabilities. It will make them think twice before going to war against you."

Damien paused for a moment.

"Two, coming after me would be a strategic mistake, a fatal one. I have associates of my own. Even if you were to somehow succeed in getting rid of me, they would wipe you out … indiscriminately." For the first time, a semblance of a smile crossed Damien's lips as he added, "Besides, it should be clear to you by now I'm not that easy to kill."

With those words of advice, the mysterious stranger left.

In his line of business, Thompson dealt with killers on a regular basis. He even had a few working for him. But something about the silver-haired man made him nervous. He couldn't quite put his finger on it, but something about him was … off. Not to mention the manner in which he had disposed of those eight seasoned bodyguards.

The room had fallen completely silent. A few shady glances bounced across the table, but no one dared speak first.

Thompson seized the opportunity to address the group and pre-empt any potential voices of dissent. He stood up, placed his hands on the table, and leaned forward. "I know some of you will have a problem with what just happened. I didn't plan for it to go down this way, but I'm sure we can all agree Fergusson's time was coming to an end. What's done is done. I'm the leader now … unless someone here intends to challenge me."

Thompson eyeballed his associates one by one, and each responded with an assenting nod—some more convincing than others, but it was sufficient for now. And not one of them protested when Thompson dismissed the group without further deliberation. They were all eager to leave this room where the body of their former boss was lying on the floor, still warm, along with the bodies of those in charge of their security.

Only Thompson and his most trusted ally remained.

"This guy just did us a big favor, Craig. But I think he's going to be a problem. We need to take care of him."

"Not yet," said Thompson.

"Are you sure?"

"Don't worry, Hendrik, we'll deal with the stranger in due time. He's obviously not a cop. And after what he just did, it's safe to say he's someone who should be taken seriously. He's also right about us needing to send a message to the other groups. And the extra cash won't hurt either. Let's play along for now. If those jobs are everything he says they are, we'd be fools to pass them up. We'll take care of him after that."

Marie Heirtmeyer woke with a start. She hadn't slept much since her friend's murder, even though she was both physically and emotionally drained. She had begun to doze off on her hotel bed when she heard a knock. She sat up abruptly and stared at the door, her mind still a little blurry as she tried to gather her thoughts.

Who could it be? No one knew she was there. Not even Jordi. And this was not the kind of establishment that offered room service. Maybe someone had knocked on the wrong door. Had she even really heard a knock?

Then another knock came, this one more insistent.

Marie slipped off the bed, grabbed the gun from her purse, and tiptoed to the door.

She stood still and listened.

After a moment, a voice called out from the other side. "Marie! Are you in there? It's me, open up!"

Marie exhaled heavily. She had been holding her breath the entire time without realizing it. She removed the chain lock and opened the door. "What are you doing here?" she said, the tone of her voice clearly expressing her discontent.

"Hello, partner!" Hans greeted her with a large smile as he nonchalantly invited himself in.

Marie shot a quick glance down the hallway and then locked the door behind her uninvited guest.

"Expecting someone else?" he asked, nodding at her weapon.

She tucked the gun into the back of her jeans. "How did you find me?"

He dropped his bag on the floor and began inspecting the room. "What can I say? I'm a brilliant detective."

"I'm serious, Hans. How did you track me here? I checked in under an alias."

"Give me some credit, will you?" he replied, now checking the bathroom.

She stomped her foot. "Stop fooling around!"

"The guy we busted six months ago on identity theft, the one we cut loose in exchange for testifying against those drug dealers. He owed us. Well, technically he owed you, since you're the one who got him the deal." Hans was now casually sifting through the closet drawer.

"Do you mind?" She walked over to him and slammed the drawer so hard Hans barely had time to rescue his fingers.

"Easy now," he said, putting his hands up in the air. "Anyway, I paid our friend a visit and asked him if he'd made a fake ID for you recently."

Marie rolled her eyes. "I should have known better."

"I know, right? You can't even trust an honest thief these days."

"And Jordi? He's the one who told you I came to Paris, isn't he?"

Hans smiled. "I asked nicely."

"I can't believe he ratted me out."

"He's worried about you, Marie. We both are."

"Why did you come here?" she asked.

"Funny, I was going to ask you the same question."

She looked away. "I can't tell you."

"Sure you can."

"Please, Hans. Go back to Berlin. This is my problem."

"What are you talking about? I'm your partner."

"I'm not here on official police business."

"I'm your partner," he repeated.

She sighed and sat on the bed.

He sat down next to her and nudged her gently. "Come on, you know I'll just stay and follow you around anyway. You might as well tell me. Does it have something to do with your friend, Schmidt?"

She turned to him with a grave expression. "Yes, and it could be dangerous."

"All the more reason for me to stay. You'll need someone to watch your back."

She kept her eyes on him a while, and then said, "OK, but only if you promise to follow my lead on this one."

He gave a military salute. "Yes, ma'am, you're in charge. Now tell me, what's going on?"

Once again Patrick Jenkins found himself in the unenviable position of having to explain yet another failed operation. He got the call minutes after touching down at Orly Airport, in the northern Paris region. He had been summoned to Leicester's office without delay.

Half an hour later, he was standing in the conference room in front of his superiors. The three listened attentively as Jenkins recounted the events that had taken place in Berlin a few hours earlier. As always, Jenkins' delivery was succinct and to the point. He gave a brief summary of the facts, leaving others free to draw their own conclusions.

"So, in your opinion, Damien has the recording?" Leicester asked.

"I have no doubt about it."

"How were they able to activate all those alarm systems simultaneously?"

"My guess would be Darius."

Nathalie Renard leaned forward and placed her elbows on the table as she stretched her snake-like neck. "Andrew didn't ask who had done it. He asked *how* it was done."

Jenkins shrugged. "If it was that easy to figure out how they're able to do the things they do, you wouldn't need them in the first place."

"I don't think I like your tone, Mr. Jenkins," she hissed.

"Come now, Nathalie, let's not bicker over such small matters," said Leicester. "We have far more serious problems. Things are progressing in a very unfavorable direction. This needs to be rectified. By the way, Mr. Jenkins, may I ask why you've returned so soon?"

"I was wondering the same thing," said Schaffer. The German was buried in his seat, hands stuck inside his coat pockets, with his head slightly tilted down. He looked like he was about to take a nap.

"Indeed," Renard agreed. "Wouldn't yours and Mr. Carson's time be better spent in Berlin, tracking Damien's group?"

"It wouldn't," Jenkins replied.

Leicester cocked his head to the side. "I beg your pardon?"

"Conventional methods are useless against those fugitives. Without the analyst to help us, we will only end up chasing shadows."

"So what do you propose?" Leicester asked.

"We might not be able to anticipate their next move, but we know what they're after."

"Yes, but we have no idea where it is," Renard sharply pointed out.

"It doesn't matter. They've only just escaped, which means we still know more than they do. I believe we can use this to our advantage."

Karl Schaffer's face came to life. "Hmm … you want to set a trap?"

"Correct. Our best chance is to confront them on our terms, not theirs."

Leicester studied Jenkins. "It looks as though you already have some idea on how to accomplish this."

"I do. I believe I've found the right bait, if not for Damien, then perhaps for the others."

"Maybe you could try being more specific," said Renard.

"There are still certain details to work out. I ask for some discretion in the matter."

Leicester thought for a moment. "Very well, we'll leave it to you."

Jenkins lingered a bit to see if he would receive further instructions. When he saw none was forthcoming, he started on his way out. But halfway to the door, he stopped and turned around. "One more thing."

"Yes?" said Leicester.

"If I come across the mercenaries, I intend to treat them as hostiles."

Schaeffer placed his left hand on the table and leaned forward. "They are of little consequence. If they've betrayed us, you may deal with them as you see fit."

"But Lucielle is not to be harmed in any way," Leicester promptly added. "Is that understood?"

"Yes, sir."

"Make sure you keep us informed of your progress," said Renard.

Jenkins' eyes narrowed. "Don't worry, Mrs. Renard. You'll be the first to know." He walked out and closed the door.

After Jenkins had gone, Nathalie Renard was left with a strange feeling of uneasiness. Something about the tone of Jenkins' last statement troubled her. She glanced in Leicester's direction and caught him staring back at her.

"I know Mr. Jenkins can sometimes give off a sort of … strange vibe," said the Briton, "but try not to read too much into it."

"I find your man quite insubordinate, Andrew. I think you indulge him too much."

"What would you have us do?" Schaffer said with a rare, albeit sarcastic, chuckle. "Replace him?"

Renard glared at the German. "I'm aware of Mr. Jenkins' unique talents. I just hope Andrew can keep him under control."

"My dear," said Leicester, "I don't believe it's possible to *control* Mr. Jenkins. But don't worry. He has his own motivations for wanting to see this mission through."

Chapter 26 – Coffee or Tea

"What are you drinking?"

It was almost 9:00 a.m. when Kincade walked into the kitchen and found Arianne deep in thought, staring blankly at a cup she was holding with both hands.

"Sorry, what did you say?"

"I asked what you were drinking."

"Tea. Would you like some?"

"No, thanks, I'm more of a coffee person."

"Up there." She pointed to one of the cupboards next to the large fridge.

Kincade grabbed the coffee packets and started brewing a cup. "Were you able to get some sleep?"

"Enough."

"Let me guess, you guys only need a couple hours of sleep per week," he teased.

"Per month," she said, playing along.

They held each other's gazes and tried to keep a straight face for as long as they could before finally bursting into laughter.

"You surprise me," she said.

"How so?"

"You seem genuinely not to mind that we're not ... normal."

"Normal, huh? Not sure what that means, really. I've seen plenty of so-called *normal* people do some pretty awful things. As far as I'm concerned, it doesn't matter who or what you are. It only matters what you do."

"Then I'd like to thank you once again for what *you* are doing, for choosing to help us."

"Don't mention it. Like I told you last night, the guys and I discussed it, and we all agreed. Besides, with your plan, we'll be able to leverage a deal out of Leicester."

"Yes, but even if everything goes as planned, it'll still be very dangerous."

Kincade shrugged. "Most of our jobs tend to land us in unpleasant situations anyway."

"This will be different," she insisted, her eyes fixed on him.

Kincade had seen that look before, back when he was in the military. Two years prior to his discharge, a General Hayward had recruited him into a black ops unit. Sometimes targets and objectives were wrapped up in so much political and diplomatic red tape that the military couldn't openly intervene.

That was when they would send in his unit. Their missions could be anything from supporting popular uprisings against oppressive regimes to fighting against government-sanctioned terrorist groups. It was all very secretive and, most of all, very dangerous. In fact, some missions were so perilous, the general would insist on asking for volunteers. Those were not, after all, officially approved operations.

Twice, Kincade had gone on such hazardous missions. He remembered the look in his commanding officer's eyes, both times, as he asked: "Are you sure, soldier?" Both times it had sounded more like a warning than a question. The general was making sure Kincade understood he could be going on a one-way trip.

And now, years later, standing in this kitchen, staring at the young woman across the counter, Kincade recognized that same look in her eyes. It was like Arianne was saying: *'It's not too late to change your mind. It's O.K. to back out.'* As though she was afraid for him, without any regard as to what it meant for her.

If Kincade and his men weren't going to help her, they would have no other choice but to fall back to the deal they had made with Leicester: recapture the fugitives in exchange for immunity from prosecution by the US military. In short, she would have a new enemy, instead of a new ally.

"You surprise me too," said Kincade.

Before she could ask what he meant, the kitchen door slammed open.

Soran strode in, followed by Sonar, Rock, and Lucielle. The young girl sat on the giant's shoulders, so he had to bend down as he passed through the doorway.

The odd quartet barged into the kitchen, shouting and arguing. Kincade tried to get a sense of what they were saying, but he could only fish out a few isolated words in the middle of the brouhaha. He was surprised to see the four them seemingly getting along so well, when on the previous night, they had all seemed to be on the verge of jumping at one another's throats.

But Kincade's surprise was mild in comparison to Arianne's shock. The young woman looked as though a bolt of lightning had dropped on her head as she stared at Lucielle, perched on Rock's shoulders.

"Quiet down!" Kincade bellowed, annoyed by the loud voices.

All four stopped and turned to him.

"What's going on?" he asked them.

"We're having a disagreement," Lucielle replied.

"Yeah," said the giant. "You remember that stupid game on the computer?"

Soran shoved him. "Hey! It wasn't stupid!"

"What about it?" Kincade asked in a jaded tone.

"The question with the boxes," said Rock. "I told you I knew it. We were supposed to switch." He poked Soran on the arm. "Which means you were wrong."

Lucielle played the drums on the mercenary's shaved head with her tiny hands. "No, he wasn't."

"Hey, cut it out!" Rock told her.

Sonar also put in his two cents. Before long the four of them were arguing unintelligibly again.

"Enough!" Kincade barked. He sighed and turned to Arianne. "Can you help me out here?"

"Uh … yes, of course," she replied, finally breaking free from her astonishment. "You're right," she told Rock.

The giant immediately boasted to Soran. "Aha! Did you hear what she said?"

Soran held up a hand and closed his eyes. "Wait for it."

"Well, I meant normally you would be right," Arianne corrected, "except it was a trick question."

"Ahem!" Soran placed his hands on his hips, stuck his chest out, and raised his chin. He looked like someone who was posing for a portrait, and who was extremely pleased with himself for doing so.

"I remember you saying something similar earlier," Kincade remarked. "Care to explain?"

"It was the woman in red," Arianne replied. "When she was asked to pick one of the two remaining boxes, she said she didn't know which one contained the riddles."

Rock squinted at her. "And?"

"That's why we didn't need to change our answer," Arianne stated.

248

"I don't see how it makes any difference," the giant challenged.

"Allow me to explain," said Soran.

He walked around the counter over to Arianne's side and grabbed three cups from a cupboard. He then placed the cups upside down on the counter and pointed to each one in turn, going from left to right. "Let's call them A, B and C. Now, imagine there's a prize under one of these cups. I don't know … movie tickets or something." He looked at Kincade. "Choose a cup."

"All right, the middle one, B."

Soran pushed cup B forward a few inches. "My turn." He flipped over cup A. "Nothing, the prize isn't here. Now, given the option, should you stick with your original choice, or should you switch to cup C?"

"Like Rock said, I should switch, shouldn't I?"

"Actually, it depends," the young man replied.

"On what?"

"On whether or not I know which cup holds the prize."

Now, Kincade too looked doubtful. "Why would it matter?"

Soran paused a moment. "OK, let's start from the beginning. I'll try to keep it simple."

Did I just get insulted? Kincade thought to himself.

"First, we need to agree on something," Soran continued.

"What's that?" Rock asked.

"Probabilities."

"This isn't going to turn into a math lesson, is it?" Rock complained.

"No, no, it'll be quick. So, a probability is the chance of something happening, the likelihood an event will occur, with the sum of all possible outcomes adding up to 100%, or 1."

"Go on," said Kincade.

"I only point this out so we can agree that we won't consider 0% and a 100% to be probabilities. For our purposes, we'll say that if something has a likelihood of 0, or 0%, then it's impossible. And if the likelihood is 1, or a 100%, then it's a certainty."

"OK, I'm with you so far," said Kincade.

"Good. Let's illustrate this point with two cups this time." Soran took away cup C, leaving only cups A and B on the table. "Same as before, there's a prize under one of those. Choose one."

"A," said Kincade.

The young man placed his hand on cup A without turning it over. "What are the chances that you picked the correct cup?"

"It's 50/50," Kincade replied.

"Correct. One way to look at it is to say that each cup carries a 50% chance of containing the prize. And also, there's a 50% chance that you'll choose the correct cup. I know it sounds like I just said the same thing twice, but I didn't. This is an important distinction. You'll see why in a second."

Kincade, Rock, and Sonar followed attentively.

"Let's start over," said Soran. "I want you to choose a cup once again, but before you do, I want you to know the prize is under cup B."

Kincade raised his eyebrows in surprise.

"What are the chances you'll make the correct choice this time?" Soran asked.

"Well, if I know where it is … it's a 100%."

"Exactly! At this point you're certain. It's no longer a matter of probabilities. In absolute terms, as long as we place the prize under one of the cups at random, each cup will always have a 50% chance of containing it. But based on the information you have, your chances of choosing the correct cup can vary. This is the distinction I was making. From your perspective, it's as if the 50% chance from one cup moved over to the other. Where it was 50/50 before, it's now 0 and 100. To you, cup A has a 0% chance of being correct, and for cup B it's a 100%."

Soran paused to give the three men time to absorb the point he was trying to make.

"Can I go on?" he eventually asked.

"Sure," said Kincade.

"All right, let's return to our original problem." Soran placed the third cup back on the table. "Just like before, in the absolute, each cup has 33% chance of containing the prize. It doesn't matter which one you choose initially, 1 time out of 3 you will have picked the winner from the start. But 2 times out of 3, you will have missed. I'll say again: after your first choice, you will have a 33% chance of being right and a 66% chance of being wrong. Then it will be my turn. And here we have two cases. One, I know where the prize is, meaning I have 0% chance of flipping over the winning cup by accident. My choice is not random, it's a certainty. If the answer is B, then I'll pick C. And if it's C, then I'll pick B. Whichever one I choose will have 0% chance of being correct. All possibilities will have moved over to the remaining cup. In short, it means if I select B, then C will have the remaining 66% chances of being the winner, and vice versa. That's why you should switch. Your initial choice has a 1 in 3 chances of being correct, whereas if you switch now, you have 2 in 3 chances of hitting the jackpot."

"So, I was right!" Rock exclaimed.

"Hold on," said Soran. "I told you there were two cases. The second is: I don't know where the prize is located either. In that case, my choice is just as random as yours. You still had a 1 in 3 chances of winning with your first pick. Only this time, I too have a 1 in 3 chances of flipping over the correct cup by accident. By turning over one of the cups, I use up 1/3 of the total chances. If my choice is wrong then the last cup will have the remaining 1 in

3 chances. To summarize, in that scenario, if you pick cup A, you have a 33% chance of being right. When I choose cup B, I also have a 33% chance of picking the winner. Therefore, cup C only has a 33% chance, just like the other two, which means there's no reason for you to switch, because all three cups are equally likely to win."

Kincade rubbed his chin. "I see … the woman in red had no idea which box contained the riddles. She made a random choice."

"Yep," Soran said, smiling.

"What if she'd picked the winning box?" Rock argued.

"Don't be silly," Lucielle told him. "She was never going to pick the winning one. It was a program. It was all virtual. The actual test was in the choice itself."

"It's very interesting and all, but erm … it seems kinda pointless," Kincade concluded. "Why have us go through those hoops in the first place?"

Soran's smile widened. "I like to think of it as a basic security check. Plus, it was fun, wasn't it?"

Lucielle rolled her eyes. "Like I said, he's a Muppet."

"Yep!" Rock and Sonar echoed in unison.

Soran frowned at the trio. "Hey! I'll have you guys know it took quite a bit of time and effort to create the website and program the game."

"That's precisely what makes you an idiot," Rock stressed.

Soran hit him on the arm. "You're the idiot!"

"Whatever," said the giant as he eyed Arianne's and Kincade's cups.

"Would you like some coffee or tea?" she asked.

"Yeah, I think I'll have some coffee." With Lucielle still up on his shoulders, Rock circled around the counter and poured himself a cup.

"I'll have some," said Sonar.

"Me too," said Lucielle, stretching her arms downwards.

Rock poured coffee into a second cup.

But as he was about to hand it up to the young girl, Arianne jumped on him like a cat. "What are you doing?" she said, the tone of her voice rising.

The giant gave a puzzled look. "What do you mean? I'm not doing anything."

"You can't give her coffee." Arianne gazed up at her sister. "And you, Luce, you know full well you're not allowed to drink this. You can have some hot cocoa if you want."

The girl pouted. "You're always treating me like a child."

"No coffee for you," Arianne reaffirmed in a stern tone.

Soran gave Rock an exaggerated look of disappointment. "I can't believe you were actually going to give her coffee. And to think you're calling other people idiots."

"Seriously," the redhead added, piling on the criticism.

"Shut up! Both of you," the giant fired back.

That got the four of them shouting and gesticulating again, each trying to talk over the others.

After exchanging a quick glance, Kincade and Arianne slowly pulled away from the tiresome bunch and made a stealthy exit from the kitchen. They continued past the dining room and stepped out onto the patio.

It was Kincade's first time admiring the landscape from the back of the house. Up until now, he hadn't really had a chance to contemplate the green fields stretching all the way to the glittering sea. He let his gaze travel across the horizon and then closed his eyes to breathe in the pure air.

Arianne imitated him. "It's nice, isn't it?"

253

"I guess."

"You should see the beach too. It's quite beautiful."

"Yeah? Maybe I will." Kincade then took in another deep breath and said, "By the way, what happened to you back there? For a minute you looked like you were about to faint."

"Did I?" She made an awkward face. "It was nothing, really."

"Good, then you can tell me."

"It's just … when I saw Luce … I still can't believe she let someone other than one of us carry her around like that. In fact, I've never seen her be this comfortable with an outsider, especially one she barely knows. It was … unexpected, to say the least."

"I admit I was surprised too," said Kincade. "After all the time Rock spent complaining last night. Look at him now."

"I know he didn't really mean it," said Arianne. "Those things he said about handing us over to Leicester. He was just frustrated."

"Yeah, he's actually a pretty good guy deep down," said Kincade, "though it doesn't always show."

"No, I can tell."

"Really?" Kincade hesitated. "Is it because of … you know, what Soran said about your intuition?"

She shook her head. "It's true I can usually sense what other people are feeling, but I didn't have to try in this case. It's easy to see your friend's true nature. Not just for me. The others can see it as well."

"Can they? Maybe that's why Lucielle is so cozy with him."

"It's not the only reason."

"No? Why else, then?"

Arianne gazed absently at the horizon. "It's because he sees her as a child. Lucielle's never really been treated like one. Not by the scientists at the Arc, and not by Leicester and his people. They all see her as an oddity or a resource, something to be studied or exploited. But your friend, Rock, is different. When he looks at her, all he sees is a young girl."

"I thought she didn't like being treated like a kid," Kincade pointed out.

"She doesn't. In fact, she hates it." Arianne paused and stared at her teacup, her eyes shimmering with a profound melancholy. "But at the same time, she wishes she were just a normal child, with friends her age and nobody expecting anything from her." She looked up at Kincade. "I'm really glad she got to meet someone on the outside who sees her the same way we do. I don't know how, but it seems Rock is able to bring out the part of her who just wants to be an eleven-year-old girl."

"The answer's easy," said Kincade. "Intellectually, he's not much older himself."

Arianne's face brightened up. "You like to tease him, don't you?"

"Believe me," he sighed, "I wish I was kidding."

"I guess it's tough being the one in charge," she teased.

"You have no idea," Kincade replied, putting on a serious face.

They laughed again.

Arianne had an infectious, child-like laugh. But she was always so serious. Although she smiled often, she rarely laughed.

"Perhaps Luce is not the only one who's getting too cozy with strange men," she joked.

Kincade raised an eyebrow, feigning offense. "Strange men, is it? You're the one who invited us here in the first place, remember?"

"Yes, I did," she replied.

Her expression turned grave as she gazed into the distance once again.

As he looked at her, Kincade did not need to ask what had prompted this sudden change. He too felt it, this vague yet persistent uneasiness over their entangled fates. The night before, when they had gone to meet Soran, Arianne had described him as a friend. And just now, she had joked they were strangers. In a way, both statements were true. But despite the fondness each had for the other, they both knew that, once the dust settled, they could easily end up on opposing sides.

As they stood in silence, contemplating the scenery, a strong breeze blew from the ocean and ruffled Arianne's flowing black hair.

Kincade stared at her as she swiped a lock of hair away from her face and tucked it behind her ear. He studied the shape of her lush lips, examined her smooth bright copper skin, and almost lost himself inside her clear hazel pupils. She was beautiful. A fact Kincade had known since Leicester had shown him her picture. But after meeting her in person, he thought Leicester's picture didn't truly do her justice.

"What is it?" she asked, noticing his prolonged stare.

"Nothing," he replied, trying to hide his awkwardness. "We should get back inside."

"Okay."

When they returned to the dining room, they were met with hectic shouts coming from the kitchen.

"Don't tell me those idiots are still at it," Kincade grumbled.

The kitchen door opened almost immediately.

True to his nickname, Sonar had heard the pair return inside and had come to join them with his noisy bunch in tow. The four of them were still engaged in a chaotic argument, with Lucielle still up on her perch.

"Quiet down!" Kincade barked.

They all froze.

"What's up with you?" said Soran.

"Don't you guys have anything better to do?" Kincade asked him.

The young man thought for a second. "Uh ... no, not really."

Unlike Kincade, Arianne looked rather amused. "Is this still about your game, Soran?"

"Nope," Lucielle replied. "We were talking about something else."

Kincade tilted his head up at her. "You call this talking? Can any of you even understand what the others are saying?"

"Sure. Why?" Rock asked, surprised by the question.

Kincade shook his head and sighed, looking discouraged. "So, what is it this time?"

"We were having a disagreement about art," said Sonar.

Kincade's cup nearly slipped from his fingers. "Art?" His eyes bounced between Rock and Sonar in turn. "Please tell me you're joking. You two have about as much business talking about art as you do talking about NASA's space program."

"It's not what you think," Sonar said. "We were having a disagreement over what constitutes art. OK, here's what happened. We were talking about something, I don't remember what exactly, and then Soran—"

"Never mind," Kincade cut him off. "We'll be heading out soon. Go grab your gear and get ready. We'll meet down in here in twenty minutes."

"Roger that!" the two mercenaries replied in unison.

"Roger that!" Lucielle echoed.

The group continued to argue as they made their way down the hallway and climbed up the staircase.

"We should get ready too," Kincade said once it was quiet again.

"Yes, we should." Arianne reached for his cup. "Here, let me take this."

He handed it to her. "Thanks."

"Go on," she told him as she headed to the kitchen. "I'll be up in a minute."

"All right," said Kincade.

He went down the hallway and up the stairs.

Chapter 27 – More Questions

The staircase led to a small lounge with a two-seater sofa and a coffee table. At one of the corners, there was a small rectangular desk with a desktop computer and two folding chairs. The room only had one window, overlooking the front of the house, and four doors leading to four bedrooms. Before Adam had helped Professor Fournier acquire this house, he had made sure it had plenty of space. In the back of his mind, Adam had probably hoped one day his children would find their way here.

Just as Kincade reached the top of the stairs, he caught a glimpse of Doc Chen entering Professor Fournier's room. At first, he shrugged and continued past the professor's door, but eventually his curiosity got the better of him.

He turned back and knocked.

"Come in," a voice said.

Kincade went in and he found Doc and Da Costa standing in the middle of the room next to the professor.

"Did you also have more questions for me, young man?" Fournier asked.

"Not really," Kincade replied. "I just wanted to know what was going on," he added, looking at his comrades.

"Actually, it's good you're here, Nate," said Doc.

"Why? What's up?"

Doc Chen was hesitant. "Well … it might turn out to be nothing, really. But something strange happened last night, and it's been bugging Da Costa and me since. We wanted to get the professor's take on it."

"How can I help you, young man?" Fournier chimed.

259

"Last night, after Arianne and Lucielle went to bed, some of us stayed downstairs to talk. We wanted to go over the plan again."

"OK," said Kincade. "And?"

"The thing is, while we were talking, the TV was on. Nobody was paying attention to it at first, but then a quiz show came on. Sonar suggested we play along. Everyone was a little tense, so I thought it might not be such a bad idea. I suggested mixed teams, thinking we should get used to teaming up since we were all going to be out in the field together soon."

Kincade thought about it. "You're right, it wasn't a bad idea."

"Maybe, but Rock and Soran wouldn't hear of it. How did they put it again? They wanted to have *the mercs versus the clones*." Doc sighed heavily. "I'm surprised how well those two seem to be getting along already."

"Yeah, they're both idiots!" Kincade summed up.

Doc chuckled. "Anyway, in the end, we went with the separate teams. Team one was Soran and Ashrem, team two was Rock and Sonar, and team three was me and Da Costa."

Kincade's head whipped around to Da Costa. "You participated?"

"Doc insisted," Da Costa replied. "He thinks I should try interacting with them more, even if it's only for a short time."

Kincade frowned. "I told you that too. How come you listened to him and not me?"

Da Costa shrugged. "He tends to be more sensible than you."

"Gee, thanks," said Kincade.

Fournier rubbed his beard as he stared at Da Costa. "You know, young man, I think this might be the first time I've ever heard you speak."

"Don't get used to it," Kincade told him.

Doc took a step forward. "Uh, guys? I think we're getting off topic."

"You're right," said Kincade. "So, you played the quiz show?"

"Yes."

"Let me guess, Ashrem and Soran wiped the floor with you."

"You'd think so, wouldn't you?" Doc promptly replied. "But in fact, they lost. Da Costa and I won. Rock and Sonar finished second."

Kincade's head cocked back in surprise. "They lost?"

"Yeah, and badly too," Da Costa emphasized.

Professor Fournier started laughing.

Kincade gave him a probing look. "What? Did they lose on purpose?"

"That's the thing," said Doc before the old man could answer. "It didn't look like it to me. I got the impression they were really trying."

"Oh, I'm sure they were," said Fournier. "You and your friends won, fair and square."

Kincade was still trying to decide whether the old man was being serious or not. "You're joking, right?"

Fournier laughed even harder. "I assure you, I'm not."

But Kincade wasn't amused. "You told us they were pretty much the smartest people on the planet. How could they lose in a quiz game? And losing to Doc and Da Costa is one thing, but if they can't even beat a couple of clueless blockheads like Rock and Sonar, then perhaps you should clarify which planet you were talking about."

"You see why it's been bothering us," said Doc.

The trio turned to the professor for an explanation, and the look on their faces told him it had better be a damn good one.

"I understand your confusion," Fournier said with a lingering smile on his face. "It stems from a common misconception."

"What misconception?" Kincade asked in a dubious tone.

"To expect smart people to be knowledgeable on a wide variety of subjects. Or similarly, to think having a broad range of knowledge automatically means that you're smart."

"Well, doesn't it?" said Doc.

"Not necessarily," the old man countered. "Think about it! How do you define intelligence? Scientists and philosophers have been struggling with this question for a long time. That's because the answer is both simple and complicated. Professor Engel defined intelligence as *the ability to understand*. It's a simple enough definition, and it has nothing to do with what a person knows or doesn't know. But it's also complicated because the ability to understand can express itself in various ways, or mean different things in different contexts. Here, the word '*understand*' should be taken in the broad sense."

"Oh, come on!" Kincade protested. "How can they be geniuses if they don't know anything?"

"I never said they didn't know anything. They actually know quite a lot." The old man adjusted his glasses. "Although, from a purely theoretical point of view, one could imagine a very smart person knowing very little. In reality it would never happen because truly smart people invariably possess great curiosity, a thirst for knowledge that drives them to learn about all sorts of things. For this reason, you're guaranteed never to meet a very intelligent person who is, as you put it, *clueless*."

Doc Chen's brow remained wrinkled under the weight of his skepticism. "Then how do you explain the clones having such a hard time answering questions from an ordinary television quiz show?"

Professor Fournier pounced on the remark. "Aha! This is precisely why it was difficult for them. You must keep in mind they've spent their entire lives locked away inside the Arc. Everything they know, everything they were exposed to, was carefully vetted and filtered. I guarantee you they know and understand more about science, technology, or philosophy than anyone alive today. But paradoxically, they are also grossly ignorant of more basic matters.

262

Things you and I might consider common knowledge, especially if there's a cultural reference bias attached to it."

Kincade's mind immediately took him back to his trip to Paris with Arianne. He recalled his surprise at her poor driving, and at her failure to recognize his ringtone. Despite his earlier reluctance, he was gradually starting to appreciate the professor's point.

"People tend to equate knowledge with intelligence," Fournier continued, "and vice versa. But that is essentially inaccurate. Having knowledge doesn't make one smart, it makes one knowledgeable. Knowledge can be acquired over time, be it with the help of a good memory, or by putting enough effort into it. Intelligence, however, cannot be learned, at least not in this sense. People, of course, grow smarter as they grow into adulthood, but even then, it most likely happens in accordance with their original genetic predisposition. Since we don't really understand how the brain works, it's impossible to be categorical on this point. And even though the wiring in our brains continues to be affected by our environment, our daily activities, and so on … how much of an effect this has on our overall potential is still an open question. Finally, I would add that both knowledge and intelligence are equally important. Only a combination of both can produce a truly exceptional mind."

"What about IQ tests?" Doc challenged.

"Those can be useful, but I consider them to be inherently insufficient."

"Why?"

"As I said, there is intelligence and there is knowledge. The problem is it's quite difficult to test one independently of the other, which, despite the best of intentions, introduces a subjective element to IQ tests. In addition, our thought processes will inevitably be influenced by a number of factors: our education, the people we've met, the places we've been, the work we've done, etc. Imagine if two people took a test and the key to solving one of the questions was the phonetic alphabet. You know, Alpha, Bravo, Charlie, Delta etc. As a military man, you're more likely to think about this answer than, say … someone like me, a civilian."

263

"Hmm … I see what you mean," said Doc.

"There are many things that will influence whether or not a particular solution will occur to a person at a specific time. It could even be as simple as a movie they saw the night before. Then there are the different psychological factors. How we feel on a given day will have a direct impact on how we perform in a test."

"You make it sound like it's impossible to tell," said Doc.

"Maybe it is," Fournier told him. "It depends on how accurate you wish to be. Like said, IQ tests can still give you an overall picture, and at the very least help classify people into distinct categories. Now I have a question for you, young man. How did Ashrem and Soran seem while they were playing along yesterday?"

"Come to think of it," said Doc, "they looked like they were having fun."

A faint smile formed on the old man's face.

"Good," said Kincade, eager to end the conversation. "I'm glad we got this whole thing sorted out." He turned to his two companions. "It's almost time. Let's all meet downstairs in ten." Then, without waiting for an acknowledgment, he left the professor's room.

Once he was outside, Kincade stopped and said to himself, *You'd think they'd all have more important things to worry about at a time like this.*

Ten minutes later, everyone was gathered downstairs in the living room.

Kincade stood in the middle of the group. "All right people, time for a quick recap. We're splitting up into two groups. The first group will go for the necklace." He turned to Lucielle. "You said it's in London, in a room three floors below Leicester's office?"

"Yes. I saw it when I went there in April last year. All of our stuff was confiscated when I was still living in the compound. So, I asked Andrew if I could go take some of mine back."

"Why didn't you use the opportunity to grab it?" Kincade asked.

"It was in Arianne's things, not mine. I didn't have access to it."

"And you guys are sure this necklace will help us locate the data card?"

"Yes," Arianne replied. "Before he left, our father entrusted it to me and said it was the key to a very important secret. He told me if anything happened to him, it would be up to Luce to decide what to do with it. I was only meant to hold on to it until she became old enough. But following an incident at the research facility, they took away all our personal belongings, including the necklace. I had no idea where it was until Luce told me about it yesterday."

"Just out of curiosity," said Sonar, "what was the incident?"

There was a brief moment of silence as quick glances were exchanged among the siblings and the professor.

Eventually, it was Fournier who answered. "Johann used a sharpened coin to kill two guards and a scientist."

"A coin?" Sonar exclaimed. "Are you for real?"

"Yes. Someone must have accidentally dropped it at some point."

"Oh ..."

"Let's get back to the issue at hand," said Kincade. "The second group will go after the woman."

"This will be a dangerous assignment," Ashrem warned. "In addition to her own private security detail, we should expect Jenkins to have someone shadowing her at all times. If they see us, they'll raise the alarm and call him."

"Indeed," Lucielle concurred. "There's also a chance Damien will target her next."

"Really?" said Kincade.

"Yes. Although he doesn't know where it is yet, Damien does know

265

about the necklace. He might try to use her to get to it."

"If we already know where this necklace is, why go after her at all?" Rock asked.

Soran facepalmed. "Weren't you paying attention yesterday? I thought you of all people would remember this part. We think she can lead us to WIAS. With the information we get from her, we'll be able to strike a new deal with Leicester, which, incidentally, is how we're going to keep you guys out of prison."

"Oh, right. Sign me up for that group, then."

"I take it you know how to get to her?" Doc asked Arianne.

"No, we don't," she said. "But there's someone here who does."

A short time later, Arianne, Kincade, and Doc headed down to the basement. They found Mark Stanwell lying on a dark red couch, watching television. When he heard their footsteps on the staircase, the assistant abruptly stood up and gazed at the trio. Usually, his captors would only come down to see him one at the time, so he was intrigued by the presence of three visitors.

The basement was poorly lit. There was a small TV in a corner, on top of a wobbly stand, and a small table, flanked by a couple of folding chairs in the adjacent corner. Across the room was a large freezer, next to a bunch of boxes filled with all kinds of junk. All in all, there was plenty of space. No bed, but the couch looked comfortable enough.

Stanwell was still wearing the handcuffs, but only around his left wrist. The handcuffs had been attached to a long rope wrapped around one of the pipes coming down the ceiling. This made it possible for the prisoner to move freely around the room, albeit within a limited range.

"How long do you intend to keep me here?" Stanwell asked them.

"Not much longer," Kincade replied.

"Really? You're letting me go?"

"Well … not now, but soon."

The prisoner gazed upon the faces of his captors with a worried expression. "Why have you all come down here?"

"We have a few questions for you."

"I won't help you!" he said.

"You will," said Kincade, "unless you want to stay here indefinitely."

Stanwell stared at the mercenary leader for a moment. Then his gaze fell to the handcuffs on his wrist. "What do you want?"

"You're Leicester's trusted assistant, right? You must know a lot about his business associates."

"I don't," Stanwell replied. "I only do what I'm told. Mr. Leicester doesn't exactly keep me informed of his dealings."

"He's lying," Arianne said bluntly.

The prisoner glowered at her at first. But then his expression changed, like he was remembering something. He gulped hard and his eyes shifted away.

"I see you know about her," said Kincade. "From what I understand, it's impossible to fool her."

"I wouldn't say it's impossible," Arianne corrected.

Kincade wheeled around. "Oh?"

"It's rare, but it's been known to happen."

"Hmm … good to know."

She frowned. "Good? Why? In case you decide to deceive me?"

"What? No!" Kincade protested. "It's not what I meant."

"No? What did you mean, then?"

"You know, I meant good as in … interesting."

She gave him a long, dubious look. "If you say so."

During the strange, off-topic dialogue, Doc and Stanwell found themselves staring at each other with a similar expression on their faces. They were surprised by the familiarity that had developed between Kincade and Arianne literally overnight.

Kincade turned back to the assistant. "There you have it, Stanwell! It's not impossible to lie to her, just pretty damn close to it. But you knew that already, didn't you?"

Stanwell didn't respond, but his brow was already glistening with sweat.

"Now, are we going to do this the easy way, or are you going to try to be difficult?"

Stanwell stared at Arianne once again and then lowered his head in resignation.

"Good," said Kincade. "Let's start over!"

Chapter 28 – Room Service

Nathalie Renard was contemplating the view from her executive suite in the prestigious Paris hotel. She could see part of the Eiffel tower from her window, including the bright revolving light at the top that shined like a lighthouse beacon.

A few seconds later, the entire monument began to glitter—each day after sunset, the Eiffel Tower is illuminated with sparkling lights, every hour on the hour.

Standing inches away from the glass, Renard stared, captivated by the scintillating display. She thought it was like watching hundreds of stars twinkling in the night sky.

Once the spectacle was over, she checked the time on her phone. It was 11:05 p.m. She closed the curtains and went over to the tall mirror on the wall.

She adjusted her glasses, plucked a piece of lint from her waist, and tugged on her black dress to straighten it.

After she was done, she examined her reflection carefully. But did not linger. The reception had already started.

The evening convention had run longer than expected. After a late dinner, Renard had snuck away to make some calls and to enjoy the quietness of her room. Attending this sort of formal event was an integral part of her job, but not one she enjoyed. She hated the fake smiles, the boring discussions, the long-winded speeches, and above all, having to dress up.

Unfortunately for her, skipping the reception was out of the question. During such gatherings, new introductions were made over late-night drinks, and important deals were struck during impromptu backroom meetings. It was an informal yet crucial aspect of her duties, one she simply could not ignore.

She did a final check of her makeup before she grabbed her purse and left the room.

Her security detail was waiting outside the door. The lead agent leaned on the mic inside his sleeve and informed the team downstairs that Mrs. Renard was on her way.

Down in the underground parking garage, two men in light blue uniforms rolled their large racks of fresh sheets and towels into the service elevator under the watchful gaze of the four armed sentries. The uniformed men kept their eyes to the ground and their caps pulled down in order to avoid facing the cameras as they entered the elevator and rode the carriage up to the first basement.

There they found two more security guards standing watch inside the corridor.

"Who are you? Where are the regular guys?" one of the guards asked in French as he eyed the two men suspiciously.

"They'll be making their run in a couple of hours," the uniformed man at the front replied. "We had to make an extra delivery because of the reception."

The guard carefully inspected the badges clipped to their front pockets. When he saw they were in order, it alleviated some of his wariness. "Your friend's a pretty big guy," he said, inspecting the towering figure at the back.

"I know. Would you believe he doesn't even work out?"

"He doesn't talk much either."

"Not really, he's mute."

The guard took another good look at the pair and then waved them through. "All right, go on."

The men in blue uniforms proceeded down the corridor. As soon as they turned the corner, they went into a staff room.

"Phew! I thought they were going to stop us for sure," said Rock, breathing a sigh of relief.

"They considered it," said Ashrem.

"What did you say about me back there?"

"I told them you were mute."

"What? Why?"

"How's your French?" Ashrem asked.

"Oh, right, good point," Rock replied. He put on his earpiece. "You guys read me?"

Two blocks from the hotel, sitting in the back of an ambulance parked on a side street, Soran was operating a set of complex communications equipment. "Yeah, I can hear you."

"I still don't like being stuck down here doing laundry while Doc and Da Costa are up there sipping champagne."

"Oh come on, this again? I already told you. You have to be invited to these things. I was only able to hack one invite on such short notice. It wasn't easy, either. I had to find a first-time participant working in the private sector and coming alone from overseas, in order to minimize the risk of anyone knowing them. The only person I could find was a Chinese businessman who recently made some money in real estate. Do you think *you* could pass for a Chinese investor?"

"He's right," said Ashrem. "Besides, neither one of us should be up there. Renard knows what I look like, and you … are far too conspicuous."

"And by the way," Soran added, "Hulin may be posing as a guest, but Da Costa had to go in as a waiter. So stop complaining."

"OK, OK, I got it," Rock muttered.

271

Soran checked the time. "Sean called in to confirm he was able to intercept the real investor at the airport. After the shot he gave him, his passenger will be knocked out for a few hours. He should be dropping off the car right about now."

"Won't the guy call the police when he wakes up?" Rock asked.

"We'll be long gone by then," said Soran.

"All right. At least Sonar didn't botch the job at his end."

"Oh, I just remembered," said Soran. "I have a jacket that needs to be dry-cleaned. Remind me to give it to you later." The young man had not been able to resist throwing in one last taunt.

"Very funny," said Rock.

Doc Chen got on the com line. "Enough, you two! We're on a mission. Stay focused."

"Sorry," said Soran. "Is Da Costa in position?"

"Yes, I'm in place."

"OK," said the young man. "I'll remind everyone of the plan. Once Hulin and Mr. Quiet get a visual on the target, we're in business. Da Costa will approach Renard and offer her a drink. That's when Hulin will give me the signal. I'll send her a text message asking her to find somewhere private and call right back. It'll look like it's coming from Leicester's phone, so she'll definitely do it. We know she's not too familiar with this hotel. According to Stanwell, she's only been here once or twice before. Since Da Costa will be standing right next to her, there's a good chance she'll ask him to point her to a quiet area. If not, he'll take the initiative. Either way, he'll suggest she go into a room near the service entrance. It's close to her table and it's inside the security zone, her bodyguards won't raise any objections. They'll want to clear the room first, but that's fine. Ash will drop his cleaner's outfit and change into the waiter's uniform stashed among his laundry. This will allow him to move around unnoticed. He'll sneak in from the staff entrance, grab Renard, meet back with Rock, and change back into the cleaner's uniform. The two of them will hide Renard inside one of their laundry carts and roll her out the same way they went in. Hulin and Da Costa will keep watch from outside the room and help with the guards if need be. We should have enough time to get her out before anyone realizes she's missing."

"Ah! You make it sound straightforward," said Rock. "What happens when something goes wrong?"

"Why would anything go wrong?" Soran asked.

"You guys are still new at this. Trust me, something always goes wrong."

"It'll be fine."

"Will it? We spent all day stalking this Renard lady, and what have we got to show for it? Nothing. For the past three hours, we've been sitting in this car, watching people go in and out of that hotel. Hell, I don't even know what we're watching for. All this because you saw her picture somewhere?"

"Calm down," Marie said without taking her eyes off the hotel entrance. "It wasn't her picture I saw. It was her predecessor's."

"All right, that does it!" Hans threw his hands up in the air and dropped them on the wheel in frustration.

"Hey, you're the one who said you wanted to help."

"I thought you actually had a plan."

"Come on, Hans, you're a detective too. The people who killed her predecessor are probably the same ones who killed the prof … Schmidt. He told me there were powerful people behind the accident of the French diplomat. Do you think those people would risk getting rid of such a public figure without making sure they could control whoever took his place?"

"Fine," said Hans. "But we need a plan. We can't keep following her around, hoping for something to happen."

"I know. I didn't expect security around her to be this tight."

"Why not go talk to her? We don't have any authority in this country, but still, I'm sure we can get a few minutes with her if we tell them it's for an investigation."

"No," Marie said in a firm tone. "It would tip them off. We have to find a way to place a bug on her."

"Are you crazy? We're supposed to enforce the law, not break it."

Marie gave him a fierce look. "I'm going to do whatever it takes. All I care about is finding the ones responsible for my friend's murder."

"We're talking about a high-ranking French diplomat, Marie. If you get caught, your career is over. I can't let you throw away—"

"Don't try to stop me, Hans. If you're not going to help, then go back to Berlin."

He sighed. "Fine, do whatever you want, but I'm staying. Somebody's got to protect you from yourself."

"Then it's settled. We'll make our move after the reception. There are too many foreign dignitaries in the hotel right now. We won't get anywhere near her with all that security. Not to mention the press is still parked outside."

"Remind me, what's our move again?"

"One of us will distract her and her guards so that the other can get close enough to plant the bug."

"Is that all we have to do?" he said in a sarcastic tone.

Marie winked. "Piece of cake."

"No, thank you." Doc Chen turned away the waiter presenting him with a tray of champagne glasses. He was standing by himself, pretending to look at his phone as he surveyed his surroundings.

The ballroom was an ideal venue for such events. It was a vast hall with golden walls, glossy wooden doors, luxurious carpets, and a high ceiling adorned with sparkling chandeliers. Round tables covered with thick white cloths were carefully arranged around the room, and there were name cards placed in front of every seat—as is customary for this type of invitation-only gathering.

The reception was gradually filling up. Its crowd was mainly composed of local and foreign government officials, and a few influential businessmen and corporate heads, some of whom had attended an economic forum during the evening and had gone up to their rooms to change before coming back down.

Doc was standing close to his assigned seat, watching for Renard. But as his gaze swept across the ballroom, he caught sight of a security guard furtively eyeballing him. He decided it was probably a good idea to mingle with the crowd. He stood out a bit on his own, not talking to anyone.

That was when Da Costa approached him, casually holding a tray of champagne flutes. Doc looked at the tray and pretended to hesitate.

"She's here," Da Costa whispered.

Doc glanced over his comrade's shoulder. "I see her. Get into position."

"One more thing. I noticed a waiter watching you a bit too … insistently."

Doc frowned. "Which one?"

Da Costa gave a discreet nod behind him and to the left. "The tall guy near the long table."

"I see him," said Doc, looking slightly troubled.

Da Costa studied him. "Something else bothering you?"

"I think one of the guards has been keeping an eye on me too."

"Do you think you've been made?"

"I'm not sure."

"Uh-oh," a voice interrupted over their earpiece.

"What is it, Soran?" Doc asked.

"Jenkins' men are among the security staff."

"What? Are you sure?"

"Yep, I recognized one of them. If they know you … Jenkins could be on his way already. We need to hurry, guys."

"Rock, Ashrem, are you getting this?" Doc asked over the com line.

"Yeah," Rock replied. "We're all set down here. Just say the word."

"Good. We'll proceed as planned. But first, Da Costa and I need to take care of a little problem. We'll let you know as soon as it's done. Get ready, everyone!"

Marie had gotten out of the black sedan and was squinting hard at something. She wasn't looking in the direction of the hotel, but rather down the street, on the other side of the large intersection.

Depending on the time of year, certain areas of Paris can seem eerily deserted late at night. The district of *la Défense* in particular, which is a business district comprised mainly of high-rise offices and a shopping center, typically appears devoid of inhabitants at this hour. Also, the police had erected roadblocks and diverted traffic away because of the reception. As a result, all the activity in the area seemed to be concentrated in a small radius around the hotel and could be attributed to the professional drivers waiting for their VIP passengers, the press members who had come to cover the event, and the police patrols. Everything else was dark and quiet.

Hans left the vehicle and walked over to his partner. "What are you looking at?"

276

She didn't reply but instead kept staring ahead, probing the shadows.

"What?" he pressed.

"In there!" she said. "I think I saw someone."

Hans leaned to the side and tilted his head to follow her line of sight. "Are you talking about the jewelry store at the end? I don't see any—" He stopped short. He too had just spotted something move inside the store. "Oh, you can't be serious," he lamented. "A robbery? Now we have to do something about it."

"We can't draw any attention to ourselves," Marie reminded him.

"I know, I know," he said as he walked back to the car. "I have a burner phone inside the glove box. I'll send an anonymous tip to the police. They're already here anyway. If it is a robbery, those guys certainly picked the wrong day for it."

He mumbled more complaints as he opened the car door, but Marie wasn't listening. She was deep in thought, with her eyes glued to the store.

Hans was right. This clearly was the wrong time and place for a robbery, a fact which should have been obvious to anyone. And yet …

All of a sudden, Marie whipped her head around and gestured for her partner to stop dialing. "Hold on, Hans!"

"Don't worry," he shouted back from the car. "Nobody will trace it back to us."

"No, no, leave it," she insisted.

He looked up at her, hesitant.

"*Préfecture de police, bonsoir,*" a voice answered at the other end of the line.

Hans gazed at his phone a moment and then hung up.

He exited the vehicle and walked back to his partner. "All right, you mind telling me why we're not alerting the police to a possible robbery in progress?"

"You said it yourself. Who would be stupid enough to rob this store, at this time?"

He shrugged. "I know. It's strange."

"It's more than strange. They're hosting a reception for government officials and big-shot CEOs in there. The hotel is crawling with security, and like you said, the police are already on site."

He gave her a sharp look. "What are you thinking?"

"I'm thinking maybe there's more to it. Maybe, whatever's going on in there is connected to the event in the hotel. Right now, we've got no clues. All I know is that Nathalie Renard is probably involved with the people responsible for Schmidt's murder. So I'm thinking maybe we should let this thing play out a little and see what happens. At the very least, it could give us a chance to get close to her."

Hans was not at all comfortable with her suggestion. "Even if you're right," he said, "it's still risky."

"I know. Look, if it comes down to it, we'll alert the police ourselves. They're right there."

He paused a long while. Then, without a word, he returned to the car.

Marie followed after him and slipped back into her seat. "Thanks, Hans."

"I just hope you know what you're doing."

"So do I."

Back inside the hotel, Doc had managed to lure the security guard who had been keeping tabs on him away from prying eyes. Pretending to admire the lavish decoration as he wandered around, he ventured outside the restricted zone and disappeared behind a staircase door.

Having lost sight of Doc, the guard hurried through the door after him.

But the urge to reacquire his target had made the security guard grow careless. As he rushed up the stairs, his jaw had an unfortunate encounter with a perfectly timed high kick, which knocked him out cold and sent him tumbling down the steps.

Doc quickly climbed down after his victim and sifted through his pockets. He couldn't find anything to suggest the guard was anything other than a member of hotel security.

He carried the unconscious man into a staff-only area, tied him up, covered his mouth with a small towel, and hid him inside a closet. Once he was satisfied the *package* was secured, Doc returned to the reception and began scanning the room.

"Da Costa! Where are you?"

"On my way, Doc."

"And the waiter who was watching me?"

"I convinced him to take the rest of the night off." Da Costa glanced back into the storage room to make sure no part of the man he had choked to sleep could be seen protruding from behind the boxes where he'd hidden him. "I'll be up there in a second."

Moments later, Doc could once again see his companion holding his tray of champagne flutes. "All right, Soran, we're on! It won't be long before someone starts to wonder where the guard or the waiter went."

"I'm all set. Just tell me when to send the text."

Having received the go-ahead nod from Doc, Da Costa meandered through the crowd, seemingly moving at random but all the while getting closer to Renard. After a few stops and turns, the pretend waiter had finally managed to maneuver himself close to his mark. He was about to offer her a drink when the sound of an alarm bell, quickly followed by a gunshot, reverberated throughout the hall.

The guests looked around uncomprehendingly.

But the security teams reacted quickly. They jarred Da Costa and the other waiters away from the VIPs and formed a protective barrier around them.

Another detonation resounded inside the hotel lobby.

The security teams wasted no time moving the more important personalities to their assigned safety areas. In the case of Nathalie Renard, it meant escorting her back to her suite.

"What's going on?" Rock shouted over the com line.

"I don't know," Doc replied. "Soran, do you see anything out there?"

"Give me a minute."

"What the hell happened?" the man shouted at his three accomplices.

"I don't know."

"Which one of you idiots shot at the police?"

"No one, it wasn't us."

"Who was it, then?"

The four men inside the jewelry store rushed to the windows to find out where the shots had come from. But all they saw was a swarm of police officers—most of them in civilian clothing—moving to surround the store. A horde of security agents also poured out from the hotel and came to swell the police's ranks.

The press, which had been camped out in front of the hotel, cautiously moved closer as well, cameras aimed and running. This forced the police to divert some of their resources to protect a few reckless news anchors who were putting their safety at risk for a scoop.

"We're gonna need help getting out of this one," said the leader of the robbers. "I gotta let the boss know." He took out his cell phone and dialed quickly.

Craig Thompson was waiting by the window of his penthouse apartment, a glass of scotch in his hand, when his phone rang. He promptly answered it. "Is it done?"

"Boss, we have a problem."

"Hmm?"

"The cops are all over us. We're still inside the store, but the place is completely surrounded. There's no way out."

"Surrounded? What happened?"

"I don't know, boss. The alarm went off."

"You morons tripped the alarm?"

"No, it wasn't us," the man protested. "We did everything exactly like the gray-haired man told us, same as the other two jobs we pulled earlier today. I don't understand why the alarm went off. Next thing I know, someone's shooting at the cops."

Thompson's voice burst through the receiver. "You opened fire on the police?"

"No, no. I'm saying it wasn't us."

Bang!

Another shot went off, shattering the windshield of a car, and causing the police to halt their advance.

"Who the hell is doing this?" the leader of the robbers shouted nervously.

But neither he nor his men had time to dwell on the question. All four of them hit the deck as a storm of bullets tore through the store.

Due to the presence of so many important personalities nearby, the police had opted to retaliate in a decisive manner.

"Josh?" Thompson shouted on the phone. "You still there? Answer me!"

No reply came.

Josh had dropped the phone among the fragments of marble and glass. He and his accomplices had been left with no choice other than to scramble for cover and return fire.

Pandemonium now reigned inside the hotel lobby as confusion grew among the guests and the staff. Taking advantage of the turmoil, Doc tried to stay close to Renard as her security detail whisked her away to safety. But he was only able to get as far as the elevators, at which point her bodyguards barred everyone from riding with them.

Da Costa joined up with him as the lift doors closed. "What now?"

"I don't know," Doc replied. "Soran, talk to us."

"It looks like some geniuses decided it was a good idea to break into one of the stores down the street," Soran replied over the com.

"You've gotta be kidding," Rock exclaimed.

"Soran …" said Ashrem.

"Yeah, I was thinking the same thing."

"Anything the rest of us need to know?" Doc asked.

"There's a good chance Damien's behind this," Ashrem declared.

"Damien? How do you know?" Rock asked.

"No time to explain," said Soran. "You guys need to bolt."

"Indeed," Ashrem agreed. "If it is in fact Damien's doing, whatever happens next, we're not going to like it."

"Uh, guys. You need to go," Soran urged. "And I mean now!"

"Calm down!" said Rock. "We heard you the first time."

"You don't understand. I just spotted Jenkins entering the hotel."

"Argh, crap!" Rock exclaimed.

"He got here pretty quickly," Doc thought aloud.

"He must have been waiting close by," said Soran.

"Are you saying he set a trap for us?" Doc asked.

"I doubt it," said Ashrem. "I think he was waiting for Damien's group. Either way, every exit will be blocked soon. If not for the trouble outside, we would probably be surrounded already. Jenkins must have rushed in here because of the shooting. Like us, he must suspect it's not a coincidence."

"All right, we're aborting the mission," Doc declared. "Rock, Ashrem, try to get back down to the parking garage and leave from there. Da Costa and I will find another way out."

"Roger!" Rock acknowledged.

As Doc stepped out of the elevator lounge, Da Costa held him back and pulled him behind one of the tall plants decorating the corners.

"Jenkins," Da Costa said, nodding towards the concierge desk.

Aside from Kincade, none of the mercenaries had seen Jenkins in person, but they could easily recognize him from the photograph Lucielle had shown them.

"We should try to sneak out through the kitchen," Da Costa suggested.

Doc nodded. "I guess it's our only option. Most of the security personnel seem to have redeployed around the VIPs, or outside, to deal with the robbery situation. There shouldn't be too many of them guarding the back entrance right now. Let's hurry, before they have time to re-organize themselves."

Blending into the hectic crowd, Doc and Da Costa managed to make it to the kitchen unnoticed. As they passed through the doors, Doc sneaked a peek back inside the lobby.

Jenkins was barking instructions at everyone indiscriminately, but the various groups lacked coordination. The head of hotel security didn't look too pleased about having to take orders from an outsider, and neither did his men.

Doc heard Jenkins ask for Renard's whereabouts. The head of hotel security gave a reluctant yet lengthy answer and motioned upwards.

Without waiting for the end of the explanation, Jenkins darted towards the elevator accompanied by a horde of agents.

They don't seem to be getting along too well, Doc thought. *That's good for us.* He and Da Costa rushed across the kitchen, shoving aside a row of cooks and waiters along the way. But as they neared the back exit, a brawny bearded guard appeared from the other side.

Alerted by the racket inside the kitchen, the guard had left his post to come see what was going on.

He immediately spotted the two men running straight at him.

Without a moment's hesitation, the guard reached for his gun.

Doc didn't hesitate either. In one quick burst, he propelled himself to within striking distance of the bearded man and knocked his weapon away with a lightning-fast kick.

Unfazed by his opponent's skill, the guard immediately threw a punch. Doc dodged to the side and followed with a counter-punch. His fist landed on the guard's nose and destabilized him long enough for Doc to set up a roundhouse kick to the temple. The heavy-looking man crumpled to the floor with a thump.

At that moment, another sentry came in. He had been wondering what was taking his colleague so long.

The second guard briefly froze when he saw the man lying face down on the floor, but then he quickly reached for his two-way radio.

He was about to call for back-up when he heard a clank coming from his left. He turned to look.

Da Costa pounced from behind a tall rack and swung a heavy frying pan at the guard's head.

There were now two black-suited men lying side-by-side on the floor.

All the while, the kitchen staff had been watching incredulously.

"Who are you?" the head chef bellowed.

In place of an answer, Da Costa pulled out his gun and waved it at the kitchen staff. "Toss me your phones and get in there!" he commanded, pointing to a metal door.

Frightened, the staff followed his orders without protest. Doc instructed four of them to carry the unconscious men in with them as they were funneled into a large storage room.

Once everyone was inside, Doc bolted the door shut. "Come on, let's get outta here," he told his companion.

The two men rushed toward the exit.

Just as they had hoped, there was no one else waiting outside—the two sentries had been the only ones posted at the kitchen entrance. Even the media vans were no longer amassed on this side of the hotel. They had all moved around to cover the attempted heist.

But as Doc and Da Costa stepped out onto the side street, they were forced back inside by a silent barrage of bullets. Luckily, they had reacted in time to avoid getting hit after they had spotted the masked men at the windows, high up in the office building across the street.

The two mercenaries were standing inside the kitchen again. They were a little shaken at first, but it wasn't the first time someone had taken a shot at them. They steadied their nerves and analyzed the situation.

"Did you get a good look at them?" Doc asked.

"No," said Da Costa, "but I'm pretty sure they're not cops … or hotel security."

"Agreed," said Doc. "Or they wouldn't be using silencers. Looks like whoever they are, they don't want to attract attention either."

"Looks like."

Doc got on the com line. "Soran! Do you read me?"

"Yeah, are you out yet?"

"No. We ran into a problem."

"What kind of problem?"

"The kind where snipers take shots at us from across the street."

"Oh …!" the young man replied.

"*Oh* is right. We need you to come and pick us up in a hurry."

"Got it. Hang tight. I'm on my way."

Doc and Da Costa ran a quick check on their ammo and took positions on either side of the door. Up until now, the firefight between the robbers and the police had provided a convenient distraction. And the earlier ruckus inside the kitchen had been covered by the tumult in the lobby and the on-going alarm outside. But eventually, someone was bound to show up in the kitchen. They needed to determine whether it would be possible to shoot their way out, should the need arise.

286

Doc unhooked one of the skillets hanging over the main counter and held it out the door frame.

When he pulled it back a second later, there were four bullets lodged inside the pan.

He presented the skillet to his comrade.

"No, thanks," said Da Costa, "I prefer my bullets rare, not well done."

"I'd like to lodge a formal complaint," said Doc—Da Costa was still in his waiter uniform. "The service here is terrible. I don't think I'll be coming back."

"What do I care? I quit anyway. The health plan in this place is a killer."

Doc smiled. "And they say you don't have a sense of humor."

Da Costa shrugged. "Hey, what do they know?"

Doc's face turned serious. Their window of escape was closing fast. "This is bad," he said.

Da Costa nodded.

Five minutes earlier …

Nathalie Renard and her entourage arrived at her suite. Two agents went in first to clear the room while the remaining four waited outside alongside her.

But when a few seconds passed and the agents still hadn't returned, Renard started getting impatient. "What are they doing in there? Should it be taking this long?" she asked one of her chaperons.

"No, ma'am!" he replied, staring at the door.

Though the agent tried to hide it, she could read the concern on his face. Then she caught the other three exchanging a telling glance and she knew something was wrong.

The four agents nodded to one another and drew their weapons.

"Please stand back, ma'am," said the lead agent.

While remaining in the hallway, he pushed the door open and called out to the two who had gone in.

No one answered.

As the lead agent leaned forward, weapon first, to try to get a better look, he was yanked inside by some invisible force.

The other guards immediately stepped back and took aim, ready to open fire.

"Psst!" a voice hissed at the end of the hallway.

Four heads turned.

A lean man stood in the middle of the corridor. He had on a plain white shirt, black pants, and shiny black shoes. Strands of blond hair covered a large portion of his face, but Renard recognized him instantly.

"Shoot him!" she shrieked.

But before the agents could readjust their aim, two large knives shot up from the floor as the man swiftly waved his arms upward like a conductor directing an orchestra. Only his was a silent and deadly symphony. Two agents were struck down as the blades lodged themselves in their chests.

First, Renard shuddered with horror at the sight of the bloodied men fallen at her feet. Then, she gaped in disbelief as the knives flew all the way back to the assailant's hands. She recoiled and inadvertently stood in front of the last agent still standing.

He shouted for her to move out of the way.

She threw herself to the side so brusquely her shoulder bumped hard against the wall. The agent's line of sight was now cleared, but the blond man had already spun around the corner, laughing.

"Are you all right, ma'am?" the agent asked, his weapon still pointed up ahead.

As Renard turned to answer him, her eyes widened in fear. She raised her skeleton-like finger and pointed behind the agent to warn him.

But it was too late.

A curvy redheaded woman in a maid's outfit smashed the agent's head against the wall as she walked past him, all the while keeping her eyes fixed on the French official.

At the end of the hallway, the blond man had reappeared and begun his menacing advance.

Panicked and confused, Renard rushed into her suite.

She quickly locked the door and fumbled inside her bag for her phone.

She found it and took it out, but her hands were shaking so much she had trouble landing her fingers on the keys.

All of a sudden, midway through her dialing sequence, she froze.

Even the shaking had stopped.

She had rushed into the room without thinking, in fear for her life. But now that her brain had had time to catch up with her instincts, she realized the absurdity of her action. The room wasn't safe either, far from it.

She dared to look back.

A tall man in a dark blue suit was standing close to her. So close, in fact, she could feel him breathe. He looked young, just like in the pictures, and would have looked even younger were it not for his severe expression. And yet, unlike his two accomplices outside, Renard did not sense any hostility emanating from him. He was certainly imposing, but he had a serene presence.

289

So after a few seconds had passed and he still hadn't made any move to harm her, she allowed herself a small measure of relief.

But Renard's reprieve only lasted an instant.

Her eyes fell on the three contorted bodies lying on the floor in the middle of the room, and fear once again tightened its grip on her.

She was so on edge she literally jumped when she heard the knock on the door.

Darius, on the other hand, appeared quite calm. He didn't move a muscle, and continued to stare at her. She traced his gaze to the cell phone she was still gripping nervously.

She understood right away.

Without a word, she turned off the phone and stuffed it back into her purse.

Darius then gently shoved her aside and opened the door for his two companions.

As Johann and Kadyna walked in carrying the dead agents, the blond man flashed a malicious grin at Renard and said, "Room service, ma'am!"

Chapter 29 – Don't Look Down

Down on the lower floors, hotel security had just finished clearing out the last of the staff. Jenkins had ordered every worker to be moved up to the first-floor lounge to make sure no intruder was passing themselves off as one of them.

In order to avoid being herded with everyone else, Rock and Ashrem had been hiding on top of an elevator carriage. Once the coast was clear, the pair slipped back inside the carriage and rode the elevator down to the first sub-level.

They returned to their laundry carts and hurried on their way back to the service elevator leading to the underground parking garage.

"Oh, crap!" Rock exclaimed as they turned the last corner. "There're three of them now."

Another sentry had joined the two previously posted at the parking elevator. He was listening on his walkie-talkie when he saw the two men in blue uniforms emerge from the corner. "Hey! Where are you two going?"

As the two men rolled their carts towards the guards, Ashrem moved ahead of his companion. "We're going down to the parking."

"Not possible," said the guard. "No one's allowed to leave until further notice. You're not even supposed to be down here. Turn around."

"But we've got more deliveries to make," said Ashrem as he kept moving forward.

"It's not my problem. Go up to the lobby."

The two uniformed men continued their advance—albeit at a slower pace—with feigned gestures of protestation. Irritated, the guards moved to surround them. The one with the walkie-talkie stepped up to Ashrem and placed a hand on his cart, while the other two moved past the young man and stood on either side of the huge guy.

The head guard reiterated his order, but with an added warning this time. "Turn around, or we'll handcuff you and drag you up ourselves!"

Rock grinned at one of the guards and, out of nowhere, delivered a vicious elbow to his nose. The giant then spun around and knocked the other guard out cold with a right cross.

Quick to react, the third guard immediately drew his handgun, but only to see it slapped away by Ashrem.

The young man then put the guard in a headlock and effortlessly choked him to sleep as Rock downed the one with the bloodied nose with a clean straight left to the jaw.

Moving hurriedly, Rock and Ashrem proceeded to stuff the three unconscious men into their laundry carts. But as they were covering up their victims, they heard a muffled cry coming from behind them.

The pair whipped their heads around and saw a maid standing at the far end of the hallway, staring at them with a shocked expression.

As soon as she saw she had been spotted, the maid swiveled around on her heels and bolted through the staircase door.

"Uh-oh," said Rock.

But before the giant could make a suggestion, Ashrem darted along the hallway at an unbelievable pace and disappeared behind the same door.

"Why have you brought me up here?" Nathalie Renard complained as she was led out onto the hotel roof.

Kadyna shoved the gaunt woman forward. "Shut up and keep moving."

Johann ventured off the flat area of the black-tile roof and onto the slanted surface. He stopped at the edge and leaned over to peer down at the foot of the building. "The shooting's still going on. Looks like our boys are putting up quite a fight."

The French diplomat gave him an interrogative look. "Your boys? You did this?"

Johann laughed. "Well, technically Damien did. He's the one who sent them."

"I have to admit," said Kadyna, "I didn't think they'd actually show up, considering all the security in and around this place."

"That's because it's hard for us to fathom how people can be so blinded by greed," Darius told her.

"I know," she said. "But still … to think such a simple plan would work."

"What do you mean?" Renard asked. "What plan?"

"Damien made a deal with the new leader of a criminal organization," said Johann. He nodded to the street below. "Those guys' boss. The deal was for us to team up with them on three jobs. We do all the research, figure out a way past whatever security is in place, and *they* supply the manpower. After each job, we split the profits fifty-fifty. Of course, we don't care about the money. The goal was always to get them here, today, at this exact time."

"Why three jobs?" Renard inquired.

"To gain their trust, of course," Johann replied. "We had to be sure they'd be here. Even hardened criminals would have serious reservations about hitting this place tonight because of the event downstairs. The first two jobs went flawlessly and were quite lucrative. That was enough to convince them we knew what we were doing. Then, we told them this last job would be the biggest score of all. We told them a large stash of diamonds would be transiting through there between tonight. They were reluctant at first, but in the end, we knew their greed would outweigh their doubts."

Renard was beginning to understand. "The gunshots … and the alarm

293

…"

Johann smirked. "It's possible our sister accidentally triggered the alarm at the right moment. And she may have fired a couple of rounds at the police to get their attention."

Darius, who had stepped away to make a quick call, re-joined the others. "Enough talk. Let's move."

As the group continued across the roof, Renard shot furtive glances around, as if she was searching for something.

"Yes," Johann said, answering the question she had been asking herself. "There were agents posted up here as well. We dealt with them earlier, though. I'm afraid no one's coming to help you."

Renard bit her lip and said nothing.

Finally, the group stopped at the corner opposite the ruckus downstairs.

"Now what?" Renard asked defiantly. "With that many agents missing from their posts, I'm sure by now my people are aware something's wrong. It won't be long before they find us. You'll never get out of here."

"I'll go first," said Kadyna, ignoring the captive's rant.

Renard forced a nervous laugh. "Go? Go where?"

Kadyna took a few steps back and turned to Renard. "Whatever you do, don't look down," she said. She winked and then dashed forward.

"Where do you think y—" Renard gasped as she watched the young woman leap off the edge to what was sure to be her death.

She kept watching, waiting for the red-haired figure to sink beneath the rooftop line. But to her astonishment, the inevitable never happened. Instead, Kadyna landed firmly on the building across the street.

The young woman had just performed a thirty-five to forty-foot jump as though it was nothing.

Renard was well acquainted with the Eritis project. She had seen the files detailing the subjects' extraordinary abilities. But reading about it was one thing. Seeing it in person for the first time was an entirely different experience. She was speechless.

Johann went next. But this time, Renard looked on, expecting him to make the impossible jump.

He did.

Renard was now left alone with Darius, who would obviously be following after his siblings. At that moment, it occurred to the French diplomat that all they had asked her for was the address of Leicester's office in London. Why bring her along, only to take her as far as the roof? Surely they knew that the second she was alone, she would run straight to the security teams downstairs.

She wasn't left to ponder the question for very long.

Without warning, Darius picked Renard up by the waist as one would a child, spun around once to build up momentum, and then hurled her off the roof.

Before she fully grasped what was happening, Nathalie Renard was flying through the night sky.

She tried to scream, but fear and shock had silenced her vocal cords. Afraid to look down, she closed her eyes as the cool wind brushed against her skin. Suddenly, she understood the meaning of Kadyna's earlier advice.

Though it had felt like an agonizingly long time, Renard had only been gliding through the air for a mere couple of seconds when her short flight came to an abrupt end. She let out a muffled grunt as she crashed into Johann's torso. The young man easily caught her and dropped her back on her feet. She was shaking, her heart beating really fast. She pressed her hand against her chest as she took a few deep breaths, all the while trying not to think about what would have happened if she had fallen to the ground from such a height.

"Careful," Kadyna chimed.

Renard looked up. Even though she had been expecting him, she instinctively jumped back when Darius landed next to her with a loud thump.

Just like that, the four of them were no longer on the hotel's grounds.

Renard almost admired the simple yet frightfully efficient way in which they had implemented their escape. The lobby was locked down. It would have been impossible to go out without being seen. But her captors had just turned this obstacle into an advantage. It was precisely because no one could get out through the lobby that no one would think to look for her outside the hotel.

That was when it dawned on her. She had been abducted.

Ashrem emerged from the staircase door, carrying the maid over his shoulder. She was struggling to get free, but the gag over her mouth prevented her from screaming for help.

"Wow, you caught her," said Rock. "I didn't think you would."

Ashrem hauled his charge over to his companion and set her down. "Listen carefully," he told her in French. "I convinced my friend not to hurt you." He nodded towards Rock. "But if you start making trouble, I won't be able to stop him. Do you understand?"

The maid gazed up at the towering figure and promptly nodded.

"Good. Then you'll be fine. Just wait until someone comes to get you."

Ashrem tied her hands and feet before leaving her in one of the staff rooms. He and Rock then rolled their carts into the elevator.

When the two men were inside the carriage, on their way down to the underground parking lot, Rock turned to Ashrem and frowned. "Did you tell her I was going to hurt her?"

Ashrem was surprised. "Oh, you understood that?"

296

"It was pretty clear from your body language."

"It's better for us if she stays put," said Ashrem.

"I get that. I'm saying you could have threatened her yourself. Why do I have to be the bad guy?"

"You're far scarier than I am. You have that … villainous look about you."

Rock gave him a good shove. "Hey! Who're you calling a villain?"

Meanwhile, outside, the drawn-out gunfight had finally come to an end. The would-be jewel thieves had all been captured, and the alarm had been turned off. The police were now in total control of the situation, and were busy keeping members of the press at bay, along with the rare on-lookers.

Inside the hotel, guests and staff members were told the emergency had been resolved.

This spelled bad news for Doc and Da Costa, who were still trapped in the kitchen. Fortunately for them, the disappearance of Nathalie Renard had given rise to a whole new commotion.

Jenkins and his men had found the bodies of her security detail inside her suite. The macabre discovery had prompted an increase in alertness, and a reassignment of security personnel around the VIPs present on the various floors. Agents could be seen rushing back and forth across the lobby, appearing and disappearing behind staircase doors and into elevators.

In spite of the on-going confusion, Doc knew that any moment now, someone was bound to realize the two sentries guarding the kitchen entrance were no longer at their post.

"There's a lot of movement inside the main hall," said Da Costa. "I'm going to check it out."

Doc nodded his approval. The increase in activity on the other side of the lobby doors was a source of concern for him as well. He kept an eye on the streets while his comrade ran to the far end of the kitchen.

Once he reached the double doors, Da Costa brushed his back against the wall and leaned down to peek through the small square windows.

"Why aren't those two idiots on com?" Carson complained as he barged into the kitchen.

Da Costa miraculously managed to step away and avoid getting hit in the face as the flapping doors slammed open.

Carson had approached from his blind spot, so he had only seen him at the last moment.

Now the two men were standing three feet apart, staring incredulously at each other.

Their hesitation only lasted a brief moment.

When experienced soldiers come face-to-face with an enemy on the battlefield, their brains switch to automatic. They don't think, they react. And in this case, both men had the same instinct: shoot first, ask questions later.

Da Costa had the advantage because his weapon was already drawn, but the short distance between them greatly reduced this advantage. Against someone like Randall Carson, this was more than enough to balance the scales.

Carson intercepted the mercenary's hand as he tried to raise his firearm. Da Costa also grabbed Carson's wrist to stop him reaching for the gun tucked in the back of his jeans.

Both men became interlocked in a sort of tug-of-war over control of Da Costa's semiautomatic.

Carson wasn't a particularly tall man, but he was wide, and he was all muscles. So it came as little surprise to Da Costa to see the barrel of his own gun slowly inching towards his stomach. A few more seconds and he would be in the line of fire.

298

Doc, who had been observing the scene from the other end of the kitchen, noticed his comrade's predicament. His first reflex was to shoot Carson. But Da Costa had his back turned to him and was shielding the target. Then, it occurred to Doc it didn't matter. He couldn't fire at Carson even if he had a clear shot. Any shots fired now would most certainly alert everyone to their presence and negate any hope they still had of escaping.

"Hey, guys! I'm coming up on the corner now," Soran said over the com line.

Finally. Doc put away his firearm and rushed towards the interlocked pair.

Da Costa too had heard Soran's voice on his earpiece and was aware of Doc's movement towards them. He clung on even tighter in an attempt to immobilize Carson until his comrade arrived.

But Carson had other plans. He could see Doc running towards them, and he had felt a renewed vigor in his adversary.

He had to do something.

He abruptly relaxed his muscles and stopped pushing back, causing Da Costa to momentarily lose his balance.

Using the split-second opportunity, Carson gave Da Costa a vicious head-butt, which sent the mercenary shuffling back a few steps.

With his hands finally freed, Carson quickly drew his firearm. But before he could fire at Da Costa, Doc threw a kitchen knife at him.

Having saw the flying blade from the corner of his eye, Carson raised his arms in a defensive reflex. Thanks to his quick reaction, he avoided a fatal injury and only ended up with a slash on his right triceps.

Seeing an opening, Da Costa put all his weight into a right uppercut to Carson's jaw and sent him tumbling over the main counter.

At that moment, an ambulance screeched to a stop in the street just outside the kitchen.

The two mercenaries immediately ran towards the exit and dove into the back of the ambulance. Luckily, the vehicle provided partial cover from the hail of bullets fired by the gunmen in the adjacent building.

As soon as he saw that both men had dived in, Soran stomped on the gas.

The engine roared as the ambulance rocketed away.

By the time Carson's head popped up from behind the counter, the mercenaries were gone.

"What took you so long?" Doc shouted at the driver.

"I was shopping!" Soran shouted back. "What do you think I was doing? The place is crawling with cops, not to mention Jenkins' minions lurking about. I had to be careful. There're not that many cars out here you know."

"Yeah, I know," said Doc more coolly. He had raised his voice more out of edginess than anger. He knew Soran was right. The young man had to be careful not to attract the wrong kind of attention. "Sorry," he told him, "and thanks for coming to get us."

"No problem," said Soran. He turned and winked. "Besides, a hero's got to make an entrance."

"Really?" said Doc. "Well, right now I'm more interested in how you're going to make your exit. I'm guessing the roads have been cordoned off because of all the shooting."

"Yep, but I'm pretty sure it'll be fine. There's a reason I *borrowed* this ambulance. I'll turn on the sirens and pretend to have a wounded man in the back."

"Don't worry, you won't have to pretend," said Da Costa in a weak voice.

Doc looked back at his comrade. Da Costa's face was pale. "What is it? What's wrong?"

Da Costa's hands were pressed against his stomach and blood was seeping through his fingers.

"Dammit, you got hit?" Doc exclaimed, rushing towards him.

"It's all right," said Da Costa, grinding his teeth together to mask the pain. "I'll make it."

"Here, let me have a look," said Doc as he gently lifted Da Costa's bloodied hands. He examined the wound carefully, and then grabbed the med kit to treat his comrade.

The wound was serious. He patched it up as best he could and thanked their lucky stars for the fact they were in an ambulance.

"How does it look?" Soran asked when he saw Doc was done.

Doc stood up and stuck his head between the front seats. "Not good. We need to get him to a hospital."

"Got it!" said Soran "But I'm worried about something else too."

Doc had never seen Soran look this serious. "What is it?" he asked.

"It's Ash. I haven't been able to reach him, or the big guy, since they headed down to the parking garage."

Doc realized he hadn't heard from those two in a while either. But there was no use trying to reach them now. The ambulance was already out of range of the hotel.

"I hope they made it out," said Soran, his fingers squeezing the wheel harder.

Doc stared at him.

The young man's expression was grave and severe. It was a complete change from his usual carefree demeanor.

In that moment, Doc had a strange feeling. It was like he was looking at a different person.

"Come on, Ash … get out of there," Soran whispered to himself.

Chapter 30 – Run

"This was the last one," said Ashrem as he stepped over the downed agent.

"Yeah," Rock replied, looking at the other three black-suited men lying on the ground.

Like their colleagues above, the four sentries in the parking garage had been adamant in their refusal to let the two men leave. With the guards stubbornly immune from all arguments, Rock and Ashrem had once again had to resort to a less diplomatic solution.

Having dealt with the last obstacle, the two men hurried to the delivery van.

When they got close to the vehicle, Ashrem started making his way around to the driver side, but he was immediately reeled back by a large hand.

"Where do you think you're going?" Rock said as he shoved the young man in the other direction. "I've seen you drive, buddy. I'll take the wheel."

Though he was a little disappointed, Ashrem didn't argue. He circled the van and jumped into the passenger seat.

As soon as he slammed the door shut, the tires started spinning on the asphalt and the vehicle drove off in a haze of smoke.

The underground parking extended over a sizeable area. Not only did it afford access to the hotel, it accommodated a number of office buildings as well.

The van navigated through the pillars, barely slowing down as it negotiated the sharp corners, until it surfaced onto an empty street two blocks away from the hotel's main entrance.

Rock was surprised to see there were no agents posted at the parking garage exit. "What happened to the guys we saw on the way in?"

"They were probably called away when the shooting started," Ashrem concluded.

"Good. It's about time we had a little luck come our way."

"We're not in the clear yet," Ashrem warned.

"Relax, you sound like Nate. I'm telling you, it's gonna be smooth sailing fro—"

Suddenly Rock lost control as a tire exploded and the vehicle began to sway.

He tried to steady it, but they were going too fast.

The van tumbled over and skidded onto the pavement until it crashed into a parking meter on the side of the deserted road.

The security officer checked every door and peered through every window of the brightly lit hallway as he performed one of his regular night rounds.

Shortly after he had disappeared around the far corner, a woman and a man crept along the hallway and stopped in front of an unmarked door. The woman retrieved a wallet-sized case from the black band around her waist and took out two lockpicks from it. She made quick work of the door lock, and the pair quietly slipped inside.

The man turned on his flashlight.

They were in a small room, with a wooden desk and a padded chair flanked by metallic drawers lined up against the walls.

"Is this the right place?" Kincade asked.

"I think so," Arianne replied as she gave a sweeping gaze around.

She had on her tight black outfit—the same one she had been wearing when she'd first appeared before him at the manor.

When Kincade had first seen her in the unusual attire, he hadn't really paid too much attention to it because of all the craziness going on at the time. He hadn't noticed how closely it traced the lines of her curves, revealing her slender and feminine body.

For a moment, Kincade was enthralled by the captivating vision, his gaze lingering on her longer than he had intended.

Arianne caught him staring at her strangely. "Is something wrong?" she asked.

He tried to act cool. "No, I was just wondering about the diving suit. I was surprised when you took off your clothes after we broke into the building. I didn't realize you were wearing that thing underneath."

His remark caught her off guard. She examined herself from top to bottom. "Oh, you mean our outfits? These are the only clothes we were allowed to wear at the Arc. They wanted to make sure we couldn't conceal anything. They were always worried we would find a way to escape despite all their precautions."

"Well, you did escape, so I guess they were right to be worried. But why still wear it?"

"… I'm not sure," Arianne replied, suddenly feeling a bit self-conscious. "We've been wearing these since we were children. I guess it just feels more natural than anything else. Do you think it looks odd?"

"Ahem! No, it's fine," said Kincade, clumsily trying not to sound awkward.

"Obviously, we'll need to get used to regular clothes if we want to blend in. But I still feel more comfortable wearing it when I'm doing something like this."

"You mean when you're breaking into the office of a high-ranking British official?" Kincade joked.

"Exactly," she smiled.

"So, where is this necklace?" he asked, focusing back on the task at hand.

Arianne pointed to a heavy metallic door, left of the desk. The door had no lock or handle and was instead fitted with an electronic pad surrounded by a glowing red light.

"According to Luce, it's stored in there, along with the rest of our belongings."

Kincade moved closer and hunched his back to examine the electronic lock. "This could be a problem." He then straightened up and checked every inch of the door and its contours. "It doesn't seem to be reinforced. We could probably blast our way in, but it's bound to raise an alarm. There's only a skeleton crew patrolling the building right now. If we move quickly, we might be able to retrieve the necklace before their back up arrives."

His suggestion was met with complete silence.

He looked back at Arianne, wondering why she was so quiet. At first, it seemed like she was gazing at him. Then he realized she wasn't really looking at anything. Her eyes were fixed in his direction, but she was staring blankly into space.

"Hey, Arianne! Still with me?"

"Hmm? Oh, sorry. Did you say something?"

"What's wrong?"

"… Nothing," she replied. "Ah, yes, the door … I'll take care of it." She pulled out a small device from another pocket of her waistband. It was some kind of electronic gadget linked to a magnetic card via a flat strip of wires.

"What am I looking at?" Kincade asked, eyeing the strange contraption.

"Something Soran and I made a few years ago."

She inserted the card into the slit below the electronic pad and pressed a button on the device. A series of numbers began scrolling rapidly on the pad's display.

A few seconds later, the red light turned green. The door was unlocked.

The two cautiously made their way into the room. It was larger than they had expected. There were two tall racks on either side of the door and five glass display cabinets evenly spaced along the length of the room. Behind each cabinet was a row of metallic shelves lining up all the way to the back wall.

"Don't you think this was a bit too easy?" Kincade said, sounding skeptical.

"What? Oh, you mean entering here. No, I'm not surprised," Arianne replied. "Leicester's office is several floors above us. He's kept our stuff all this time, but as far as he's concerned, there's nothing of value here."

Kincade studied her a moment. Twice now, she had seemed distracted. He approached her and said, "Come on. Something's clearly bugging you. What is it?"

She sighed. "I keep thinking I should have gone with the others."

"We've been over this. You and Lucielle are the only ones who know what the necklace looks like. Are you suggesting she should have come here instead of you?"

"Of course not. But ... what if Jenkins is there?"

Kincade frowned. "Help me understand something. You guys are freakishly strong, right? Then how come you're so afraid of Jenkins?"

"I don't know ... I'm not afraid. I just ... I've always had a bad feeling about him."

Rock heard a voice call to him as he was coming to. It sounded like Ashrem, but he wasn't sure. Images flashed through his mind. He remembered a loud popping sound. He remembered trying to steady the van after it abruptly dipped to the side. He also remembered banging his head on something, something hard.

He heard the voice again. And he felt a hand on his shoulder, trying to pull him back to consciousness. He shook off the grogginess and willed himself back to partial awareness.

His head hurt like hell, and the wheel was pressing hard against his chest, making it painful to breathe. He turned his head and saw Ashrem crouching next to him. The young man appeared to have been left unscathed by the crash. He was leaning over the giant, checking for signs of injuries.

"I think we blew a tire," said Ashrem.

"You're OK?" Rock asked, in a tone conveying more surprise than concern.

"I'm fine."

"Of course you're fine," Rock sighed, holding his head in his hands. Suddenly it struck him that Ashrem was upside-down. But when the giant looked around the vehicle, he realized it was in fact he who, like the van, was in an unnatural position.

"Can you get out?" Ashrem asked.

The giant grunted as he tried to wriggle his body out of its awkward position. But it was much harder for his bulky frame to maneuver within the enclosed space. The door on his side was stuck, and the wheel greatly impeded his efforts. "Argh! I can barely move!"

Ashrem placed his hands on the wheel, his muscles stiffened, and in one abrupt motion, he ripped it off the dashboard. "How about now?"

"Much better," Rock said, breathing easier. "Thanks."

"Come on, we have to move."

"Yeah, go on. I'm right behi—"

All of a sudden, the front passenger door flew away with a loud snap.

308

Startled, Ashrem turned around.

Then he too flew out through the opening, like a pilot ejecting from a fighter plane.

"What the hell!" Rock exclaimed. He called out to his companion, but there was no reply. He could, however, hear faint grunts and other muffled sounds.

After a jarring contortionist's routine, the giant managed to slither out of his metallic trap. He crawled headfirst out of the passenger window and promptly rose to his feet.

He saw Ashrem engaged in a brutal struggle with a brawny opponent.

It was Jenkins.

The two men were grappling with each other in a contest of strength.

Rock assumed the outcome would be a foregone conclusion. He had witnessed first-hand Ashrem's surreal physical abilities.

But after observing the two men for a while, the mercenary was forced to acknowledge the unimaginable, yet undeniable, conclusion: Ashrem was losing!

Rock was shocked. And he wasn't the only one. Ashrem looked like he was struggling as much with his opponent as he was with trying to understand how he could be so clearly overpowered. The young man found himself sliding back from Jenkins' irresistible pressure, until he literally ended up with his back against a wall.

Pure strength wasn't going to do it. It was time to try a different approach.

Ashrem delivered a well-timed low kick to Jenkins' inner leg. It was enough to destabilize the brutish soldier. The young man used the opening to land two quick hits in succession: a right upward elbow to the chin, followed by a left palm strike straight to the face.

As his opponent staggered backward, Ashrem attempted to put some distance between them. But Jenkins wouldn't let him. He slammed Ashrem against the wall with such violence it forced the air out of the young man's lungs. Jenkins then quickly followed with a mean straight punch.

Even though Ashrem had not fully recovered, he was somehow able to narrowly escape the hard fist rocketing towards his face.

Jenkins' punch missed its target, but the impact against the wall was so strong it cracked the surface and left an impressive dent in its wake.

Ashrem dived to the side and used his momentum to roll on the ground and rise over fifteen feet away.

It wasn't far enough.

Deceptively agile, Jenkins chased the young man with a stepping side kick, his foot ramming into Ashrem's back as he was standing up. It was a blow of such violence it sent Ashrem tumbling at Rock's feet.

Relentless, Jenkins closed in on his fallen adversary. But as he bent down, his hand clutched in a fist, preparing to deliver the finishing blow, Rock greeted him with a heavy uppercut. The direct hit on Jenkins' chin caused him to shuffle back a few steps. Rock quickly followed with a powerful shoulder charge, introducing Jenkins to the pavement.

As he lay on his back, Jenkins raised his head and looked up at Rock, as though he was only now taking note of the giant. It was clear from Jenkins' expression he had not often been knocked to the ground in such a fashion.

What in the world was that? Rock asked himself as he bent down to prop Ashrem up. He glanced back at Jenkins. *This guy's one tough bastard. It feels like I just hit an elephant or something.*

Ashrem was in awful shape. He was badly bruised and was coughing droplets of blood.

"You don't look too good," Rock told him. "Don't worry, I got this." He tapped the back of his waist, looking for his handgun.

It wasn't there.

Crap! It must have fallen inside the van. "OK ... maybe I don't," said Rock.

Jenkins rose back to his feet and wiped the blood running from his nose—a result of Ashrem's earlier strike—with the back of his hand. He stood there, glaring at the pair with blazing hatred in his eyes.

Teetering, Ashrem took a step forward and said to his companion, "Run!"

"Hold it! Stay where you are!"

Darius' group had just exited from the building when a woman's voice shouted the order at them. They stopped and turned around.

Standing no more than twenty feet away, a woman and a man peered at them from behind the barrels of their guns.

"Who are you? Where are you taking her?" the woman asked, nodding at Renard.

"Hold on," said the man, "first things first. Was it you we saw flying across buildings? How did you do that? I didn't see a wire."

"Here, let me show you!"

Out of nowhere, Johann appeared behind the pair. He grabbed the man with both hands and flung him far and high.

Darius and his siblings had spotted the two stalking figures before stepping out onto the dark street and had laid a simple trap for them.

"Hans!" Marie shouted. She watched her partner crash ten feet up into a street pole before dropping face down onto the ground.

She was dumbfounded.

The blond man had tossed Hans in the air as though he was a plastic dummy.

Shaking off her surprise, Marie promptly turned her weapon towards her partner's assailant. But she didn't get a chance to use it.

Moving at lightning speed, Johann closed the gap between them and wrapped his hand over hers as she held her gun.

Then, he tightened his grip.

Marie cried in pain as her fingers were squeezed against the handle of her own gun. But through her pain, she was once again baffled by the stranger's incredible strength.

Alarmed by the cries of his partner, Hans spurred himself back into action. He pushed off the ground and began looking around for his firearm—he had dropped it upon hitting the pole.

Johann saw what Hans was doing. He let go of Marie's hand and turned to face her partner.

Marie dropped to her knees, moaning in pain, and her gun slipped from her fingers as she nursed her throbbing hand.

At that moment, she noticed an object glittering in front of her eyes. It was a knife. It had a large blade with a small row of dents on the dull side near the hilt. She also saw something else. A wire. Almost transparent. Like a fishing wire sticking out from the base of the knife's handle.

Then, Marie's gaze was drawn back to her partner as he returned to his feet.

He had found his gun. But as he leveled it, the blond man launched the knife into his chest.

"No!" Marie shrieked as she watched Hans collapse into a miserable heap.

Frozen in horror, she saw the blond man wave his hand.

The blade jumped out of her partner's chest and raced along the pavement in a trail of sparks before shooting off the ground and flying back into the pale creature's claw.

Marie stared with shock and disbelief at Hans as he lay inert in a pool of blood.

What had just happened? Was any of this even real?

But the reality of the situation was about to literally drop onto the detective.

Marie felt a strange sensation on her forearm, like rain falling on her skin one drop at a time, only warmer. She refocused her gaze and turned her head slightly.

Less than ten inches from her face, she saw the knife again. It was now covered in her partner's blood. She raised her eyes at the man holding it. He remained planted on the spot, as if waiting for something. She saw the demented blue eyes staring down at her, and the evil smirk distorting his face like a grotesque mask.

Marie's eyes fell on the knife once again before jumping back to her partner.

Hans … I'm so sorry, she lamented to herself.

In an explosion of anger and guilt, the detective sprang to her feet and punched the blond man in the face as hard as she could. But when her fist impacted the creature's face, Marie felt something was off. The mask … it felt different … harder than she had expected.

With his thumb, Johann wiped the blood from the fresh cut on his lip. "Hmm, I thought you'd be going for the gun." He looked embarrassed, like he wasn't sure what to do next. But as he eyed the blond woman, his expression changed. "Wait a minute, I know you. You're that detective from Berlin. What are you doing here?"

Marie's shock grew even further. He knew her. How? He didn't look familiar at all. She examined him in turn, trying to place him.

Out of the blue, Johann burst out in laughter. It was a cruel, horrible laugh. "Don't tell me you've come all this way because of the old man."

The old man ...? Professor Karpov. Marie's eyes stretched into circles. "You know about the professor? Do you know who killed him?" she heard herself ask.

"I should," he replied nonchalantly, "since I'm the one who did it. I sent the old man to his grave, and not a moment too soon if you ask me."

She recoiled in horror. "You ...? You killed him?"

"Trust me, he had it coming." The killer gave Marie a gentle tap on the shoulder. "But I can't take all the credit. After all, we wouldn't have found him without you."

But Marie wasn't listening anymore. *First, the professor ... and now, Hans.*

She only had one thought on her mind.

She shoved the monster with both arms, and this time, she did reach for her gun on the ground.

She picked up the weapon with her left hand and aligned the barrel with the monster's head. But she wasn't able to get a single shot off before Johann knocked her weapon away with a backhanded slap.

Marie watched the gun slide on the ground all the way next to Hans.

But she never saw the knife.

She only lowered her eyes because of the faint sound she had heard. When her gaze mechanically homed in on the source, she saw the tip of the blade less than an inch away from her blouse.

A shiver ran through her body.

She could have been stabbed. She could have died. She would have died, had it not been for an unexpected intervention.

Up until then, the man and the woman standing next to Renard had not said a word, nor moved a muscle. They had remained silent spectators to the drama unfolding before their eyes. Which was why Marie was stunned to see the other man from the mysterious group now standing next to her, gripping his comrade by the wrist. He had prevented the blond man from thrusting his knife into her midsection. He had saved her life.

Johann snapped his hand back and brandished the bloody knife in front of his brother's face. "Darius! Getting in my way again? I already warned you about doing that."

Darius responded in his ever-placid tone. "I don't know why Damien let you kill Professor Karpov. But I will not allow you to do the same to this woman."

"Why do you care? She means nothing to us."

"You know as well as I do she meant a lot to the professor, a man who cared for us like his own children. What other reason do I need?"

"Ah!" Johann scoffed. "You are as misguided as Ashrem and Arianne if you really believe this nonsense. Karpov was just as guilty as the rest of them. To him, we were nothing more than test subjects ... freaks to be experimented on. Adam was our father."

"And yet, it was Adam who saw fit to entrust our well-being to Professors Karpov and Fournier."

Johann shrugged. "He didn't have a choice."

"You're welcome to your opinion," Darius retorted. "I have no intention of debating this matter with you, nor do we have the time. We need to leave, now." He turned to Marie, who had been listening in silence, trying to make sense of the strange conversation. "Go," said Darius. He nodded to the inanimate body lying at the foot of the lamppost and added, "There may still be time to save your friend if you hurry."

"Time? You mean ...?" Marie rushed to Hans and carefully rolled him over. His wound looked serious, but he was still breathing.

"Marie ..."

"Hans, you're alive," she breathed in relief.

"You're not … *cough* … getting rid of me like … *cough* …"

"Don't speak. I'll go get help, OK? Hold on, partner. I'll be right back. Hold on!"

Marie spotted her gun next to Hans and mechanically picked it up as she got back to her feet. She then hesitated, worried about leaving her wounded partner alone with the killer and his accomplices. But the group was already walking away from the scene. Her gaze lingered on Professor Karpov's killer. He made for a very tempting target. She eyed her gun for an instant but her concern for Hans was stronger than her urge for revenge. She shoved the gun inside her belt and ran towards the hotel.

"Why did you save this woman who was threatening you earlier?" Renard said to Darius.

The young man ignored her and kept walking.

"You're worried about Mitsuki, aren't you?" Kadyna asked, noticing the concern on Darius' face.

"She should have been here by now."

"I know," said Kadyna. "I wonder what's keeping her. It's not like her to be late. Then again, you're the only one who's ever had a clue about what goes on inside that little head of hers."

"Run!" Ashrem warned a second time.

"Don't be stupid," Rock told him. "I'm not going to leave you here. Anyway, I don't know what the deal is with this guy, but I think we can take him."

"No," Ashrem replied as he stared at the menacing figure. "We cannot."

Without a word, Jenkins pulled a gun out from inside his jacket. He then removed the clip, emptied the chamber, and tossed the weapon aside.

"Why did he do that?" Rock blurted out. "Wouldn't it be easier to just shoot us?"

"He wants to kill us ... to kill me, with his bare hands," Ashrem said in a grave voice. "I don't know why, but for him ... this is personal."

For the second time, Darius stopped and turned around, and gazed in the direction of the hotel, a heavy frown etched on his face.

Kadyna stared at her brother in silence. His current image was a far cry from his usual placid expression. She had rarely seen him look this worried. "I'm sure Mitsuki's all right," she eventually said. "Her escape route was mapped out long in advance."

The redhead's reassurances did little to ease Darius' concerns. His eyes remained fixed straight ahead as he gazed into the distance.

"How long are we going to stand around here?" Johann complained.

"Shut up!" Kadyna told him.

"You two go on ahead with her," Darius said, glancing at Renard. "I'll meet you back at the apartment."

With that, he walked away from the group, leaving their prisoner with his two siblings, and disappeared down the dark street.

Made in the USA
Coppell, TX
05 March 2022

74501203R00194